When The
Rooster Crows

Spencer Butler, Sr.

ISBN: 9781976763441

This is dedicated to Melvina…
My 8th, 9th, and 10th Wonder of the World.

Spencer

CONTENTS

INTRODUCTION

The weather-beaten cedar fence, metal swing, and old oak tree had shared generations together. They had seen seasons come, and seasons go. The huge oak tree stood tall, strong, and proud; the roots were deep and well anchored. The leaves were green in the Summer and russet in Fall. The acorns would tattoo the ground with regularity. The oak was the epitome of strength and endurance and towered over all the other trees in the neighborhood. The oak tree was rightfully respected, and deserved to be in the Bible.

The metal swing hung from one of its massive limbs and invited one and all to come visit and rest. The trio, tree, fence and swing, were trustees of secrets, joy, merriment, and laughter. But, when the rains came, raindrops of excruciating pain would drip from the leaves onto the swing and roll down the fence's face.

When the Roses, Azaleas, Lilies, Daffodils, and Fig tree were in bloom, the beauty, and splendor of the yard, rivaled the Garden of Eden. The grass was lush green and healthy. Boxwood hedges lined the walkway leading from the backdoor of the house to the cement patio surrounding the oak tree. My grandfather built the house. My father and his two sisters were raised there. When my grandparents died, my father, having made his mark on the world, bought his sisters' interests in the property and had it renovated. In time, as fate would have it, I became the owner.

My mother had a spiritual connection with that section of the yard. To her it was 'Sacred Ground' and when sitting there, she felt the entire Host of Heaven smiling down on her. If she had anything important to discuss with anyone, he or she were escorted to the backyard swing — that was her office. There were many days I'd look through my window and see her sitting on that metal swing reading the Bible. Now and then I'd hear her softly singing, and there were times I'd observe her holding her head in her hands, silently weeping. Many years would pass before I'd learn the source of her sorrow.

As I sit here on the very swing where my grandparents and parents sat before me, with the old oak tree as my umbrella, serenaded by the whistling of the leaves and the chirping of birds, I'm reminded that I'm in the twilight of my years. My memory is not as keen and sharp as it once was.

Yet, a force as strong as that old oak tree is compelling me to tell my family's story.

I am always amazed at people who can recall events that occurred when they were four or five years old. How they can remember the first tooth they lost, the name of their kindergarten teacher, and the names of their classmates in primer school, are mysteries to me.

Anyway, my mother, whose name is Mira, was convinced the human body was not designed for meat consumption. She would say often, "Fish, fruit, and vegetables, are brain foods."

One thing from childhood that stands out in my mind is wearing short pants. I hated short pants. I had a pair for every color in the rainbow.

While dressing me, my darling mother, seeing my discontent would say, "When you're nine years old, Joshua, you'll not have to wear shorts again."

Holding my face in her hands she'd kiss me, smile and softly say, "I promise."

After rubbing Vaseline on my legs, she'd pat me on my butt and send me on my way. I have no idea what my age was when that conversation took place, nor what the age of nine had to do with the equation. The only thing I knew for sure was a millennium passed before my ninth birthday.

Try as I may nothing much comes back with any degree of clarity. My memories resurface in fragments. Fragments such as my mother singing me to sleep, Uncle Joe standing in the backyard talking to the moon — he had a mental disorder, being overcome with sadness at the movies when the cowboy rode away, kneeling by my bed as my mother taught me the Our Father Prayer, and the awful taste of Castor Oil.

Many images and events come in and out of focus. While I find it impossible to put an age on these impressions, one thing I'm sure about, certain about, have no doubt about and can be specific about is this July 7, 1948, I was nine years old, and I never, ever wore short pants again. Never!

CHAPTER 1

My name is Joshua Edward Lange. I am the youngest of four children. There's Rodney, the oldest, Gilda, Melanie, and myself, in that order. There was an eighteen-year difference between Rodney's age and mine but the distance could not be measured in years. It was much greater. Our father's name was Robert Anthony Lange. Our mother's name was Mira Marie Gardner-Lange. Our mother is the only person who called our father, Robert. To everyone else, he was Mr. Bobby. This story is about my family, the Lange family. My family was… Well, you be the judge.

Twenty-four hours a day, three hundred and sixty-five days a year, the neon lights, flashed, Bobby's Café, Bobby's Café, there would be a slight pause then they'd flicker, Meet Me At Bobby's Café. That was the name on the marquee, but to everyone in Central City, Bobby's Café was known simply as, 'The Place'.

'The Place' was a middle-of-the-road diner. It specialized in Red Beans, and Rice, Backbones and Greens, Pig tails and Cabbage — don't forget the Corn bread, Chitterlings, and Ox tails would always taste like more. Bobby could prepare a Sirloin Steak, Porter House, or T-bone that would make your mouth water. But, his battered fried chicken would make your heart sing. Everybody in the downtown area of New Orleans knew 'The Place' and knew Bobby Lange even better.

Every now and then an elderly white man who resembled Santa Claus, minus the beard, would visit the café. Because Bobby's facial expressions seldom changed, it was difficult to tell if he were happy or sad to see this gentleman. His driver would wait out in the car. The kids on the block would gather around to admire the automobile. It was truly an eye-catcher. It was a black Fleetwood Cadillac, custom-made. It had horizontal bars and catwalk grilles on both sides, with tear drop taillights. It was a sight to behold.

The gentleman's name was Francis Anthony Francino. He was a crime boss in the State of Louisiana and parts of Mississippi. Bobby began working for Mr. Frank, as he was known, when he was eighteen. It was a relationship that would bring Bobby power, influence, money, unbelievable grief, heartache and pain.

Mr. Frank had aged. He now wore thick-rimmed eyeglasses and walked with a cane. Though small in stature, he still made an impressive presence. He sported an expensive gold bracelet with a miniature 8-ball dangling from it. Besides his wedding band and watch he wore no other jewelry.

When his associates would inquire about the significance of the little ornament attached to such a beautiful bracelet he simply would smile, toy with the tiny 8-ball and say, 'Ask me no questions and I'll tell you no lies.'

He was never seen without it. In the corner booth of the café was another sight that could not be ignored. Bobby and the old man looked like night and day. As they sat conversing, it was obvious their relationship had history.

As my brother, Rodney entered the dining area from the kitchen, the old man seeing him yelled, "Rodney! Come here boy!"

Smiling from ear to ear and lavishing in the recognition, he rushed to the booth.

Rodney gave a slight bow and said, "Hello, Mr. Frank. It's good to see you, Sir."

After exchanging a few pleasantries, Rodney politely excused himself. As he walked off Bobby said, "Rodney, fix a box of chicken for Mr. Frank to take with him."

"Good thinking, Bobby." The old man said.

As I came out of the supply room, the waitress said, "Joshua, Mr. Bobby wants you in the dining room."

Setting the supplies down, I walked slowly to Bobby's table; all the while wondering what I had done wrong.

As I tentatively approached the booth, Bobby said, "This is Mr. Frank, Joshua."

Relieved that I wasn't going to be reprimanded, I managed a smile and said, "Nice to meet you, sir."

Mr. Frank had skin spots on his hands that I found unsightly. Not wanting to shake his hand I placed mine behind my back.

I heard Bobby saying, "Yes, he's getting big. He's doing okay in school. No, I don't think he'll be good in business. He's not a go getter like Rodney."

I wanted to extricate myself from this awkward situation but didn't know how.

So, it was a blessing when Alvin, who worked in the kitchen said, "Excuse me Mr. Bobby, Joshua is needed."

As I walked off I heard the old man say, "Listen to your Paw boy and you'll go a long way."

I didn't respond.

Bobby and Frank spoke of many things; how beautiful the café was how the neighborhood was changing, how far Bobby had come in the business world, how well he was respected and how he stood head and shoulders above many business men in New Orleans. As they sat many topics were covered, but the incident that had cemented them together for life was not mentioned.

Bobby would never forget the chilling words Frank told him years ago.

"Should you ever speak a word of what took place here tonight, the pain you'll endure will cause the dead to weep."

The death of two innocent men, and a third one in prison for life, would follow Bobby to his grave. When the visit was over, Bobby walked Frank to his car. As his bodyguard held the car door open, he eased into the backseat.

Smelling the box of chicken Rodney prepared for him, he smiled and said, "The best fried chicken in the South."

As an afterthought, he exclaimed, "Take some time off from counting your money Bobby and relax."

He waved, rolled up his window and was gone.

After they had driven off, Bobby remained standing on the corner. Lost in thought, he was oblivious to people speaking as they passed. Looking half a block down Tremain Street where his property started and half a block up St. Bernard Avenue where it ended, he smiled. Not bad for a colored kid who, dropped out of high school, to take care of his disabled mother. While congratulating himself, he was suddenly flooded with a sea of sadness.

As he hung his head and walked into the café, he thought to himself, "What a price I had to pay."

When colored entertainers came to New Orleans to perform, the four places they were sure to patronize were Dooky Chase, Hayes Chicken Shack, the Dew Drop Inn, and Bobby's Café. They may have been the celebrities, but they all made Bobby seem like a star, bringing him gifts, requesting their picture be taken with him and giving him free tickets to their concerts. They all wanted to be on Bobby's good side for they knew in time they would need him.

When there would be a musical in the city, the performers would party into the wee hours of the morning. Often, they'd get arrested for drunkenness, disorderly conduct, and creating a public nuisance. Not wanting the negative publicity and not wishing to waste time returning for a court date, their managers would contact Bobby. Bobby would have the matter resolved immediately.

It was common knowledge in the downtown community that if you went to jail call Mr. Bobby. He had the power to get you released. The ministers in the area could not understand why a businessman like Bobby would stoop to help pimps, prostitutes, con-men, and thieves.

When they'd question him about such practices, he'd say very tersely, pointing heavenly, "If those 'Incorrigibles' as you call them, are unfit to walk among us, take it up with your sponsor."

He'd hold the door open and say rather gruffly, "Good day, gentlemen. I have a business to run."

'The Place' was always open and always crowded. Bobby saw no reason to close. He'd say, 'People are hungry and I'm here to feed them.'

Extra waitresses were always needed for breakfast and lunch. The café was located directly on the corner of St. Bernard Avenue and Tremain Street. Next to it were the barbershop, the cleaners, and the pool hall. On Tremain Street, at the end of the diner, was the fish market.

Bobby's cleaners was two doors away from Reynolds' "Fold N' Press" laundry. It wasn't there at the beginning. Before opening his business, Mr. Reynolds asked Bobby if he ever intended on opening such an outlet on the

Avenue.

Bobby responded in the negative saying, "Reynolds, I don't know diddly about that line of work. Open your laundry. You have my blessings."

Upon seeing the business, Mr. Reynolds laundry generated, Bobby changed his mind and opened his cleaners two doors down. When Mr. Reynolds could muster the nerve, he confronted Bobby.

Trembling, he asked, "How could you open a laundry next to mine when you gave me your word you wouldn't?"

Showing no concern, Bobby said, "Competition is good for business." Leaving Mr. Reynolds standing on the corner.

In little or no time, Bobby's laundry was doing as much, if not more business than Mr. Reynolds' laundry.

CHAPTER 2

The police who patrolled the area gave the local businessmen hell for little or no violations. Excessive force was used on their customers, and false arrests were common. Words like respect and dignity had no substance whatsoever. Those seeking equality found it only in the graveyard. The police knew Bobby very well and with whom he was connected. They didn't enter his café on unofficial business nor did they harass his customers. If Bobby was standing outside and a patrol car passed they'd stop and chat with him, even as a child, I found it noteworthy that they never called him "Boy" or "Uncle". It was always "Mr. Bobby".

As dangerous and unpredictable as the outlaws and hoodlums were, they never caused a problem in his establishment. They knew that one word from Bobby could get them released from jail. One word could get them arrested. With one, word, if need be, they'd find themselves in the emergency room of a nearby hospital. The law and the lawless protected Bobby. He was respected and insulated. In all the years he was in business, he was never threatened, robbed, nor had any crime related problems. Bobby, his family, and customers were safe on Tremain Street and St. Bernard Avenue.

Across the street from 'The Place' was the St. Bernard Project. It was the largest and most dangerous in the nation. It was a haven for pimps, prostitutes, con-men, hustlers and criminals of every kind. It was also home to hard-working, God-fearing, decent human beings. I don't know how, but many young people found a way out of the St. Bernard project to become highly productive citizens.

Along the Avenue, the foot traffic, buses and automobiles never stopped. The vendors and peddlers were extremely loud and colorful. There were bars, taverns, a record shop, grocery stores, a hardware store, restaurants, and a goodwill store. There was a distinction in the area that no other neighborhood could claim.

With so many different personalities in the vicinity, problems and confrontations were unavoidable. Morning, noon, and night something was always brewing. The best course of action was to keep your eyes open and your mouth shut. For example, Rev. No- Goode, I can't remember his name, was the pastor of New Faith Baptist Church. He dropped his wife off at the airport. In a hurry, to "blacktop" something he didn't wait to see her off. She missed her flight and took a cab back home.

Upon entering her house, she caught the Pastor and Sister C. Moore Butte, shaking the sheets. A few moments later, the chariot swung low and swung sweet carrying the two lovebirds to their nest up in the sky.

Then, there was Joe Miles. He was living with Linda Banks. He wouldn't work, so she threw him out. Instead of getting in his broken-down truck and cutting his losses he tried to make a stand.

Knowing his boys on the corner were witnessing what was unfolding, he yelled so they could hear, "That's alright bitch, one day I'm gonna catch ya wit ya drawers down."

With a sheepish grin and feeling victorious, he stepped into the vehicle. His moment in the sun was short lived because Linda shouted back, "Da day ya catch me wit ma drawers down, ya rubber-dick Mothafucker, will be a good day for ya ta kiss ma big black ass."

Bobby was not open to advice or suggestions from anyone. His word was the last word. Only two people could hold his attention: Mr. Frank and Rodney. When he spoke, which he did only when necessary, it was with a harsh commanding tone. He was a demanding employer and with me an impossible father. Why he treated me as he did, I have never known. For many years, I have pondered that question. To this day, it has remained a mystery. He was forty-eight when I was born, going on crazy. I must have been a total disappointment to him. He gave me the impression I was a problem. If I had a penny for each time he called me dumb, lazy, trifling, or stupid, I could build a mountain out of insults. I didn't have a clue as to how to please him. When he'd berate and scold me, without pause, I'd go into myself. I'd daydream, and where Bobby was concerned I dreamed a lot.

After experiencing one of his angry and violent tirades, I'd go to my secret secluded spot behind the café. I spent many hours sitting there — alone and dreaming. I'd envision a day when Bobby would need my help. Of course, in my dreams, I'd be the only one he could call on. He'd be in unbearable pain and emotional discomfort. His misery would be beyond words. He'd plead and beg for my assistance and support. In his moments of distress and tribulation, his voice wasn't rough and demanding. It was sad and pitiful.

He'd call out my name, 'Joshua, please help me. Don't walk away, son I need you.' Void of all pride and dignity he'd fall on his knees and cry.

As I'd walk away feeling triumphant, I'd hear him screaming, 'Come back, Joshua. Please don't go.'

Finally, with his spirit in shambles, he'd utter the words he could never verbalize, 'I love you, Joshua. I love you.'

That was all a long, long time ago. I was just a child. How could I know I would hate myself, the day my dreams all came true.

I have no good memories about working at 'The Place'. I hated every moment. My job was to keep up with the dishes, pots, and pans. They never stopped coming. At the end of the tour, my hands would be so sore from being in soapsuds I couldn't unzip my pants to pee.

I never spoke much around Bobby or Rodney for fear of saying something wrong. I was so accustomed to one of them pouncing on me until I thought it best to remain silent. Every blue moon I'd tried to join in their conversation. Whatever input I offered must have been wrong because Bobby would look as if the mere sight of me repulsed him.

He'd shake his head as if he were trying to discard something in it and shout, "Boy, do you ever intend to grow up?"

Rodney would laugh uncontrollably. He was much older than I and truly a piece of work.

CHAPTER 3

The friends I made in high school included Daniel Brumfield, James Curtis, Jerry Cotton, and Louis Peterson. The girls were Elizabeth Jenkins, Gladys Turner, Amanda Perry, Anna Hunter, Barbara White, and Cindy Hudson. We made a pack to remain friends forever. Around school, we were known as 'The Group'.

The girls all lived in the St. Bernard Project.

James and I sat next to Liz in the classes we had together. She was always prepared and carried us in class. We called James 'Count' — that was short for 'No Count'. No one outside 'The Group' was privileged to that information. We called him by that name because he was always broke. He never had any smokes, and he never knew the answers on our tests. His short comings here and there actually didn't matter. He was our friend, and when things really mattered, he truly counted.

Because of Bobby's reputation, my friends and I were free to roam the St. Bernard Project's courtyards day and night. We were not bothered by anyone. Strolling through the courtyards, the older guys were always calling out to us. "What's going on Lil' Bobby?", "Hey Lil' man, how's the cat hopping?", "Ya know what Bobby, a hot piece of ass, and a cold glass of water, will kill ya.", followed by laughter.

Because we were young and innocent the prostitutes got a kick out of teasing us. As we walked by one might say, pointing to her body, "Ya rabbits want some of dis?"

Another might cup her breast and ask, "Wanna take dees home with ya?"

We were more afraid of them than we cared to acknowledge. The project is an environment unlike any other. To survive, you need to be educated in the ways of the street. The first law is never bringing undue attention to yourself, blend in — don't stand out. Walk with confidence but not arrogance. Look and observe, but don't stare. Listen with your third ear, hear what's not being said and run only if you must, but remember, flight invites pursuit. If something seems too good to be true, it generally is. Let it be. Keep your intentions to yourself. If you feel compelled to act — do so. And don't ever, forget, the project is like the Titanic; it's not a safe place to be.

Elizabeth Jenkins lived with her mother, in the project, in an upstairs unit. The apartment was cleverly decorated. It became 'The Group's' headquarters. Liz's mother's name was Rita. She was down to earth and extremely liberal. She gave and expected respect. She'd settle for nothing less. Without being told, we knew we had to call her Miss Rita, or Miss Jenkins and we did. Liz called her mother Rita, not Momma.

Miss Rita was a happy-go-lucky kind of person. She was very young and had been a single parent since Elizabeth's birth. She enjoyed going out and having a good time. And while she dated often, no man was ever known to stay overnight at her apartment. When expressing herself Miss Rita cussed a bit — well, a lot. She had a way of connecting nouns, pronouns, and adjectives that sounded poetic. She was raw and uncooked but pure as rain. She never cussed us. She saved her colorful vocabulary for her friends. Even though Miss Rita laughed loud and a lot, it was obvious life had stepped on her a time or two.

When it became apparent 'The Group' would be spending an excessive amount of time at her house, she read the rules to us. With a beer in one hand, a cigarette in the other and giant curlers in her hair, she spoke very seriously.

Looking at each one of us individually she said, "As long as you respect me, Liz and our home, you're welcome here. I expect you to conduct yourselves like young men and young women."

Taking a drag off the cigarette and pausing to sip her beer she continued. "You are to keep your minds on your books and nothing else."

She stressed 'nothing else' and we had to be out of her house by nine o'clock on weekdays and by mid-night on weekends. One of us, or all of us could always be found by Liz's house.

The girls in 'The Group' were a complete joy to be around. They were truly special. They were fun-loving and spirited. Each one had a little quirk in her make-up that made her precious and unique. For instance, Barbara White fell in love with a new fellow every other week. The new fellow was the one, he was so fine, that is until the next seven days had passed.

Cindy Hudson would wait until the teacher said class dismissed to ask a question. Someone in the rear would throw something at her, and she'd be offended.

"You all are so immature and childish," she'd scream, storming out of the classroom.

Amanda Perry was worse than Cindy. At least we understood Cindy's questions. Her timing was just off. No one ever knew what the hell Amanda was talking about. She once asked a student teacher if she could expand upon the different approaches to the following philosophies: Epicureanism, Idealism, Existentialism, and Materialism.

Gladys Turner had the distinction of being the shortest student in school. She was also short in comprehension. She was never quite sure what was meant by what was being said.

"Excuse me, Mr. Medulla. When you said, we should be able to complete the field trip in two shakes of a lamb's tail, are we to measure that in hours, days, weeks, years or what?"

Elizabeth Jenkins was the class demonstrator. Whenever a question was asked, and we all sat there looking unwise and otherwise, the teacher would have Liz explain the answer. And she would.

On Saturdays, my hours at 'The Place' were from seven to three. Alvin, the other dishwasher, would relieve me. Nothing ever changed. Bobby would complain, scream, and yell like some kind of nut case and Rodney would glance in my direction and laugh. He was always laughing.

Rodney was the oldest. He was a junior. Why everyone called him Rodney, I haven't a clue. He and Bobby got along like two peas in a pod, a hand and a glove, like a straw and a Coke. They were one and the same. They belonged together. Rodney was the only person who could make Bobby laugh. He found the foolish and ridiculous things the boy said hilarious. Anything Rodney said, Bobby would believe and Rodney told him plenty.

If Rodney said, 'Bobby, the mouth of the Mississippi river wears lipstick.' He would beg Rodney to tell him what color.

He would keep Bobby informed of my every move. Everything I did, he reported to Bobby. Believe me, as I grew older I began to do enough to keep things interesting. He derived a great deal of satisfaction from ratting me out.

He'd say things like, 'Hey, Bobby, you'd better talk to that boy. He's drinking. He's smoking. He's running behind those tack head girls in the project, and he's playing dice in the courtyard.'

You'd think he was concerned about my well-being, but he wasn't. When Bobby came down on me, Rodney enjoyed watching me squirm. I'll never know what he found so funny, Bobby coming down on me, or watching me squirm. Of course, Rodney was right on all counts. Everything he reported was true. I was now fifteen years old. I was smoking, drinking, gambling, and running the street. Once Rodney reported, I was guilty; Bobby never asked my side of anything. At those times, he'd begin yelling and screaming as if he had lost his mind.

Poking me in my chest with his finger he'd shout, "How many times do I have to tell you to keep your ass out of that damn project? You will listen to me or else. If I catch you smoking, or drinking that will be the last thing you'll do. You're too damn stupid; that's your problem. You're wasting your time going to school. Look at me when I'm talking to you."

Shoving me out of the kitchen I'd hear, "Get the hell out of my sight."

Over by the work table, seasoning chicken, Rodney could be heard laughing.

Again, I'd find comfort in my dreams. I'd think of all the things I would do to Bobby when my day came. Just as sure as water is wet, roses are red, and bluebirds fly my day would come. He was wasting his time telling me to stay out of the project. It was like telling the sun not to set, the tide not to roll out to the sea, a rooster not to crow at the break of dawn, and it's like saying half the truth is not a whole lie. It's impossible.

When I turned fifteen, the girls gave me a party at Liz's house. Everyone was there. There was a huge birthday cake with the words, "Friends Forever" written on it. Fried chicken, potato salad and other goodies were ordered from 'The Place'. It was July 7, 1954 I'll never forget that night. I took my first drink that evening and fell in love.

15

On the corner of Galvez and Music Street was a neighborhood grocery store. It sold just about everything meat, poultry, eggs, bread and liquor. It was open six and a half days a week. Customers were always complaining about the meat not being fresh and the produce being spoiled. Because credit was granted, they patronized the store and prayed they wouldn't get poisoned.

There was just about as much litter inside the store as outside. It appears it was against company policy to sweep or apply a fresh coat of paint to the interior or exterior of the building. Young men in the area, not having much to do, could be found at night singing on the corner. They'd chip in and buy a gallon of Vino and commence singing. As soon as the wine kicked in they'd become loud and argumentative.

Peter Capo, the owner who lived alone above the store, would raise his window, and yell, "Get your asses off my corner and stop all that damn noise."

To which one of the guys would reply, "Go jerk yourself off you old perverted bastard."

Dan, Jerry, Count, Louis and I would steal from Capo's store — every day we stole something. Dan loved peach pies. I loved Almond Joys. So, on the way to school we'd steal two of each. We had a system that never failed. Peter Capo had run the store for as far back as I can remember. He was a fat little stump of a man who spoke with a heavy accent. His religion must have frowned on shaving because he seldom did. He was filthy as a pet pig. He wore the same dirty apron all the time. He had a full set of dentures that must have been fitted for his apron pocket because they were seldom in his mouth.

He didn't like the young men in the neighborhood nor did he allow them in his establishment. He thought of them as hoodlums whose mouths should be washed out with soap.

Placing his hand on my shoulder, he'd say, "They are not like you and your friends, Joshua. You all don't cuss or steal from me."

Peter Capo may not have liked the young boys in the area, but he couldn't keep his eyes off the young girls. When no customers were in the store, he'd pull out a box of pornographic pictures. With a twinkle in his eyes and drooling, he'd talk as if he had dated each woman intimately. While viewing photos and placing his hand under his apron, the conversation would always turn to the girls in the area.

"Joshua," he'd ask excitedly, "Is January, February, or March giving it up?"

Nervously, he'd say, "Tell me all about it."

First, the only thing the girls gave me and Dan was advice and what train we could take to find it. But that didn't matter. I would tell big bald-faced lies on the girls. Whoever he wanted to know about now became the slut of the day. While I held Capo captive in the "Virgin Islands" lying on the girls, Dan would steal him blind. The girls, on the other hand, didn't like going to Capo's store alone, because as they put it, 'That man looks at us funny.'

On the way to my birthday party Count and Jerry stopped by Capo's to steal a pack of cigarettes. While Count fabricated stories about the girls, Jerry stole the smokes and for the first time stole a pint of Early Times Whiskey. It wouldn't be the last. The party was on the way we were having a good time eating and dancing. Gladys and Count, who were always teasing one another, were at it again.

"Hey, y'all guess what?" Gladys laughingly yelled out, "Miss Clark put Count out the class because he said, McDonough High School was named after a farmer."

She fell back on the sofa kicking her legs and guffawing. Not to be outdone, Count responded with, "That's alright. Short as you are you'd make a damn good Urologist."

Then Gladys said, "That's the kind of Doctor who delivered you when your mother was pregnant."

On and on it would go. We truly enjoyed one another's' company.

Miss Rita who never socialized with us stuck her head in the room asking that the cake be cut. She wanted to take a slice to a friend along with some chicken and potato salad. The party was about to come to an end when Jerry remembered he had hid the pint of liquor behind the sofa. Retrieving the bottle of Early Times, he placed it on the kitchen table.

Knowing that what we were about to do was wrong, we were filled with unbelievable anticipation. The bottle sat there like the Belle of the Ball, the Grandmaster of the Parade, the Star of the Show and the Main Attraction. Fueled by a rush of adrenaline and doubt, we poured equal amounts of liquor into five glasses.

We raised the glasses high and said, "Friends forever."

The alcohol was strong. It caused us to cough and gag. Still, with trembling hands, we refilled the five glasses.

That drink, for me, was the beginning of a love affair. It became my mistress. When I was with her, she respected me. She made me feel good about myself. She never once called me lazy, dumb or stupid. She made me feel as if I were somebody. The only problem was, I wanted to feel like somebody all the time.

I began to live up to, or down to, Bobby's expectations. He said I was stupid. He was right. I spent most of my time on the street. He said I was dumb. Right again. I was failing in school. He said I didn't have the sense I was born with. Guess what? I was acting like a moron. And, he said I'd never be shit. How right can one man be? I was going down the sewer headfirst. My mother was constantly talking to me about my destructive behavior. I'd promise her to do better only to do worse. She never yelled at me. She spoke hardly above a whisper. She didn't scream or call me names or cuss. She always left me feeling guilty. I had no defense for her. She spent a tremendous amount of time defending me.

I was beginning to spend a lot of time by Liz's house. Since I was doing so poorly in class, Liz felt I would benefit from studying with her after school. She was convinced I had a chance to graduate. I found Liz easy to talk to. I knew she was smart. That was a given. After all, she had the highest-grade point average in school. She was fascinating and would haunt my reverie for years.

While walking home from school with her, I began to learn a lot of little things about her I didn't know. I discovered that she was a mental warehouse of insignificant information.

Out of the blue, she'd say, "Joshua, did you know", and she'd start grinning, "the Nobel Peace Prize depicts three naked men with their hands on each other's shoulders?"

"Are you kidding me?" I'd ask in disbelief.

"No, it's true. And glass doesn't wear out. Guess what else? Jiffy is actually a unit of time and Mona Lisa has no eyebrows."

Then as if she had just thought of something truly amazing, she'd stop walking, look at me excitedly and asked, "What is the most popular name in the world?"

"Everyone knows the answer to that." I said smiling, "It's Joshua."

"No, no, no my brown eyed handsome friend." She exclaimed. "It's Muhammad." She'd nudge me, and we'd continued walking.

18

Elizabeth was very friendly and extremely popular. She was tall and slender. Her brown eyes, while dancing, hid a pain that ran deep. She wore her hair cut short.

Miss Rita would tease saying, "You'd better let your hair grow, or one of those funny girls will ask you for a date."

All the guys at school didn't care how she wore her hair. She had the entire package. I began looking forward to our walks and study time together. By observing and listening to Liz's cares and woes, I got a good read on her. While she projected an air of confidence, in reality, she was conflicted, insecure, vulnerable and confused. I didn't know why but emotionally Liz had a serious problem.

CHAPTER 4

Just when Rita thought the melancholy and pensive moods were over the moods would resurface. It had been awhile, but those moments of intense sadness had returned. Elizabeth entered Rita's room and stood by the side of the bed. She was trembling and afraid.

She said, "Momma, may I..." before she could complete the question Rita patted the bed inviting her to lie down.

Liz slid into the bed and snuggled close to her mother. She put her arms around her child and held her close.

Miss Rita was well-aware that the neighbors looked down their noses at her. They couldn't understand why she would allow teenagers to fraternize at her home unsupervised. They'd ask themselves, why did she allow kids a free run of her house? They never questioned Rita. Her manner and disposition held them at a distance. By no extension of charity could Rita be regarded as a saint. She was well acquainted with the laws of life. She refused to apologize for her lot. She felt that it was the Lord's job to judge her.

Rita wasn't naive, unpretentious, transparent, or gullible. After her mother had died of an overdose, she moved in with her aunt and her common-law husband. She was ten years old. She felt uncomfortable being near him because he was always trying to touch her in forbidden places.

Soon after reaching puberty, she learned a man's brain did not rest

20

between his ears but resided elsewhere. At the age of fifteen, she became sexually active.

When she fell in love with Charles Webster, she was seventeen years old. He was twenty-three. Five months into the relationship she became pregnant. It was then she learned he was married. She couldn't believe that she had been that blind. Sitting in a worn and tattered chair; in a two-bit motel, she felt as alone and frightened as the roach she observed scurrying around the squalid floor seeking safety.

Charles' first reaction was one of suspicion, followed by doubt, and distrust. As he hurriedly stepped into his pants, through tear filled eyes she expressed her love for him. His only words of support were, "How could you be so fucking careless?"

More concerned with finding his shoe than in the matter at hand, said with a cutting edge to his voice, "I didn't bargain for all this fucking shit."

And in the very next breath shouted, " I hope you're not trying to pawn it off on me. I wasn't born yesterday. You need to get rid of it." He growled.

As he walked out of the two-bit motel he slammed the door, that was the last time Rita saw or heard from Charles Webster. That was sixteen years ago. He and his family moved to Albany, New York. With the help of Mr. Izalla, an elder at New Haven Baptist Church, Rita made it through her pregnancy. With assistance from Miss Ernestine Jackson, down at the welfare department, she got a job at a downtown department store. She's been employed there since before Elizabeth's birth.

Rita's gut feelings were the young people that frequented her house were decent and respectable. She had no need for undue worry. In fact, she was happy and delighted they were there because without warning Elizabeth would be overcome with strong feelings of sadness and mood swings. Not knowing who or where her father was haunted her. She could not process why he abandoned her. Why he never tried to see her, and finally, why he didn't love her. Her deep-seated conviction was that if her own father didn't love her how could anyone else love her. Rita believed that having Liz's friends around would keep Liz from focusing on herself. The last thing she wanted was for her child to sink into a deep depression. As far as what the neighbors thought, her position was simple; she'd be bending over — because it makes kissing easy.

Lying in the bed holding Elizabeth in her arms, she could hear her whimpering. At these moments, seeing Elizabeth in such distress and discomfort, it was all Rita could do to hold on to her own emotions. For the last thing, she wanted was to project her feelings onto her child. Rita braced herself for the moment of truth was near. She had never known it to fail.

Then with a heavy sigh Liz flinched and asked the one question she always wanted to know the most about. "Momma, please tell me about my father?"

And there, in the darkness, holding her daughter in her arms she'd tell her about her father. She'd tell Elizabeth only what she thought she emotionally could process. In time, all her heart-breaking inquiries would be satisfied. She'd learn that the flaw was not in her character, but elsewhere.

In time, she'd learn to accept life on life's terms — with, or without her father's love. No matter how strong Rita pretended to be, one thing always caused her to fall apart, during those precious moments Elizabeth never called her Rita — she called her Momma.

As Liz and I entered the apartment, we immediately began studying for a history exam. Sitting next to me on the sofa, she smelled like the first day of spring. She had a pair of green shorts on with a yellow blouse tied in a knot under her rib cage. She wore open-toe sandals, and her legs were crossed at the ankles. The history book was open on her lap. She was reading out loud for her benefit as well as mine.

"Isabella was abused by several masters as a young woman. Isabella said she saw visions and heard the voice of God. As a woman of God, she traveled throughout the North speaking against slavery. Isabella was her birth name, but Sojourner Truth was her name of fame."

Looking at me and smiling Liz said, "You're not paying attention. You haven't heard a word I said."

Pushing me playfully she yelled, "I'm talking to you, Joshua."

Impulsively I placed my hand on her thigh. She did not move. Her skin was smooth as oil. I felt welcome. Slowly and tentatively I fondled her breast. She rose from the sofa and stood by the open window. Silence invaded the room. The only sounds heard were those radiating from the courtyard.

Without looking at me, she said, "I think you'd better go." I was anchored in the moment and could not move. Standing by the window with her arms folded and her back to me she was the epitome of female beauty. I could not take my eyes off her. She was exquisite. She was impressive. She was living poetry standing before me. Where had I been? It was like seeing her for the first time.

Unable to endure the silence any longer I said, "Elizabeth, I..."

Before I could say another word, I heard, "Joshua, please go."

What's the big deal, some might ask? All you did Joshua was touch the girl's thigh. My response to that is this: A touch can mean more to one person than another. Because of that touch I began to realize that Adam was doomed from the start. The second Eve placed his hand on her heart all bets were off. Because of that touch I came to know that while Samson may have been a man of barbaric fury and terrifying strength, in the arms of Delilah he was only as strong as the weakest man. In time, I would learn to forgive Marc Anthony for deserting his army in the heat of battle to return to the comfort of Cleopatra. And, in a few years, I would understand the true meaning of the song "Ebb Tide".

As I walked down the stairs from Elizabeth's apartment, in the next unit, someone was playing a song by the Ink Spots. I could hear them singing:

"Two lips must consist,
And do more to be kissed,
Or they'll never know what love can do..."

CHAPTER 5

From day one, Rodney was Bobby's pride and joy. My mother didn't want a junior in the family. But, Bobby insisted, and against her better judgment, she named him Robert Anthony Lange, Jr. Rodney was his nickname. There were four children in the family, but in Bobby's heart, there was room enough for only one — Rodney. From a very early age, Rodney knew he was favored. As a child, he was unruly and difficult to manage.

When our mother would punish him because of his behavior he'd scream, "I'm going to tell my Daddy!"

And Bobby would question the necessity of the penance. It mattered little what my mother said or did. She could not get Bobby to see or understand that by upholding Rodney's actions and undermining hers he was doing the child a grave injustice and would live to regret it. She'd explain that a house divided could not stand. Her words fell on deaf ears.

When Rodney would interact with his classmates he was bossy, selfish and domineering. He would bully the weaker kids into doing things his way. If he couldn't get his way by manipulative measures, he'd use might. There were no limits to which Rodney would go to further his personal agenda as he grew older. His wishes, his wants and his desires came first. Because of the lack of discipline in his life and the excessive attention Bobby lavished on him, he became hopelessly self-absorbed and self-centered.

In Rodney's mind rules did not apply to him. As Rodney became a man, the indulgent attitude he presented to his peers and classmates carried over into his adult life. His destructive behavior became part of his social and business world. His philosophy was, do unto others before they do unto you.

Bobby could not be convinced to dispense any type of discipline towards Rodney. Whenever Mira would approach the subject, Bobby would hold his hand above his head and scream, "He's a boy. I'm raising him to be a man, not some kind of Jinny Woman."

And as he'd storm off he'd shout, "Damn it to hell! Stop vexing me, Mira!"

She would try to reach Bobby by quoting passages from the Bible. She'd read, "The surest way to discourage children is to treat them unjustly and unfairly. And one of the surest ways to be unjust is by practicing favoritism."

She explained to him that Isaac and Rebekah each had favorite children. Isaac loved Esau, but Rebekah loved Jacob. This resulted in such strife and deceit that Esau sought to kill Jacob and Jacob had to flee his home. When she had finished, she waited patiently for a response.

Disgusted and aggravated he'd shake his head from side to side and with a puzzled look ask, "What the hell does that have to do with me?" He'd take the sports section from the newspaper and go into the bathroom.

The young lady's name was Irene Hawkins. She was from a middle-class family who resided on Bayou Road. Irene was a petite, attractive, sweet, mild mannered young woman. She was introverted and extremely shy. Soon after she and Rodney began dating, she became pregnant. After waiting 4 months for Rodney to tell our parents about the pregnancy and he couldn't find the courage, she took matters into her own hands and informed the family. Shortly thereafter, they were married. They rented a room, kitchen and bath on Dumaine and Tonti Street.

Upon hearing the news from Irene, my mother was brokenhearted. She sat in the backyard swing crying. They were just children she thought and their futures were in jeopardy. Knowing how irresponsible Rodney was, her heart went out to Irene. She wiped the tears from her eyes and placed the problem in the hands of the Lord.

When the situation was explained to Bobby, he began bragging to the men in the neighborhood. With his chest poked out, he'd grin and say, "My boy ain't no child no more. He has dropped his anchor in the sea of love. I'm here to tell ya my son is a man. He's a man I tell ya."

Because he was Mr. Bobby, the men smiled in agreement. Bobby had been working for Mr. Frank for many years. He knew that he owned a building on St. Bernard Avenue and Tremain Street. Since the building was located in a predominantly colored neighborhood, Bobby thought it would be an ideal spot for Rodney to run a vegetable, fruit and shoeshine stand. After talking it over, Mr. Frank gave his blessings. Rodney went into business.

In a little or no time, he was doing exceptionally well. To my Mother and Sisters' delight Rodney proved good at operating the business. He enjoyed maintaining the stand. He derived a great deal of pleasure rearranging the fruit after every sale. He worked overtime keeping the produce looking fresh and appetizing but, more than anything else, he enjoyed short changing the customers.

Rodney and his enterprise became a common fixture on the Avenue.

Years later, Mr. Frank put the corner up for sale. Bobby bought it and opened the Café. Rodney became the manager of the eatery and was in seventh heaven.

A few months after Irene gave birth to a beautiful girl, she visited momma unexpectedly. After fixing Irene a glass of Lemonade and a piece of Apple Pie, Momma took off her apron and sat across from her. Rubbing her finger around the edge of the glass, Irene began by apologizing. Her voice cracked as she spoke. She explained how awful she felt for having to bring such a distasteful matter into her home and, please forgive her.

Choosing her words very carefully she continued. "Mrs. Lange, I'm here asking you and Mr. Lange to speak to Rodney."

Fighting back the tears she expressed, "Rodney had not been paying the rent on time. He comes in all hours of the night and some nights he doesn't come home at all."

She paused a moment and said, "He slaps and cusses me sometimes. I can't talk to him anymore without him getting angry. I just don't know what to do."

"Abuse does not stop like that." She explained, snapping her fingers. "If he hit you once, there's a good chance he'll hit you again."

Holding her hand, momma told her that she and her daughter could not continue to live under those conditions. She advised Irene to think about separating awhile until they could work things out.

With her head down gazing at the floor, she said, "Mrs. Lange I'm pregnant again. I love Rodney. I don't want to leave him. I just want him to be the man I know he can be."

My mother rose from the table feeling a rage brewing in her heart. She took a face cloth from the closet and dampened it. She gently wiped Irene's face. Holding her to her bosom she assured her she and Bobby certainly would talk to Rodney.

With her arms around Irene and swaying gently, she told her she was not alone. "Don't ever forget that I'm always here. You're family."

Because of the urgency of the matter, Momma could not put off discussing such an important issue with Bobby. Later that evening after supper, she asked him to accompany her to the backyard swing. Not knowing what was on her mind, he thought it best to do as requested. He cursed under his breath as he felt a slight chill pass through his body.

Bobby knew the day he met Mira that there was something peculiar about her. It was something about her eyes and her manner that he found attractive — that was when they first met and began dating. As the years rolled by that same demeanor and those same eyes began to cause him to feel uneasy and bothered. There were times when a cold flash would rush through his body chilling him to the bone, especially when Mira was upset with him. My mother's name was Mira Marie Gardener-Lange. She was an impressive woman who stood about five-seven. She was beautiful, mesmerizing, and charismatic. She would have been described as a high-yellow Negro woman in her childbearing years capable of house, field or any type of work deemed necessary.

If Solomon was the wisest man, my mother had to be the wisest woman. If you ask me, I'd say she was more prudent than Solomon. She was wise enough not to do half the ungodly things he did. She was a walking, talking proverb.

She often could be heard saying, "Keep your eyes on the one who brings bad news."

"If you love the cow, you had better love the calf." "The devil is in the details."

And, "The Lord will make a way — If you only believe."

The neighbors all thought she was gifted. Bobby thought she was full of shit. Gifted or not, if the devil resided within you, her gift was of little use.

Bobby sat in the swing rocking slowly. He knew something heavy was on her mind because he had those damn chills. He sat there uneasily wishing she'd get this over. Mira stood before him trying to organize her thoughts. She decided not to mention anything about how he had failed to discipline Rodney. She knew to do so would only make him angry and defensive. To prevent that, she would only discuss the present set of circumstances. Slowly and deliberately, she related what had taken place during Irene's visit. She left nothing out. She explained how hurt and alone Irene felt and how hard it was for her to ask the two of them to intervene.

She concluded by asking, "How do you think we should proceed?"

Motionlessly he sat. He seemed more interested in the bees pollinating the Azaleas than in what had just transpired. He scratched his head and began patting his foot.

Leaning back in the swing he asked matter-of-factly, "Are you crazy? Are-you-crazy? If you think for one second, I'm going to interfere in Rodney's personal business, you have flipped your lid."

Raising his voice he continued, "No man has the right to tell another man how to run his affairs. Rodney is a man. When are you going to realize that? And, if you think I'm going to tell him how to treat his woman, you're crazier than I thought."

By now, Bobby was nervous and extremely irritated. He asked angrily, "Why are you siding with that girl instead of your own blood? The trouble with you is you don't know a damn thing about raising a boy. And, I'll tell ya another thing, " he shouted, "Joshua will never be the man Rodney is. You can bet your bottom dollar on that."

Mira could not believe what she heard and witnessed. This arrogant display of ignorance and hostility was beyond all comprehension. She did not know the man sitting in the swing. He was not the same man she had been willing to follow to the ends of the earth. He was not the man who could make her eyes twinkle and her heart sing. He was not the man who had the power to make her soul take flight and, he was not the man who had awakened feelings within her she had never known.

She was forced with the sad realization that Bobby was becoming like those men he worked for... Mr. Frank and his associates. She accepted the fact that birds of a feather flock together and we gravitate toward our own.

He had become cold, cruel, insensitive and heartless. He was like them. It was obvious to Mira that Frank had a tremendous amount of influence over Bobby. So much so that it was getting to the point where he couldn't urinate without asking Frank which hand he should use to unzip his pants.

Mira could not get through to Bobby. He was unreachable. His mind was like that tree they sing about. It was planted by the river and would not concede. He sat swinging back and forth and humming. He felt another chill and cursed under his breath. Realizing he was lost, instead of anger, she felt pity for him for he was unable to see what fate awaited. When she began to speak, she was composed, and her voice was soft and controlled. Her words seemed to resonate from a place yet to be; a station far away in a distance land.

Putting her hands in her apron pocket, and in a foreboding voice said, "Robert, write this on your heart. Just as the eagle rules the sky and the sun sets in the west, you'll pay dearly for what you're doing to Rodney."

With a sigh, she continued, "Hear every word I say Robert, and if you are wise you'd take heed. The very eyes with which you cast upon Rodney with favor will be the same eyes that will view him, one day, with a heart filled with hate. Yes, Robert, I said hate. The repulsion you'll experience at the mere sound of his name will eat away at you. You'll awaken to days of pain and heartache only to retire to nights of loneliness and regret. Sorrow and despair will be your constant companions. Rest will evade you and peace and contentment will desert you. You are blind Robert, and refuse to see."

His failure and unwillingness to see the error in his judgment filled her with sorrow and anguish, she softly said, "May God have mercy on you and our misguided child."

She got down on her knees and tenderly whispered. "Please, talk to Rodney. He'll listen to you. I'm begging you. Go to him. Please, please give my child a chance."

Having spent herself and not knowing what else to say or do, with a heavy heart, she slowly walked back to the house. Upon reaching it, she stood in the doorway weeping. She took one long look back at Bobby and gently closed the door.

Bobby sat leisurely swinging back and forth. He couldn't understand or believe the things Mira uttered. She was just like the rest of those so-called Christians. They talk about love on one side of their mouth and hate on the other. He thought to himself, how could she talk about Rodney and hate in the same breath. The way he saw it, this was nothing but a bunch of bullshit. The woman had lost her mind. Yes, that's it, he thought. She was insane.

At that precise moment, a cold chill passed through his body causing him to shiver.

By the time Rodney turned twenty-seven, he and Irene were the parents of two beautiful girls, Savannah and Brooklyn. By now, he gave up the vegetable and fruit stand and was the manager of Bobby's Café and he made sure everyone knew it. Rodney left home on a cold and windy morning and never returned. He saw his children sparingly. Not willing to support them financially, Irene reported him to the State. He was forced to pay twenty-five dollars a week. He never paid a penny more.

CHAPTER 6

As a young girl, my sister Gilda was a tomboy. Her nickname was Miss Johnny Wopp. She hated being called that. While most girls her age were playing hopscotch, and jumping rope, she could be found in the lumberyard riding horses. Gilda was a double threat. She could fight and she enjoyed fighting. She fought girls as well as boys. The gender was of little concern to Gilda. Mrs. Brooks, a good neighbor and friend, was forever telling our mother to have a mother-daughter talk with Gilda.

To which our mother would respond, sweetly, "Everything in time. Let her be."

On her thirteenth birthday, momma bought Gilda a brand-new outfit, a pretty dress, earrings, a purse, and a beautiful pair of shoes with a low heel. After dressing, she was pretty as a prom queen.

Smiling at Gilda's makeover, momma asked, "Now that you are all dolled up, where would you like to go?"

While swinging her purse above her head, and jumping up and down, she exclaimed, "I know. I know. I wanna go to the Rodeo."

Again, our mother sighed deeply and said, "Everything in time. Let her be."

One evening Gilda ran into the house after school very excited. Unable to contain herself, she cried, "Momma, momma, guess what? I'm on the high school football team."

Momma looked at her, all the while thinking how healthy, happy and innocent her little angel was. She slowly raised herself from the rocker, closed the Bible she had been reading, took off her glasses and set them on top of the 'Good Book' extended her arms and invited Gilda saying, "Come here, sweetheart."

She took the football from under her arm. Then she gently removed the oversized helmet from her head. Holding Gilda in her arms, she whispered, "You're so precious, and I love you very, very much."

Gilda softly replied, "I love you, too, momma."

With her arm around Gilda's shoulder, they walked happily to the backyard swing. It was time.

Bobby may have thought Mira was weird and peculiar, but many sought her counsel and cherished her advice. They saw her as a God fearing, strong willed, no nonsense woman, one courageous enough to stand up to Omari Ayo, the High Priest of Voodoo, without flinching. The day he sprinkled Gofer dust on her doorsteps, her reputation in the community was cemented forever.

The Ayo family lived on Annette and Johnson, in a large two- story frame house. Behind giant sized trees and overgrown bushes which hid the house. There was a long cement walkway that ran from an iron gate to a broken quarry tile porch. Candles burned nightly giving the dwelling an ominous, eerie and mysterious presence.

The Ayo family consisted of Omari, his wife Dahlia, and their daughter Rashada. They practiced the religion Voodoo and were well known around the city of New Orleans. On weekends, people of all persuasions would come from various parts of the Parish to participate in the ceremonies, prayers, dancing, and rituals. Many came seeking love potions; others came needing tonics to cure certain ailments. Then there were those who sought to have a hex removed or one assigned. Whatever the reasons, a celebratory crowd, was always present.

The word Voodoo would strike fear in the hearts of many residents in the neighborhood. That was because their knowledge of the religion was limited or misunderstood. Many individuals didn't know Voodoo was never designed to frighten or bring harm to anyone. Europeans, who distrusted anything African, introduced the idea of cruelty.

The chanting and loud drumming would go on until the wee hours of the morning. There were times when it would start on Friday night and continue until Monday morning with few pauses in between. Of course, many of the neighbors found these gatherings to be disruptive, inconsiderate, disorderly, and downright disrespectful. But, because they feared Omari Ayo and what they thought he could do, no one would outwardly complain.

For a handsome fee, Ayo guaranteed his spells for all occasions. For women who were unable to pay for portions or tonics, Ayo, with a gleam in his eyes and a smile, would gladly make other arrangements.

Almost all the kids in the neighborhood knew better than to call Gilda 'Miss Johnny Wopp'. She'd fight anyone who dared call her that awful name. Still, some insisted.

While walking home from school one evening with her classmates, Rashada, Ayo's daughter, began teasing Gilda.

She began chanting, "Johnny Wopp, Johnny Wopp, ahoy, ahoy. Johnny Wopp, Johnny Wopp, you should've been a boy."

She ignored Gilda's many requests to cease the name calling. Refusing to comply, Gilda hit her in the face with her lunch pail. With blood gushing from her nose, Rashada began running home. By running, she bled more profusely.

When Gilda related, what had happened, momma decided to pay the Ayo's a visit. She thought it best for Gilda to apologize. Our Mother knew the Ayo's only by reputation and did not relish meeting them, but in her heart, she realized this was the best resolve. She did not condone violence in any form and would decide Gilda's punishment after hearing Rashada's side of the story.

While humming, Ayo took a long swig of gin from the bottle. As he swallowed, the alcohol burned his throat. He set the bottle on the kitchen counter and continued mixing what his followers thought was Gofer dust. Gofer dust was generally made from graveyard dirt and other elements from the Earth. True believers are convinced it has magical power. Omari's Gofer dust consisted of Baking Powder, Salt, and Red Pepper. The pepper was for color. As he shook the contents to get an even mix, he laughed to think those ignorant sons-of-bitches really thought this shit had power.

He choked and coughed as he took another drink.

People in the community went out of their way to stay in Ayo's good graces. The last thing they wanted to do was to make him angry. They tiptoed around trying to please him. The attention along with the many favors and gifts they lavished on him was due in part to a lack of knowledge and fear. Ayo was aware of this and used it to full advantage.

He was run out of Opelousas, Louisiana for selling so called Love Potions that did not produce the desired results. When it was discovered, he was nothing but a con-man with a fake accent he and his family had to flee.

An elderly Cajun man had been having trouble maintaining "Lead in his pencil". Tired and frustrated by the lack of potency, he sought Ayo's help. He purchased love potion after love potion; none produced the desired result. Ayo assured him that if he were patient, took the love portions, sat in the Sun, sang love songs to the Moon, did Junny-flips, and danced in the rain, he'd be fine. Meanwhile, his consultation fees kept increasing.

After a period of time, the poor soul began to realize that Ayo was stringing him along. Those so-called Love Potions were not going to revitalize 'Mr. Happy'. Upset and angry, he went looking for Ayo with a pitchfork. When word reached Ayo that he was about to become a batch of crackling, he knew the jig was up.

He hurriedly picked up his wife, from the seafood plant where she was employed, his daughter from school, and like thieves in the night they fled to New Orleans.

Arriving in the Crescent City, his fake accent became more pronounced. He bought a wig consisting of dreads, wore beads and dressed in predominantly African attire.

He then informed everyone that he was from Jamaica. He began selling oils, ointments, and potions. As soon as people began to flock to his residence he proclaimed himself the high Priest of Voodoo.

In little or no time, his reputation began to spread, and people began to worship him. He was revered, and he wallowed in the adulation. Rose petals were dropped on his lawn. Notes were pasted on his fence, and favors of all kind were requested. Dolls with names attached were thrown on his porch, and candles of all shapes and sizes were left burning on a makeshift altar in front of his residence.

Ayo found the attention intoxicating and addictive. He couldn't get enough. His ego was as big as an elephant's ass. Everyone kissed the ground he walked on. Everyone that is, except Bobby Lange or as Ayo referred to him, "That motherfucker over on Pauger Street."

Ayo was offended and insulted because Bobby had never acknowledged his presence in the community. He was sick and tired of hearing Bobby's name mentioned. "Call Mr. Bobby, he can do this. He can do that. Mr. Bobby said — Mr. Bobby did — "

"Fuck that nigger. He ain't shit." Ayo thought as he poured another drink.

Ayo had never met Bobby face to face. He had only seen him from a distance. He didn't like Bobby and didn't cotton to the idea of Bobby going out of his way to get criminals released from jail. The nigger must be fucking crazy, he reasoned. He couldn't understand why Bobby wouldn't listen to the Ministers when they begged him to discontinue assisting those no count ass hoodlums.

Ayo resented how those young outlaws would get full of weed and alcohol, and walk past his residence shouting obscenities. "Mr. Zulu, throw something over the fence to make my dick

hard. Hey mon, how much is bullshit selling for today?"

While urinating on a tree on the sidewalk, one would yell, "Oh, Boogy Mon, come take a look at my Mo-Jo stick." They would do an imitation African dance while singing, and then move on.

The way Ayo saw it; those weed-headed bastards had no respect for themselves or anyone else. And as far as he was concerned, those niggers could rot in jail — fuck'em. Taking another drink from the bottle of gin, he began packing the Gofer

Dust for transportation. He was obsessed with Bobby. As he put it, "That nigger was too big for his britches. He had to be cut down to size" — and he had a plan.

His plan was simple. He'd begin with Mira, or as he called her, that nigger's wife, Mora, Moro, Mira or whatever her fucking name was. He was not pleased at all that Mira was not receptive to him and his wife. Who in the world does she think she is — Queen Ann or somebody? She was too into herself in his opinion.

While grabbing his crotch and laughing he was convinced Mira, Mora, or whoever, would melt like butter once she had been introduced to his magic wand. With his hand inside his trousers, he couldn't wait to get her under his spell. After all, he figured she was just another whore with sophistication.

When Ayo would run into Mira at PTA meetings, the Supermarket or Civic outings, she'd speak in passing, but she'd never stop to chat. What is it? My wife and I are dog droppings or something. He found her reserve to be downright objectionable, and her uppity manner and disposition infuriated him. Another thing that nagged at him was no one could be as real, genuine, and wise as everyone said she was. The way he saw it, she was just another stuck-up high yellow bitch.

One thing Ayo could not deny, Mira was a fine woman. Thinking about what it would be like making love to her, caused a stirring in his pants. He wondered what in the world did a nigger the likes of Bobby Lange do to get a woman with all that ass — and class. Whenever he'd see Mira, his fantasies would take flight. His eyes would lock in on her shapely legs, the curve of her hips, her beautiful breasts that seemed to stand at attention, her velvet skin, and how her buttocks resembled pistons as she walked. He'd pawn his soul to get next to her.

Many women had come to Ayo in good faith, troubled, and seeking guidance. Realizing how frightened and vulnerable they were, he'd taken advantage of them. They'd become confused, disconcerted, and befuddled. Not understanding the complexities of their emotions, they'd find themselves totally dependent on him, and he'd manipulate them like puppets. He couldn't wait until he had Mira under such a spell. He'd have her eating out of his hands and jumping through hoops. He had no way of getting close to the Lange family, but since Gilda and Rashada had an altercation, the time had presented itself.

He drank the last of the gin and discarded the bottle. As he stumbled around the kitchen, he began singing. He picked up the phone and called his cronies. They all knew the routine well. Come in full dress, put on a good show, and get paid well.

Ayo dressed hurriedly. He put on his multi-colored floor length gown. Tied his Do-rag around his head to hold his dreads in place and put on his fake gold bracelets. He painted his face with black grease paint and streaked it with white lines. Admiring himself in the full-length mirror, he laughed out loud. His yellow teeth stood out against the black facial paint. His ominous appearance, he thought, made it easy to understand why those simple-minded niggers trembled at the sight of him.

In his backyard, where the rituals were held, he took the five-foot harmless snake out of its tank. Smiling at the reptile and talking to it as if it were a baby, he draped it around his shoulders. After today, he said to the snake that bastard Bobby Lange and his entire fucking family will kiss my ass to get along. He picked up his Mo-Jo stick and wobbled out of the yard. He waited on the porch for his cronies to arrive.

Mira tapped on the bathroom door encouraging Gilda to hurry. She wanted to resolve this matter regarding Rashada so she could return and finish cooking. She turned off the stove. She didn't think it would take long to settle. Walking through the house with an urgency and Gilda on her heels, she paused in the foyer. She did a quick once over in the mirror. Satisfied, she opened the door to exit. She was surprised and amazed at the sight that greeted her. Ayo and twenty or so of his people were standing in the street facing her home. For a moment, she thought they would be great in an African movie. She could not fathom what was going on — drums began a powerful rhythmic beat. The dancers followed in time.

They were clapping and chanting. As the tempo increased, so did the excitement and furor of the dancers. The women swished their skirts, jumped, and leaped wildly as if caught in a frenzy.

The women were dressed in white blouses and oversized outfits. Their braids were laced with a variety of beads while large earrings dangled from each ear. Bracelets complimented the ankles of their shoeless feet. The men were scantily clad with grass skirts, grease paint, beads and dreads. Each carried a Mo-Jo stick, snake, or drum. They were loud, colorful, and dramatic. The drums and chanting could be heard blocks away.

To Ayo's delight, the crowd was gathering in the street. He smiled for he knew this was good for business. The crowd was familiar with Omari Ayo and his voodoo. They were aware that when he and his band of believers took to the street in full regalia, a serious hex was about to be assigned to someone or to someone's entire family.

My mother had heard that when Ayo and his people confronted someone in this fashion it was because the spirits were offended.

"These people must be kidding," she thought. "Don't they have better things to do?"

She wondered if this had anything to do with Gilda. Gilda was instructed to remain in the doorway as she approached Omari Ayo in the middle of the street. The chanting and drumming was deafening. The snakes, mode-of-dress, dancing, and drumming were all designed to intimidate. Ayo relied on a person's belief system, without that he could do nothing.

Ayo raised his Mo-Jo stick and silence fell over the gathering. He made a sign of some kind and yelled something unintelligible.

A few chosen members began frantically running around Mira's house sprinkling Gofer Dust. It was placed in doorways, sills, an literally on the doorsteps. The spectators didn't dare venture to close for fear of getting Gofer Dust on their person. To believers the dust would cause a powerful hex that only the high priest could eradicate. The mere thought terrorized them. They began praying that no long-term misfortune would befall a nice lady like Mrs. Lange or her family.

Mira stood before Omari Ayo perplexed and extremely irritated at the spectacle unfolding before her. She approached him with utter disbelief. He must be deranged she thought. As she neared him, she felt the negative vibrations and in his blood shot eyes, she saw what no one else had ever seen — fear. Suddenly, Omari Ayo was afraid of this woman. Ayo had never been this close to Mira. He was immediately troubled and worried. He found something about her presence extremely disturbing. Try as he may, he could not meet her gaze. He knew as his heart began to palpitate that she was not looking at him, but through him. Her eyes were hypnotizing like those of a wild undomesticated animal, one that could see, smell and sense, one's innermost fears. He began to quiver trying to conceal what he knew to her was obvious.

Ayo was aware of one thing, although it had worked for many years; his con was ineffective this afternoon. Having dispensed the Gofer Dust, his aids returned to their stations. They were accustomed to Ayo's being more vocal and animated. Today, they found him to be confused, troubled, and uncertain. Ayo began to perspire excessively. The black and white paint began to blend together. He looked ridiculous and almost humorous. He was nervous and wished he had another drink. His mission now became one of saving face. He couldn't allow this woman to prove him a fraud.

Clearing his throat and trembling, he stepped closer to Mira. He could not rid his brain of how gorgeous a woman she was. How he wished she were this close to him under different circumstances. He spoke softly. He couldn't risk his followers hearing the irresolution and weakness in his voice. He couldn't afford having them witness how ill equipped and spineless he really was. Pointing to Gilda in the doorway with his Mo-Jo stick he could feel himself trembling.

In a feeble voice, he uttered, "That child is possessed by evil spirits."

His mouth was dry as cotton. The salt from his sweat began burning his eyes. "She assaulted an innocent child unprovoked."

Raising his voice trying to show control, stated, "The spirits must be satisfied."

A loud chant went up followed by a short rhythmic drumbeat. Finding a parcel of courage, he held his Mo-Jo stick high and shouted meekly, "She must be punished. The Gods are angry."

The chanting began again and stopped.

Momma couldn't believe what she heard. The alcohol he reeked of had evidently driven him mad. She had wanted to discuss this in a civil manner, but this idiot masquerading as a clown had taken it to another level.

She took a deep breath and looking at his sweaty face said tersely, "I'm sorry the spirits are angry. Give them a nip of what you've been consuming and I'm sure that will pacify them."

His eyes widened, and his heart began to pound. No one had ever spoken to him so disrespectfully. He opened his mouth to speak, thinking better of it, said nothing.

My mother pointed her finger and in a commanding voice said, "If you never understand another thing in life, understand this. You are not to say, or do anything to my daughter. Not today. Not tomorrow. Not ever. Do you understand me?"

She could smell the booze and the awful scent of the grease paint. She was ashamed of what she was about to say.

Spitting the words out like fire, she whispered. "I'm sure you've heard of the people Mr. Lange works for. They are a lot like you. And like you they deal in powder."

"The difference is," she said frowning, "they use gun powder.

Like you, they are known to cast a spell or two, the problem is their spells last for all eternity."

Stepping back and placing her hands on her hips she took a deep breath. Measuring her words, she said harshly, "As final as death is, I assure you, put your hands on my child and you'll prefer death by their hands instead of mine."

Omari Ayo was standing like a deer caught in the headlights of an automobile. He had completely underestimated the strength and depth of this woman. Her conviction and resolve was the likes of which he had never seen. He was defeated with no honorable way out.

Mira stared at this poor excuse of a human being. He was more pitied than scorned. He was nothing more than a two-bit con- man that profited from the fears of others. He had no conscience; therefore, remorse was foreign to him.

His undoing was he had mistakenly bought into all the stories that circulated about Mira in the community. There were those who sincerely believed that Mira had the power to see into the future, heal the sick, and feared nothing or no one. In the process, he had become a victim of his own belief system.

Without a doubt, Mira was a prudent woman; wisdom personified. She read what a Chinese General once said, "Build your enemy a Golden Bridge." Whenever possible give your enemy a way out and allow him a chance to maintain his dignity and honor.

Sensing Ayo didn't know how to extricate himself from this predicament, against her better judgment, she decided to help him save face.

In a controlled voice, she whispered, "Do as I say. Hold your stick above your head and shout: All is well. All is forgiven. All has been rectified. The spirits are pleased."

In a trembling voice, he did as instructed.

As the chanting and drumming started, Ayo stood before Mira sweating and confused.

Still unable to meet her gaze, said in a voice filled with spite,

"You are a high-yellow bitch from the bowels of Hell. You are the Devil himself."

With her arms crossed, she smiled but said nothing.

After Ayo and his band of followers departed Momma walked down the alley to get a broom. When she returned to sweep the Gofer Dust off the steps, Gilda had taken her finger and written in the powder... I hate school.

When Bobby was told that the voodoo people from Annette

Street had paraded, he simply asked, "What's that fraudulent asshole up to?" Without waiting for an answer, he picked-up the newspaper and headed for the backyard swing.

In the following years, Ayo's reputation began to spread like ants on a sugar cube. His activities, and the successful sales of his potions forced him to seek larger accommodations. He moved out of the neighborhood and into the French Quarter. Before long, Omari Ayo was famous. From as far as Europe people came to take part in his rituals and sessions. The sale of his oils, ointments, and potions, which were sold worldwide; made Omari Ayo a wealthy man.

CHAPTER 7

Having discovered alcohol, I began drinking a little and missing school a lot. My buddies were indulging a bit but, Dan and I began running wild. We couldn't get enough of the street.

I may have missed school a day or two, but I couldn't miss working at 'The Place'. Being there was never a walk in the park. I had to contend with that lunatic Bobby and his darling son, Rodney, and that was never an easy row to hoe. Bobby always seemed sad. It was as if he were pulling the world around his waist by a chain. Even Bobby's laughter seemed dismal, that is, when he allowed himself to be amused. Most of the time, you could find him ranting and raving like a mad dog. Whatever his problem was, I certainly couldn't spell it. When I'd report to 'The Place' to do my penance, I kept to myself. I spoke only when spoken to. I'd wash my pots, dishes, and pans. I would sail far, far away on an ocean of soapsuds, and I would dream. Unhealthy dreams, but dreams none the less. It was a sin the things I wanted to do to Bobby.

Rodney, on the other hand, couldn't stop laughing. He found everything about me to be hilarious. I never knew I was really funny. He never knew how much I wanted and needed his friendship. I held out hope after hope that one day we'd act like brothers. I wish I could have said to my buddies, "My brother and I went to a basketball game." "My brother is teaching me to drive, or my brother and I went fishing."

We could have learned a lot from each other. For unexplained reasons, it was not to be. He treated me the same, as Bobby did, like a worn-out shoe. He hit me only once. I'm ashamed to tell you what I did, but he never put his hands on me again. If I did something he didn't appreciate, he'd tell Bobby, and Bobby would come down on me like a ton of bricks.

My sister, Melanie, was the youngest girl in the family. She was like the wind, a free spirit. She was one of those individuals you meet now and then whom everyone can get along with. Her heart was twice the size of Alaska, and if Alaska is doubled the size of Texas, it goes without saying she had heart. There wasn't a selfish bone in her body. She was kind, loving, compassionate and all the good stuff. She was intelligent and analytical. While I was too young to understand what she was talking about it didn't matter, it sounded like sweet music to my ears.

Of all the instruments, she could have played in the school band, she chose the drum. Looking back, I suppose she wanted

to set the beat to which she'd march. Melanie lived her life by the Golden Rule. She practiced doing unto others, as she'd have them do unto her. She loved and respected her family dearly. She even had the ability to make Bobby smile now and then. Smile. Not laugh. She was only human, not a miracle worker.

She and Gilda were exceedingly close. Our mother's love guided and directed her. It provided her with a sense of belonging and real worth. Because she was loved, she learned to love and respect others.

The young man's name was Roy Lee Jordan. He was engaging and charismatic. In an offbeat sort of way, the girls found him handsome. Standing at six-two he was the color of a ripe plum. He weighed about two hundred pounds and walked with a limp. The limp was due to a compound fracture he suffered jumping off the back of a moving truck as a youngster.

As a child, Roy Lee was bad news. When in grade school, he'd pick on the other kids. He'd take their lunch, their lunch money, their skates, or anything else worth taking. By the time he entered high school, he had learned how to shoplift from the department stores. Stealing and strong-arming became a way of life. Besides beating and teasing the weaker boys, he'd subject them to a wide range of degradations and abuses. By the tenth grade, his education was complete. He dropped out of school.

He was aggressive and violent. He showed no signs of guilt or remorse. He felt his violent acts and whatever he did was justified. Because of his behavior and the petty crimes, he committed, he'd find himself in the parish jail. The maximum time he'd serve was six months. While serving one such sentence, Roy Lee was processed with a young man named Oscar Lewis. Oscar had delicate features and was considered good looking. He was small in stature and to Roy Lee's delight, fragile and afraid. He smiled knowing the boys on the tier would be happy to see a pretty little thing like Oscar.

A 'fish' or 'fresh meat' as new inmates are referred to is always welcomed by a perverted group of convicts. A stay in prison is more tolerable if you associate yourself with a gang, it's almost impossible to survive without being affiliated or connected — no man is an island. This was a totally new experience for Oscar. He had never been to jail. He was a fish out of water. He was not wise to this way of life. And, if the truth were told, he shouldn't have been there. He was charged in an automobile accident that was not his fault. The public defender was more concerned with maintaining his personal drug habit and was not adequately prepared to defend Oscar. Consequently, he was given six months to serve.

As Roy Lee and Oscar entered the cellblock, the catcalls and whistling began. Roy Lee was well known by the State and had run the street with most of the inmates. He was not a 'fish', and he was nobody's "fresh meat".

"Welcome home, Roy Lee", they began yelling, "Yo bed is ready, Sir." Followed by loud laughter, "What took ya so long ta come home?"

"We is sure glad ta see ya."

"Where do ya want yo mail delivered?"

"Would ya like a wake up call, Sir?" That and more was heard above the noise.

At the sight of Oscar, they began to go wild screaming, stomping and yelling in unison, "She's mine. She's mine. She's mine."

One deep voiced inmate cried out, "My pride and joy — look at the butt on dat boy!"

Agreement rang throughout the tier. Greetings of all kinds were directed at Oscar "I love ya, girl."

"Come to daddy ya sexy thing."

And, "Da Lord is my Shepord and I sees what I want."

It was loud and seemed as if the screams, clanging, and taunts would never end. Oscar would not last a night in this animalistic environment. As they said, he was fresh meat, and animals love meat.

Never in his life had Oscar been so frightened, alone, helpless, and defenseless. Whatever problems he had encountered in the past, help was always in reach. Here, he was on his own, nowhere, and no one to turn to. He was a drowning man in an ocean of fear and despair. He felt hopeless and desperate. If he was raped, and most likely, he would be, disclosure to his delicate psyche would be worse than the crime. He would never be able to face Ramona again should that happen.

Every inmate wanted a piece of Oscar. They began to harass and sweat him at every turn. Each one had a sexual proposition for him to consider.

As they would get near him they'd whisper, "Either it's me fish, or it's everybody. Be mine and I gon protect ya."

Licking his lips and smiling another said, "I'm gon ride dat ass 'till da cows come home."

One inmate with four of his front teeth missing offered, "Ya be nice ta me fish, and I'll be nice ta ya." Winking he added, "Ya know what I mean?"

One burly inmate with a scar running diagonally across his face stood next to Oscar. He raised his shirt exposing a jailhouse shank.

He whispered, "When da lights go out, it will be ma dick or my shank. The choice is yo's sweet thing."

Oscar was filled with horror and frightened beyond words. He began to tremble uncontrollably and became weak. His stomach began to bother him. He became dizzy and thought he would faint. Not being able to defend himself made him feel ashamed and humiliated. Of course, he would try and fight them off, but in the end, he knew they would prevail. With that realization, he felt less than a man. Unbelievable damage was being done to the image he had of himself. Emotionally and psychologically, Oscar was in critical condition. He was a tortured soul.

Trying to use the phone to call his wife Ramona, he had trouble dialing the operator he was shaking so badly, he'd hit two or more numbers at once forcing him to try again. He had difficulty breathing and swallowing. His nervous system was in overdrive.

He couldn't steady himself and his teeth began to clack. Fighting back the tears he was bordering on a break down. Suicide was considered.

Roy Lee had been in and out of prison enough times to be well acquainted with the rules of prison life. He was aware of how the inmates pounced on a helpless 'fish'. They used fear, intimidation, and harassment day-in and day-out until they broke him. He had seen guys on the street who were the neighborhood terror, but behind bars they were reduced to performing wifely duties.

Realizing the time was right, Roy Lee eased next to Oscar. Seeing how traumatized he was, smiled and said, "Relax, I'm ya friend. I'm not like dose freaks. I don't roll dat way."

Roy Lee ran the tier. When he was seen talking to a 'fish', the other inmates knew to back off and not to interfere. His reputation on the street and in prison was well known and respected.

Talking a bit more forcefully and commandingly said, "For twenty dollars a week I can keep dem off ya ass, and guarantee ya safety. Have someone deposit that amount into my prison account each week and ya won't have ta go to the infirmary for stitches.

Can ya handle dat?"

Oscar nodded in the affirmative.

Roy Lee smiled and said, "Dare's da phone fish. Get busy."

Oscar had his wife Ramona to do as instructed. As Roy Lee promised, no one bothered Oscar. He did his time in relative peace.

Melanie was a nurse at East Jefferson Hospital. She also filled in at 'The Place' from time-to-time. She was a substitute who allowed the waitresses and cashiers to have time off. The customers loved her, and she was fond of them. Somehow, she managed to tiptoe around Bobby and was Rodney's two bits change.

While updating the menu one summer day, she met Roy Lee Jordan. She was taken by his personality immediately. She later explained that she was attracted to his charm, confidence, and good looks, that she felt a strange type of security when with him. They began dating right under Bobby's nose. Before you could yell, "Ham on rye, hold the mayo" they were married.

When Bobby got the news, he hung his head and said, "Heaven help her. She's gonna need it. She is dumb, stupid, and crazy."

When Momma was informed, she said a silent prayer and gave the two of them her blessings. She then invited Roy Lee to follow her to the backyard swing.

Through a crack in the backdoor, I had a clear view of the two of them.

They both stood by the swing. Whatever Momma was telling him, didn't meet his approval. It was obvious. His body language exhibited signs of arrogance and defiance. His hands were on his hips. His head was tilted to the side. He kept shifting his weight. He didn't seem the least bit interested in what Momma was saying. Suddenly, he punched the fence and walked out of the yard down through the ally. For a moment, he resembled the devil in blue jeans. Momma sat down on the swing, filled with sadness; she placed her head in her hands and began weeping.

Several years would pass before I would learn the content of the conversation that took place between she and Roy Lee. He would have been wise to heed Momma's counsel.

Bobby had no use for Roy Lee. All he'd say to him was good morning, good evening, and goodbye. Nothing more. Nothing less. Momma accepted him as family. She'd let him know he was in her prayers. She constantly reminded him, "In all things keep God first."

My sisters and I treated him like a brother. He was included in all family activities. We sincerely enjoyed his company. We thought he enjoyed ours. I would come to learn that what I took for enjoyment on Roy Lee's part was tolerance. I think my family bored him.

Rodney was on the same page as Bobby. He would say for anyone to hear "I wouldn't trust Roy Lee no further than I could throw him."

We were not naive. We were well aware of his history with crime, the law, and his street activities. Bobby wouldn't let us forget it for a second. He could not accept the fact that his baby girl, a "Lange" mind you, would marry such a man. Despite Roy Lee's background and Bobby's protestations, my sisters and I didn't hold anything against him. We respected Melanie and her choice. She had our sincere love, support, and blessings.

For the first few years of the marriage everything seemed to be peaches and cream. They were the epitome of marital bliss. They had a spacious two-bedroom apartment near the bayou. It was smartly decorated and comfortable. She was a nurse working at Jefferson Hospital, and he worked in a mattress factory. Their future was bright. It appeared to be filled with hope and promise. They were young. They were in love, and they were happy.

Without warning, the winds of change began weakening the foundation of the world they were building. For reasons Melanie could not comprehend, Roy Lee began missing work. He was given several warnings then he was suspended. He had ample time to be regular in attendance, which he wasn't, so he was terminated. Roy Lee was back on the street breaking the law. When Melanie would try to talk and reason with him, he'd explode. He'd throw his hands up in the air screaming obscenities, and like an immature child he would storm out the house slamming the door. He would be gone for hours — sometimes days.

Verbal abuse escalated followed soon by degradation. He then began questioning her fidelity, criticizing her, calling her unforgivable names and blaming her for his mistakes and misfortunes. Everything wrong in the western world, according to Roy Lee, was Melanie's fault. His accusations and anger intensified and turned into pushing, shoving, and then hitting. He'd hit her in places where the bruises and marks would not be visible. In a short period of time, he had total control over her.

Melanie preferred to suffer in silence than allow her family or friends to know the horrible conditions she was enduring. Living in an atmosphere of fear, intimation, and unpredictability, her self-worth and confidence began to erode. She began to develop anxiety and panic disorders. At times, she would question her sanity. She tried her best but couldn't prevent his violent outbreaks.

One night, Roy Lee began berating and cussing Melanie. She was unresponsive — she did not act, speak, or move. She did absolutely nothing. She completely ignored him. Her indifference was more than his fragile ego could process. It sent him into an explosive rage. Hissing like a snake, he began cussing her using every expletive known to man. In a state of unprovoked rage, he retrieved the .357 magnum revolver from the hall closet and held it to her head.

Acting like a wild animal and spitting out word-after-word of profanity, saying viciously, "Give me one good reason why I shouldn't blow ya fucken brains out?"

She did not move a muscle. He grabbed her by her throat with his left hand, and holding the revolver above her left eye screamed, "Do ya think I'm stupid, do ya? I know ya been fuckin' round."

Because he was choking her, it became difficult to breathe or swallow. She broke away, and as she tried to run he hit her in the back with the butt of the gun. The force of the blow sent her stumbling face first into the bedroom wall. She tried to arch her back to ease the pain. A second blow found the same mark as the first. The pain was excruciating and unbearable. Her legs went numb, and she slid slowly to her knees still facing the wall. An aching, throbbing, sharp, piercing sensation was traveling a mile a second throughout her entire body. Her body cried out for relief. The pain and agony was constant. She wanted the brutality to end. Oh, how she wished it would stop. Every inch of her body was pulsating; muscle spasms began to run rampantly through her.

She wanted to beg him to halt this brutal assault, but experience taught her that doing so would excite him causing him to intensify the violence. Weeping with a shattered spirit she accepted her fate. Nothing mattered to her now. Everything worth holding onto was gone. Her pride, dignity, and self-respect had been annihilated. This was her "Cape Coast Castle" — her door of no return. She felt dehumanized and empty as a drum.

On her knees facing the wall where she had fallen, she took the Bible off the night stand. Clutching the Holy Book close to her bosom in a voice void of all emotion she murmured, "Enough is enough. Please kill me."

Not hearing what she had said, with an open hand he slapped her violently and shouted, "What da fuck did ya say?"

Hysteria entered; permeating the depths of her soul and she began banging her head on the paneled wall. She couldn't stop. Breathing heavily, she began heaving and screaming, "Kill me." Over and over, louder and louder, she cried, "Kill me. Kill me." She fell over on her back convulsing and screaming those awful words.

Fearing the neighbors had heard the assault and called the police, Roy Lee ran off into the night. When Mr. Milton Webster, the landlord, found Melanie, she was prostrate on the bedroom floor trembling, shaking, and saying repeatedly, "Please kill me."

Mr. and Mrs. Webster lived next door. Now and then, they would hear Roy Lee arguing. It didn't seem much out of the ordinary. They charged it to just a lover's spat. They saw no reason to intervene. They were quite fond of Melanie. From the first day, she inquired about renting the apartment, she and "Moxy" as Mrs. Webster was called, became instant friends. They would talk incessantly and frequently exchanged recipes, plus every so often Melanie was asked to baby-sit the Webster's six-year-old granddaughter.

As close as the two of them were, Moxy noticed a change in Melanie. She would say to Mr. Webster, "Melanie seems unhappy. She seems to be avoiding me and doesn't seem to have time to chat anymore. Something just ain't right."

To which Mr. Webster would offer, "Mind your business, Moxy. Don't you dare interfere in those young people's affairs. Whatever it is, it will all come out in the wash. Do you want that last piece of fish?"

Tonight, was different, Roy Lee was more intense, loud and exceedingly obscene. He sounded as if he were deranged. Mr. Webster couldn't believe the language he was using. His first impulse was to call the police as Moxy suggested. As he picked-up the receiver, he heard Melanie screaming, "Kill me. Please, kill me." He slammed the phone down and rushed to Melanie's apartment with Moxy on his heels.

Mr. Webster considered himself a God-fearing man. He was Deacon over at Mt. Zion Church, and he took his church related duties very seriously. He studied the good book daily and would not entertain those who questioned its validity. There was something about Roy Lee's presence that rubbed him the wrong way. He had caught Roy Lee in a lie or two and knew he hung around with some unsavory characters over near the park. None of the young men who sat on the grass shooting the breeze were employed. One thing Mr. Webster knew for sure was, idleness is the devil's workshop.

Mr. Webster, after entering the apartment and seeing the state Melanie was in, cussed under his breath and asked forgiveness at the same time. He picked her up and sat her on the side of the bed.

Her small body was shaking uncontrollably. Melanie stammered and stuttered repeatedly between sobs, "I can't — take — anymore. I — can't — take — anymore."

She sat on the side of the bed shivering as if freezing. As Moxy wiped the blood from her nose, she began saying hesitantly, "Please don't call the police. Please don't call the police."

Realizing no bones were broken Moxy instructed Mr.

Webster to retrieve the bottle of vodka from their apartment as she continued to wash Melanie's face with the warm basin of water.

Moxy enjoyed a nip or two every evening after dinner. While her husband, didn't drink he didn't prevent her from doing so. She always kept a bottle of vodka in the house. She drank vodka because she believed it didn't smell as loud as bourbon. At church, she was constantly sucking on mints. She drank vodka for everything that ailed her. If she had a cold, flu, toothache, or was in pain, vodka was her medicine of choice. She often told the doctors, all some patients needed was a stiff drink, and someone to share it with.

She diluted the alcohol with 7 Up and after about an hour and three drinks, each one stronger than the last, Melanie began to collect herself.

Mr. Webster left the bedroom while Moxy helped Melanie to change out of the bloody clothes so she could shower. When she was presentable, he asked, "Is there anyone we can call? Is there anything more Moxy and I can do? Can we take you anywhere?"

Melanie answered in the negative to all questions. As she wiped a small bit of blood that trickled down her nose, she blurted out, "On second thought, there is somewhere you can take me."

Melanie had often heard Mira say to Mrs. Brooks, "Wise is the woman who has a dollar for a rainy day." She'd smile and say, "It's called highway money."

Coming from Mira, Mrs. Brooks found that hilarious. Finishing the last drink Moxy had given her and feeling a little sure footed, Melanie picked-up the Bible from the floor and kissed it.

Finally, understanding the words of wisdom, Mira had imparted, she said softly, "Thank you Momma, thank you." Then shook the Holy Book. Fifteen one hundred dollar bills she had hidden fell onto the bed.

The next morning, when Roy Lee returned home drunk and full of smack, Melanie was nowhere to be found. She had taken up residence in San Diego, California; miles and miles away from the city that care forgot. Roy Lee went ballistic when it became apparent that Melanie had left. He was so livid that all he could think of was what he was going to do to her when he got his hands on her.

"I'm gonna break every bone in her fuckin' body. I'll teach her a lesson she'll take to da grave."

Roy Lee began looking over his shoulder. He may have been one banana short of a bunch, but he was smart enough to know he was in danger. For he knew deep down in his soul, Bobby would have people looking for him and if found his life wouldn't be worth a plug nickel. After all, he thought, once that Motherfucker found out how he had been treating his precious daughter, he'd have hell to pay.

He'd cross that bridge when he got to it, at the moment; he had his hands full trying to locate Melanie. He began harassing her good friend

Paula Holloway; they had been friends since grade school. If anyone knew her whereabouts, Paula would. When she refused to talk to him, he threatened her. When she called for her husband who was in another part of the house, Roy Lee cussed her and ran off. He kept an eye on the Lange's house from a distance at different times of the day and night. Seeing nothing out of the ordinary made his blood boil. He was obsessed with finding Melanie; he could think of nothing else.

When Bobby was informed of how Melanie had been treated by Roy Lee, he was irate. Sitting on the side of the bed, patting his foot, he had difficulty controlling his anger. Bobby was furious, not because of what had happened to Melanie, he felt she got what she deserved. His thinking was, she should have known better than to marry an ass-hole like Roy Lee, a two-bit hustler who wasn't worth a dime in Chinese money. He was angry because of the lack of respect Roy Lee's actions showed towards him. Bobby wanted him found.

Ready to issue his orders, Bobby angrily snatched the phone from its cradle. As he did, Mira entered the room. She knew what he was about to do. Standing at the foot of the bed she sighed.

Mira began talking in a way that he found disturbing. Whenever she lectured him about getting his life right with God, he'd feel uneasy. Or when she said she was praying for him and those shady associates of his on Tulane Avenue, a cold chill would rush through his body. There was not a man alive Bobby was afraid of. He could hold his own. If he had been weak or timid, Frank would have had no use, or respect for him. Yet, there was something about Mira that literally scared him to the bone.

With her arms crossed and without blinking she said, "Hang up the phone Robert."

Not wishing to deal with her, he said tensely, "Go away woman. This is business. I don't have time for your nonsense. Go away."

"Hang up the phone." Mira said again.

Paying no attention to her, he dialed the phone while talking to himself. "I can't believe that piece of shit had the audacity to disrespect me that way. Well, that's O.K. I will personally deal with Mr. Roy Lee."

While dialing the phone he continued talking, "That fool must be on something mighty strong — mighty, mighty strong. Well, I'll tell ya one thing he's gonna need it to dull the pain. When I finish with him, he won't have a hand to hold his dick to piss with. I'm cutting both of them off. And

I do mean off." He shouted.

With the phone in his hand and vengeance in his heart he heard Mira say, "Robert, for the third time, hang up the phone. There will be no more violence. You will not harm a hair on Roy Lee's head. Do you understand, Robert?"

She said sorrowfully, "Roy Lee's every step is being directed by Satan. How much more do you wish for him to suffer? You will let him be. Let him be."

Bobby felt cold.

Mira sat down on the bed with clasped hands in her lap and staring at the floor she wiped a tear from the corner of her eye. With a heavy heart and sadness in her voice, said, "Melanie will be alright. It will take a little time for her to recover emotionally, but, when she does she'll be stronger for it."

Mira explained to Bobby and the rest of the family that Melanie was safe and well. She was presently residing with her aunt Inez in San Diego, California, working at the city health center and, all things considered, was doing well. As soon as she could find suitable living accommodations, she'd be moving.

Bobby knew the law of the street demanded that he avenged this matter. He would be perceived as soft, fearful, and weak if he were to stand idly by and do nothing. Given his way of life, he could not afford to allow that to happen. What did Mira know? She was always talking a lot of religious mumbo-jumbo. She had no idea how things were perceived and dissected on the street. His mind was made up. When Roy Lee was found, he'd never be able to clap his hands again.

Roy Lee didn't know where else to look for Melanie. It was as if she had vanished from the face of the earth. He checked out all her friends, her job, her relatives' comings and goings, he didn't know where else to look. Roy Lee was tired, broke, hungry, and in need of a fix. It had been a day or two, and his nerves were raw. He had been living on the street and needed a bath.

Mr. Webster, the landlord, demanded the back rent, because of how he treated Melanie, he showed him no mercy. Unable to come up with the rent, he was evicted. All his worldly possessions were placed on the sidewalk. Without warning, the rain came and ruined everything. He had pawned his clothes, jewelry, and everything else of value to the drug dealers.

So, nothing was left but the furniture. He was going to offer that up, but now, it wasn't salvageable.

Roy Lee was going in circles. He had to get his hands on some money. He needed a fix. Standing by a tree urinating he had an idea. It was extremely dangerous but one he had to take. He would go to the café and check the work schedule. Melanie filled in now and then. That might tell him something. Under the circumstances, he knew Bobby wouldn't expect him to show his face near 'The Place'. With an attempt at a smile, he thought he was on to something.

Being careful not to be seen, Roy Lee stood in the courtyard across from the café. He didn't see Bobby's truck or Rodney's Cadillac. He had to be sure they were not there. He walked, half- ran to Jim's Superette. Using the phone, he asked to speak to Mr. Bobby or Rodney Lange. Neither one was available. He had his answer. The coast was clear.

It was a very cold February night. The north wind was blowing as if irritated. The chill in the air made it seem colder than it was. There was a fine mist, which meant rain wasn't far behind. The sidewalks and streets were wet. The cars that passed made a searing sound as the tires made contact with the asphalt. There were very few people on the street and the ones that were hustled and bustled by trying to get indoors. The hookers who were always walking the Avenue were nowhere to be seen. The record shop, barbershop, and hardware store, were closed for the evening. Looking around once or twice, seeing the coast was clear, Roy Lee started walking towards 'The Place'. He felt a lot of things, but he didn't feel cold. He pulled his cap down, raised his coat collar, and increased his trek.

CHAPTER 8

Every Tuesday night, from eight p.m. until midnight, was sweetheart night at the café. Whatever meal you ordered your sweetheart's meal was free. The two meals had to be comparable. There were always customers waiting to be seated. Roy Lee entered the restaurant walking at top speed. He was on a mission, and his life was in extreme danger. With that knowledge, he made a dash to the night manager. 'The Place' was jam-packed. Customers were everywhere, and the waitresses were moving at the speed of light. Combinations of sounds were heard; music from the jukebox, knives and forks hitting porcelain, orders being called into the kitchen, the cha-ching of the cash register and the buzz of customers engaged in conversation. Hannah, the night manager, was standing by her post observing the employees.

When Roy Lee approached, she couldn't believe her eyes and could not believe how awful he looked or the foul odor emanating from him. Before he could say a word, she lowered her voice, speaking very confidentially she advised him of the danger he was in. She hurriedly explained to him that no one knew where to find Melanie. Mr. Bobby had people combing the city looking for him, and he'd better leave because Mr. Rodney would be coming on duty any minute.

Storming out of the café, Roy Lee was like a mad dog. Like never before he needed a hit. So, filled with rage and anger at not finding Melanie, and needing a fix, he was about to erupt. His only thoughts were where can she be and finding some money. He was a walking keg of dynamite. His heart was racing and his nerves were shot. His net worth in his pocket was thirty-seven cents.

As he was about to exit the 'The Place', sitting in a booth near the jukebox was Oscar Lewis and his wife Ramona. Roy Lee and Oscar's eyes met simultaneously. Roy Lee gave a cunning smile and nodded his head for Oscar to meet him outside.

"Are you Ok My-O?" asked Ramona. "You look as if you've seen a ghost."

"My-O" was her pet name for Oscar. She would tell her friends the first time they made love she couldn't stop saying 'My- O, My-O'. And for the last four and a half years he had been her ever-loving 'My-O'. Oscar had heard that fate could be cruel and unforgiving, but this was unbelievable. To him this was totally unfair and undeserved. He nervously played with his fork, stammered a bit and finally said he'd forgotten his wallet in the glove compartment of the car. He kissed her hand and asked her to order for him. With an awkward grin, he said he'd be back in a jiffy.

On that unusually cold February night, Oscar Lewis began to sweat. As he stepped outside, the cold night rushed to greet him. He shivered while pulling the collar of his jacket up around his neck. With his hands in his pocket, he looked up and down St. Bernard Avenue. Except for a bus with few passengers, he saw nothing. The corner was well illuminated, and the neon lights flashed "Bobby's Café" repeatedly. The mist had turned into a light drizzle. Oscar thanked his lucky stars for not seeing Roy Lee. He turned to re- enter the café.

Just as his hand touched the doorknob, he heard, "Hey, fish. Over here." Roy Lee was standing across the street by the hardware store.

The side of the store was on Tremain Street. It was closed and extremely dark. Roy Lee could not risk being seen. As Oscar crossed the street, his spirits dropped to the pit of his stomach. He couldn't help but wonder what in the world could he possibly want.

As he approached Roy Lee it was not with the same fear and the helplessness he experienced in jail. This was the free world, and if he thought Oscar feared him, he had another thought coming. Not knowing what to expect, Oscar was not afraid but apprehensive, more annoyed than angry. He did not at all appreciate his privacy being invaded this way. If

Ramona had not been with him he would have ignored the invitation to meet him out front. But, under no circumstances did Oscar want him near Ramona. He saw Roy Lee as a human contaminant and he did not want Ramona's space compromised.

As Oscar neared, Roy Lee began grinning like a Cheshire cat. Smiling, as if to beat the band, he extended his arm to shake hands. Oscar not responding kept his hands in his pockets. Roy Lee then tried to stir up old memories as how he protected him when they were locked down. Oscar stared at him coldly without uttering a word. Peeved by Oscar's reception he wasted no time getting to the point. He saw a man walking in their direction. He kept his eyes on him.

Realizing he was no threat he continued saying, "I don't mean to sweat ya fish, but I need a few hundred dollars and I need it tonight."
Oscar let out a grunt type of laugh, and said, "What's that got to do with me? That's a personal problem."

Roy Lee was homeless. He was standing out in the rain, cold, broke, in need of a fix, and desperate. Roy Lee was fuming due to Oscar's attitude. He hadn't figured on him being difficult. His
nerves were getting the best of him. He didn't have time for Oscar's attitude. He needed some money, and he needed it in a hurry. He couldn't risk committing a crime and getting caught because his next offense would send him to Angola penitentiary. He may have been a whale in parish prison but in Angola he would have been just another 'fish', and he knew it.

Nervous and irritated, Roy Lee wiped his hand across his mouth and began breathing laboriously. He had about all he was going to take from Oscar. If he wanted to play hardball, then hardball it would be.

Pointing his finger in Oscar's face savagely saying, "Listen up ya lil' punk-ass motha-fucker, either find me some money tonight or I'll tell that hoe ya with all ya fuckin' business. I'll tell that bitch the way ya was fucked in jail. Yeah, dat's right."

Agitated and impatient he continued, "I'm not here for no bullshit. I'll tell her dat da niggers on the tier passed ya round like bad news. And dat ain't all, I'll tell her dat dey had ya on yo knees and…"

Oscar threw his hands up stopping Roy Lee. He knew for a fact this animal was capable of such lies. He couldn't believe this was real. If he were dreaming, he wished he'd awaken. For this was an unbelievable nightmare.

It had been about four years since Oscar was in jail. He thought all those old memories were gone forever. He shook his head again in disbelief. Everything was just beginning to break his way. It was as if life had built him up to tear him down. From a mental and emotional perspective, Oscar's stint in prison cost him dearly.

When Oscar was released from prison, he sank into a depression. Those moments of helplessness and hopelessness he experienced while incarcerated would not let him be. The stress along with the guilt was constant. He felt useless and worthless.

Many nights, Ramona would reach for him with welcoming open arms, then feelings of inadequacy and deficiency would ruin the tenderness of the moment. His self-esteem, self-worth, and self-image were all in serious jeopardy. He would sit on the side of the bed holding his head in total frustration. With Ramona holding him tightly, his tears would fall like rain.

Those times when Oscar would have bouts of performance anxiety, Ramona would hold him close to her bosom and reassure him of her love. She'd whisper tenderly, "My-O, this is just another river we have to cross — and we shall."

With her warm body close to his, she'd remind him that her love for him could never die and in a voice ever so tender she'd say, "I'm here, My-O, I'll always be here for you. Be patient My-O and try to relax. I know in my heart-of-hearts we'll make love again. I'll always love you."

Kissing him she whispered, "This too shall pass".

Oscar was convinced that he could survive without oxygen, water, shelter, or food. He didn't know how, but remove those elements from his life, and he would find a way to survive. But, to live without Ramona's love and respect was a total impossibility. It could not be done. Oscar loved Ramona, and Ramona loved Oscar. The love they shared was an "Annabelle Lee" kind of love.

It was more than love. He was her lifeline. He was the left ventricle in the heart of her existence. Oscar awakened earlier than usual one morning, his mind a million miles away on many unimportant things.

As Ramona slept, he leaned over and kissed her on her bare shoulder. He sat on the side of the bed and said his morning prayer. He took a deep breath and entered the bathroom. He turned on the shower, and while waiting for the water to warm-
up, he hummed a tune then stepped into the shower. As the water

commenced, tattooing his body a feeling that had been dormant began to resurface. A stirring began in his soul penetrating every cell in his body. A fire of passion ignited within him with such force, it could not be ignored.

Without drying himself and forgetting to turn the water off, he rushed to the arms of Ramona leaving wet footprints in the carpet. That morning, as Ramona had promised, they made love again. Oscar was reborn, refreshed and renewed. Once again, Oscar soared with the eagles. He led the Iditarod in Alaska. He ran with the bulls in Pamplona, Spain, and he finished Le tour De France. Because of Ramona's love, patience, and understanding, Oscar felt whole again — complete and fulfilled.

Sitting on the side of the bed Ramona heard him whisper, "Thank you, Jesus. Thank you, Jesus. Thank you, sweet Jesus,".

Standing by the hardware store in the dark, cold, and rain, Oscar stared at Roy Lee in disbelief. He wondered what had gone wrong in his life to cause him to be bitter, cruel, and ruthless. He said dejectedly, "I can help. I'll get whatever money you need."

Oscar was not naive. He knew this shake down was just beginning and would never end. Still, peace descended on him like he'd never known, a slight smile even donned his lips. For at that very instant, he knew everything was going to be all right. The future looked bright and full of promise Ramona's love had made him stronger than he ever thought he could be.

He said again, "I can help. I know where I can get some money."

As they walked across the street to his car, he said again, "Don't worry, everything is going to be all right."

They entered the car and drove east on Tremain Street. Not taking any chances of being recognized, Roy Lee slouched down in the seat. Realizing Oscar was beginning to play ball he smiled and relaxed.

Patting Oscar on the shoulder condescendingly said, "I don't mean to sweat ya fish. It's jist dat I'm having drawers trouble. My old lady's fucken up on me and ain't no trouble like drawer's trouble. Ya understand where I'm coming from don't ya fish?"

Oscar glanced over at him and nodded, "Sure, man." He said, "I understand."

Oscar was not at all familiar with downtown New Orleans He lived across the lake in Slidell, Louisiana. He had come to the café to thank Bobby for being so helpful in aiding him in resolving a legal problem. Plus, he wanted to share some good news with Bobby. One, he had gotten the job he applied for, and two, he and Ramona, were expecting their first child in a few months. He was overjoyed. A while back Oscar took a test with the telephone company and passed. Two months from that date he had to report for orientation. Further instructions were to be forwarded. That was five months ago.

Receiving the notice from the telephone company caused him great tribulation and distress. He knew when a background check was done, his criminal record would be discerned, and he would be terminated. He had been employed at the Belfast Supermarket in Slidell as a stock clerk. One day at lunch he explained his dilemma to Ross Thomson, the chief of security. He put Oscar in touch with Bobby. Bobby put him in touch with Allen Adamo, and for eight hundred and sixty-five dollars his record was expunged. Not having that sum of money, he borrowed it from Bobby at twenty-five cents on the dollar.

Oscar and Roy Lee had driven one block. He had no idea where he was going. At the stop sign on the corner of Tremain and Burnside Street, he looked both ways and for no particular reason decided to turn left. In the middle of the block, between Tremain Street and Tulip Street, he pulled to the curb and stopped.

Roy Lee upset by the delay asked angrily, "What the fuck ya stop for?"

With a voice, gloomy and pensive Oscar replied, "I have to piss."

Roy Lee nervous and irritated bellowed, "Make it snappy. I got things to take care of."

Standing at the rear of the car Oscar surveyed the surroundings. Burnside Street looked like a third world country. The houses were all dilapidated and boarded up. It looked as if no one had inhabited those houses in years. Burnside Street was being used as a community dump.

Trash, rubbish, garbage, refuse, and debris of every kind littered both sides of the street. The temperature was beginning to drop. It was extremely cold, dark, and dreary. It drizzled off and on. The street was deserted. As far as the eye could see there was not a soul in sight. Oscar stood like a statue watching as the wind blew a tin can down towards Tremain Street.

As he contemplated what he was about to do, a tear stained his face. With a sadness originating in the pit of his stomach and radiating throughout his body, he took a deep breath and opened the trunk. He hesitated as if second-guessing himself. Satisfied with the decision he had made, he unfolded the bath towel. Under his breath, he cursed Roy Lee for being the conduit of this quandary.

He took one last look up and down the Street and picked-up the snub nose .38 Special. The gun was colder than usual.

Sensing something was wrong Roy Lee stepped from the car impatiently. Seeing the gun in Oscar's hand he became furious. Tensing his muscles like a wild animal about to pounce on its helpless prey, clenching his teeth, menacingly said, "Why ya Lil bitch-ass — "

Before he could complete his thought, a shot rang out disturbing the silence of the night. Far away in the distance, a dog could be heard whining. The bullet splintered Roy Lee's clavicle. The velocity from the bullet spun him half way around but he didn't fall. With a look of surprise, followed by stark raving fear, he tried to run. Three more rounds were fired each found its mark in the upper portion of his back. He fell face down on the asphalt choking on his blood.

Looking toward heaven, Oscar whispered, "Please forgive me."

As Roy Lee lay convulsing, Oscar fired again. The bullet entered his ear shattering everything in its path. The dog in the distance began to wail as the rain came down in waves.

Sitting across from Ramona in Bobby's café, Oscar speared an olive from his salad and fed it to Ramona. Thinking what a difference she made in his life, said, "I love you so very much, and need you more than you will ever know. You are my world and everything in it."

Feeding him a piece of her steak she winked and replied, "You're my kind of man My-O. Say that again."

Then clutching her stomach, suddenly she exclaimed, "My-O, My-O guess what? I can feel the baby kicking."

As Oscar and Ramona prepared to leave the café a customer rushed in excitedly explaining to Hannah, the Night manager, "Someone's been wasted over on Burnside Street. They think it is drug related."

The rain had ceased as they stepped onto the sidewalk. When the news of Roy Lee's death reached Momma, she was distraught and brokenhearted. She was sure the account reported by the newspaper was entirely inaccurate. His criminal history was exposed, but she was wise enough to know that the investigators had missed the mark as to why he was killed. Although she couldn't prove it, something in the recesses of her soul told her it was a crime of passion that had been motivated by the power of love.

Mira did not delay informing Melanie of Roy Lee's unfortunate demise. When the phone rang, Melanie was sitting at her dressing table combing her hair. She had gone to church early that morning. After the service, she spent time in the fellowship hall drinking coffee and conversing. She stopped at the supermarket, on her way home, to gather a few needed items. Something was troubling her, but whatever it was she couldn't put her finger on it.

Picking up the phone hearing Mira's voice she happily exclaimed, "Hello, Mother. How nice of you to call."

Without hesitating, Mira hastily explained the tragedy involving Roy Lee. After pausing to digest the news, Melanie said, with a quivering voice, "Mother, may I call you back in a few minutes?"

"Will you be alright?" Mira nervously inquired.
Beginning to tremble Melanie responded, "Yes, Mother. I'll be okay. I'll call you back shortly."

Melanie retrieved the long-handled hairbrush from the dressing table, but instead of brushing her hair she quickly set it back down. It reminded her of the times Roy Lee had hit her with a similar one. Seeing her reflections in the mirror she was flooded with an avalanche of emotions.

Mira had advised her repeatedly to find a way to release the negative energy that was eating her alive. She would quote verses from the Bible, suggest passages for her to read, and remind her to pray without ceasing.

"Do this Melanie," she offered, "And the Lord will enter your heart and restore peace to your soul."

She heard every word Mira said, but they had no meaning or substance. For in her reality it was the hatred and disdain she harbored for Roy Lee that had sustained her. It became her strength. She was obsessed with vengeance. She wanted harm in the worst way to visit him. She prayed to live long enough to see him wallow in the pain, fear, humiliation, and misery he had subjected her to. Let him experience the feeling of being trapped like a caged animal... defenseless, and helpless, at the mercy of a cruel, vicious, and unforgiving captor. She found comfort in wishing him to suffer in ways words couldn't describe. She was consumed with hatred and unable to see the harm it was doing to her. Before her next heartbeat, forgiveness would find her. She would have an epiphany and the pleasant memories spent with Roy Lee would trump her darkest moments.

With tears streaming down her face, blurring her vision, through this haze, she saw Roy Lee in the mirror. He was struggling to give her something. Leaning close to the mirror she realized it was an olive branch. The Romans considered the olive branch a symbol of peace. In the Bible, it was brought back to Noah's Ark by a dove indicating the flood was over. He was violently weeping and talking incoherently. The only word she could understand was the word 'wrong'. She heard him say 'wrong' several times. She could not make sense of anything else he said.

After dabbing her eyes with Kleenex, the only reflection in the mirror was hers. Suddenly, she remembered what had taken place at Church that morning. As her heart began to palpitate she recalled the Pastor's invitation to anyone wishing to join the fold. An old man stood and slowly walked to face the congregation. He was about six feet tall, with a dark complexion. He gave the appearance of traveling one time too many, to places where angels are never found. He began by begging the Church's' pardon. Weeping he was pleading to be reinstated. The old man's education had obviously been abbreviated for he had difficulty expressing himself. He spoke of his many transgressions and his sinful past. Words did not come easily to him, but his honesty and sincerity echoed throughout the Chapel. After about fifteen minutes, looking directly at Melanie he concluded by saying in a voice that shook the rafters of the Sanctuary.

"Ma sistas and broders, all I can say is, wen ya done, done, wrong... ya jist done, done, done, wrong. Please ask da Lord ta fo- give me, cause I done, done wrong."

Melanie sat before the dressing table mirror for a spell. Her mind traveled back in time returning rapidly to the present. Computing all the things that had transpired, the good, the bad, and the otherwise. As she said a silent prayer, a slight smile made its way to the corner of her mouth. Putting her fingertips to her lips she placed a kiss upon the mirror. The flood was over. As her heart began to sing and her spirit began to soar, she picked up the phone and called her mother.

Bobby was kept informed of who was doing what on the street. In Roy Lee's case, the outlaws didn't have a clue. At least that's what they said to Bobby. The general consensus among the street rats was, Bobby had it done. Of course, they wouldn't dare say that to Bobby.

The buzz was, "Man, da nigger was doggin' Bobby's daughter, kicking her ass night and day. Bobby had enough and put an end ta dat shit."

A few years ago, when Mira invited Roy Lee to join her by the backyard swing, she said this, "Roy Lee listen carefully. If you are wise, you won't take these words lightly. You are being forewarned. Should any harm come to Melanie, by your hand or deed, I promise you, you'll curse the day you were born."

CHAPTER 9

It was Thursday morning. The breakfast rush at the café had ended. The waitresses were scurrying around getting prepared for the lunch crowd. Rodney was shouting orders like a drill sergeant. He kept the employees, hop, skip, and jumping. The ministers having scheduled an appointment with Bobby arrived and were directed to a corner booth. Instead of four for the conference there were six. Bobby instructed Mary Ann, the waitress, to bring a pot of coffee. Bobby took a chair and joined the meeting.

After pouring himself a cup of coffee, Rev. Bateman, the Pastor of Epiphany Church of Christ, was the spokesman. He was a huge man who had never missed a meal. When he spoke, his voice was as deep as the ocean. Clearing his throat, he took a sip of coffee, and began speaking.

"Mr. Bobby," the sound of his voice made the earth shake, "on behalf of each one of us, and our congregations, we extend to you and your family our deepest sympathy regarding the senseless murder of your son-in-law a few months ago. Crime is running rampant in our community, and we are here again asking you to discontinue helping and assisting criminals to get released from jail. It's our understanding no one has been arrested in the case of your son-in-law. Is that correct?"

Bobby did not respond.

"For all we know sir," he said peevishly, "One of the very people you've aided could be the culprit."

Bobby crossed his legs and pretended interest. Rev. Bateman having gained a bit of confidence continued.

"You're in a unique position. You can do wonders for the community. As you know, Mr. Bobby, times are rapidly changing."

Bobby took a deep breath and wondered how long this sermon would go on.

Rev. Bateman paused a second and gathered his thoughts. "There's a lot of talk going around about integration. No, it won't be here anytime soon, but it's on the way. And what does that mean?" Thumping the table several times said in a sing-song voice,

"It means — we — have got to be — ready. And I submit to you this morning, sir, our young folk are not ready. Far too many of them have no respect for themselves or anyone else? They have no discipline in their lives."

Raising his voice a tad said, "Spare the rod and spoil the child. That's what the good book says."

Bobby looked out the window of the café and said nothing.

His knowledge of the Bible was limited. But, as a youngster, he often heard his mother, who did not believe in physical punishment, say, "That statement may well be often quoted but it could not be found in the Bible."

Pouring another cup of coffee, he stopped to add cream and sugar. He took a quick sip, which burned his lip, then went on.

"The kids today, more than ever before, need direction, guidance, purpose, and," he shouted, "...discipline. Yes, Mr. Bobby, they need to be held accountable. Too many of our young people are running wild. I ask you, who are their role models?"

Without waiting for an answer said, "I'll tell you. Dope peddlers, pimps, con-men, and outlaws."

Bobby looked down at the tile floor, rubbed his head, and wondered to himself, 'Don't these hypocrites ever change their tune?'

"Mr. Bobby," he concluded, "we don't mean you any disrespect, but you're doing your people a disservice by enabling them in a life of crime. You're getting them out of jail is encouraging them to disregard the law and all authority."

With an air of satisfaction, he smiled and said, "Rev. Todder will continue."

Bobby had every man at the table in his back pocket. He had never met

Rev. Todder. He had been the assistant Pastor in Baton Rouge, Louisiana, and now was taking over the Pastoral duties at New Hope Baptist Church on Miro Street. It had one of the largest congregations in the area. Rev. Ralph had been the Pastor at New Hope but had recently died. Bobby had made huge contributions to New Hope. He helped with the building fund, bought choir robes, and an organ. He was always sensitive to the needs of Rev. Ralph and his congregation.

Every minister at the meeting had benefited from their relationship with Bobby, and most of his favors had nothing to do with Church issues. He had been instrumental in getting summer jobs for many of their young members, had taken care of parking tickets, and helped in obtaining building permits. When their wives would have meetings or parties he'd give them huge discounts.

He also made personal loans to them when their applications were denied, and charged them very little interest on the money borrowed.
Then there was Minister Eddie Blunt, he never said much at these meetings one way or the other. In fact, he'd never attend these gatherings if the other ministers didn't insist that he did so. He was embarrassed to be in Bobby's presence. Late one night, while parked on Lake Shore Blvd., he was arrested along with his female companion. He was committing a sexual act in the back seat of his car. He couldn't afford to have that knowledge made public. He would have been stained and tarnished for life.

He called Bobby from central lock-up, crying on the phone, "Mr. Bobby, Mr. Bobby, please, please help me. I'm in serious trouble."

He was so nervous Bobby couldn't understand a word he was saying. After calming him down to get the particulars. Bobby turned it over to his associates, and nothing ever came of it.

In return for his many favors and contributions rendered, Bobby expected favors in return. When an election rolled around, Bobby's associates informed him about the candidate they were supporting. He would share that information with the Ministers, and of course they were required to encourage their followers to vote likewise.

As Bobby, often would say to them, "It's nothing more than one hand washing the other."

Rubbing his chin and shaking his head, and with a heavy sigh Rev. Bateman said, "Now, I'd like to introduce Rev. Todder. I think you'll find what he has to say very interesting."

Rev. Todder was a tall thin man with a heavy mustache. His suit was well tailored, and his shoes were name brand. He sported two gold rings, a wedding band and an expensive watch. If there was one thing Bobby knew... it was jewelry, because many of the professional gamblers in the area would pawn anything of value to Bobby when they were on a losing streak: rings, diamond stickpins, and watches. Rev. Todder was a very impressive looking man. His congregation was twice the size of the other ministers. He had been briefed as to what to expect, and he was confident he had met Bobby's kind before. In Rev. Todder's mind, Bobby was just another colored man who was fortunate enough to get a little dirt under his fingernails, and now intended to use his people to keep it there.

The way Rev. Todder saw it Bobby was nothing more than a bottom feeder. Instead of sitting to talk, Rev. Todder decided to stand. Standing and looking down on Bobby gave him a sense of superiority. He hadn't spoken a word when Bobby labeled him arrogant, conceited, and demanding.

Bobby smiled thinking, 'This asshole is in for a rude awakening.' Bobby took the small note pad he kept in his apron pocket and began to write. He beckoned for the waitress, gave her the note, telling her to give it to Rodney.

Standing with one hand on his hip and sheets of paper in the other, Rev. Todder said authoritatively, "Gentlemen, we've wasted enough time. Bobby," the 'Mr.' was deliberately omitted, "let's get to the point. You will discontinue using your power and political connections to get criminals released from jail. No longer will we sit back and allow these violators to be sent back to an unsuspecting and under protected community."

Straightening his tie, he rambled on, "You've been asked several times by these men of God to stop the madness only to have this request ignored. Well Bobby, I'm not asking, I'm demanding you cease this insanity."

The other ministers shifted in their seats a bit uneasy at Rev. Todder's abrasive and imperious tone. They all knew where and how their bread was buttered, and as much as they would like Bobby to curtail his leniency towards the undesirables in the community, they realized it was not to their advantage to lean too hard. For after all, Mr. Bobby wasn't just another colored man, he was powerful and connected to some extremely dangerous people.

Rev. Todder spread his arms and said, "I can't speak for their congregations, but, as for my members, we are done talking, trying to get you to do the right and Godly thing. We have decided to act."

Feeling in control and showboating for his fellow ministers he threw the sheets of paper in his hand on the table.

Aggressively patting the stack of papers, said dryly, "These are signatures of the members of my congregation. We will begin canvassing the neighborhood for more. Then, we will march in front of this café until you comply with our demands."

Slamming the table with his fist, shaking the cups and saucers asked, "Do you understand?"

Bobby looked at him coldly but said nothing. Rodney returned to the table whispered something in Bobby's ear and handed him several sheets of paper. Glancing at the documents Bobby decided to respond.

"Gentlemen," he said flatly, "I'll take your request under advisement."

"In that case Mr. Bobby," Rev. Todder emphasized the 'Mr.', "my congregation and I will march until we close this establishment down. Maybe then you'll get the message."

Rev. Bateman, realizing Rev. Todder may have gone too far, chimed in. "Gentlemen. Gentlemen. Maybe we can all…"

Before he could complete his thought, Bobby spoke abruptly. "I thank you all for coming but my position regarding this matter is solid as a dollar. I said it before, and this is the last time I'll say it. I will help those I can, whenever I can and however I can. I am not a court of law. I am not a judge. I am not a jury. Good day, my friends, this meeting is over."

He rose, walked to the door and held it open.

As they were filing out, Rev. Bateman wanted to say something, but thought better of it and said nothing. Each minister smiled and shook Bobby's hand perfunctorily. It was obvious to them that Bobby was far from pleased. They seldom saw him smile, but today he was a block of ice.

As they stepped out of the café, Bobby called out, "Rev. Todder, may I have a word with you in private?"

He looked at his fellow clergymen and felt special for being singled out proudly said, "Of course, Bobby, of course."

For he knew, in his heart, it was just a matter of time before a foolish man like Bobby saw the light. He grunted softly in satisfaction.

As Rev. Todder positioned himself in the corner booth, Bobby poured him a cup of coffee and pushed the cream and sugar towards him. Bobby thanked him for taking a moment to speak to him alone and assured him that they would reach common ground.

"After all," Bobby said, "we both want peace and harmony."

Smiling for the first time that afternoon Bobby asked, "Didn't a wise man say, we must learn to live together as brothers or we'll perish together like fools?"

Rev. Todder stared at Bobby but didn't utter a sound. He was thinking to himself, "I wish this ignoramus would speak his peace so I can go on my way."

Bobby adjusted his eyeglasses and set the sheets of paper Rodney had given him on the table. He said in a confidential tone, "You're new here, Rev. Todder. You may have heard, there are very few doors I can't have opened. My arms are long, very long. They can reach in many directions."

Bobby shook his head, smiled slightly and continued. "All I want is to be like the man they talk about in that poem. You know the one."

He looked up at the ceiling as if it were written there.

"It says something about: Let me live in a house by the side of the road."

Bobby hesitated to try to remember. He scratched his chin and said, "Where the race of men go by. The men who are good and the men who are bad; as good and as bad as I."

Smiling broadly, which was rare for Bobby, he added, "Yes, Sir. Yes, Siree, that's how I try to live my life — in a fair, non- judgmental fashion. Live and let live is my philosophy."

Reaching across the table, Bobby patted Rev. Todder on the arm in a brotherly sort of way and said, "You're a man of God. You know better than anyone that sinners have a future and saints have a past."

Drumming the table with his fingers, Bobby resumed in a voice filled with memories he wished he could forget, "Life doesn't treat us all the same. Some of our sisters and brothers got lost along the way and, unfortunately, they'll never find their way home."

Shaking his head and feeling the weight of the burden he had to carry, said, "There are those whom life has treated with kid gloves. They've never known adversity; therefore, they've never been tested. The truth is Rev. Todder, there are those who believe we are all divinely connected."

Sighing heavily and spreading his hands he concluded, "That's my purpose, Rev. Todder, to be a friend to man. Nothing more. Nothing less...

And that includes you. I can help you in so many, many, ways."

Bobby leaned back in the booth, acknowledged a couple entering the café and continued. Shaking his finger from side to side said pointedly, "This talk about marching in front of my place, protesting and causing dissension is a No. No. People talk Rev. Todder. They take things out of context. My associates and I shun publicity at all cost, especially the negative kind. I'm asking you to give this some serious thought before acting."

Feeling they had reached an understanding Bobby extended his hand in friendship. Rev. Todder ignored the gesture.

Rev. Todder frowned and forcefully stated, "I despise everything you represent. You are a gigantic sore on the face of the Colored Race. Personally, I don't want, nor do I need anything from you. I detest being in your company. You are a sad excuse for a human being."

As he rose to leave he said emphatically, "I've made my position exceedingly clear — do as requested, or I'll run you out of business. Good day, Bobby."

"Allow me another minute of your time, Rev. Todder. I have something you'll find interesting." Bobby said bitterly.

The note Bobby had passed to Rodney said: Information on Rev. E. G. Todder. Tell Adamo it's urgent. Need ammunition. Bobby began to read from the sheets of paper Rodney had given him. He relayed Rev. Todder's social security and driver's license numbers to him. The Reverend's eyes widened as he looked at Bobby in total disbelief.

Bobby read on, "Your name is Eugene Gregory Todder. You graduated from the Seminary in Baton Rouge, La. in 1945. You married Darlene Wagner in 1944. You have two daughters: Carla, seven and Bernice, five. Your address in Baton Rouge was 2131 Beaumont Blvd. You were Assistant Pastor of Fairview Baptist Church. You are currently Pastor of New Hope Baptist Church here in New Orleans. The Church is presently adding six hundred additional square feet to your home to accommodate you and your family."

Tomorrow morning, Rev. Todder", Bobby said folding the sheets of paper and placing them in his apron pocket, "all construction will cease. The building permit will be found invalid, and until my associates get a favorable response from me, work will not continue."

Nervous and visibly shaken at this severe invasion of his privacy, Rev.

Todder asked, "What's the meaning of this? How could you acquire my vital information?"

Looking directly at him with eyes as cold as a well digger's ass, Bobby sneered. "I told you. My arms are long."

"Now that we understand each other," Bobby said, while deliberately taking the cup of coffee from Rev. Todder, "this is what you'll do. You'll inform your congregation that this talk of marching and protesting in front of my establishment will be delayed until further notice. And every time it's mentioned you'll keep postponing it until they find another cause to champion. Do you understand me?" Bobby asked, trying to control himself.

For the first time, Rev. Todder saw the viciousness in Bobby's eyes and was frightened.

Trembling badly, Rev. Todder managed to ask, "And if I don't?"

"In that case," Bobby said tapping the sheets of paper, "not having your living quarters completed will be the least of your worries".

Hurt and violated, on the brink of tears Rev. Todder asked, "What kind of animal are you? How can you live with yourself? You are to be pitied."

Rev. Todder slid from the booth disheartened and discouraged. His spirits in disarray, said hardly above a whisper, "The God I serve does not sleep. Nor does he slumber. Just as sure as a dog returns to it's own vomit, and a hog having been washed returns to wallow in the mud, your day will come. You may feel victorious today, but days of torment await you. That smirk will be replaced with bitter tears. Tears that will run down your face like water from a broken spigot. And when that day dawns, and it shall, you'll call on my God in a voice so sad it will cause the angels to weep and mourn. For your sake, I hope he hears you."

Then with a heavy sigh said, "Good day, Mr. Bobby. I'll never bother you again. There is really no need too. The demons in your heart will lead you to your destiny."

Unable to contain himself, Bobby screamed, "Get- out. Don't ever come near me again."

CHAPTER 10

I was working in the kitchen rotating the food in the freezer and refrigerator. One of the cooks had not come in to work, so we were shorthanded. Bobby was about to blow a gasket and the lunch crowd had started trickling in. Knowing he was upset, I tiptoed around him. The ministers had gotten on his last nerve, and he couldn't control himself. He was yelling and cussing more than usual. Alvin, the other helper, was nowhere to be found. He spent most of his time in one of the rooms smoking dope. Heaven help him if Bobby ever found out. Needing a garbage can for the discarded food I went to retrieve one. As I walked out of the kitchen, Bobby ran behind me screaming.

"Where in the hell do you think you're going? Get your lazy ass back in the kitchen."

Without waiting for an explanation, he raised his hand to hit me. I caught his hand in mid-air. I twisted his arm down to his side. I held it there a few seconds longer than necessary. I wanted him to feel my strength. His eyes were big as silver dollars. Just as he was about to cry out in pain, I released him. He was shocked and confused.

Holding his right shoulder with his left hand he mumbled through clenched teeth, "Get your ass out of my place."

I took off the apron and threw it on the ground.

Bobby was a very complicated and contradictory man. I saw him do some unbelievable good deeds for many, many people. I also witnessed him commit some unforgivable, unconscionable and unthinkable acts. He was a cow who would give a good bucket of milk then kick it over.

Because he treated the outlaws with kid gloves and gentle hands, one would think he did that out of fear. Nothing could be further from the truth. They feared Bobby and the people he was connected too.

Whenever his behavior regarding anything was questioned, he'd simply say, "When you're talked about, you're thought about."

I walked down the Avenue not wishing to speak to anyone. I entered Jim's Superette, bought a bottle of wine and stole a pack of cigarettes. I spent the rest of the evening with Liz listening to records. Elvis Presley's "Heartbreak Hotel" was a mega hit that crossed color lines. Other popular songs were Chuck Berry's "Maybelline", Fats Domino's "Blueberry Hill" and Ray Charles' "Mess Around". Black folks have been gyrating and shaking their butts since the beginning of time yet, collectively it was said that no one ever shook like Elvis the pelvis. It was that Tarzan concept once again. One white man in a jungle of blacks and he was the "King".

Bobby didn't stop screaming like a preacher at a Baptist convention, but he never hit, pushed, or put his hands on me again. In fact, he hardly spoke to me following that incident. The only method he had of controlling me was fear. Once that was taken away, he was lost as to what to do with me.

What I felt and thought concerning Bobby was not healthy, and I was aware of that. Still, I would not rest until I made him feel the pain and humiliation he had subjected me to. And when my day came — Heaven help him. I hated him with a passion.

Upon graduating, Elizabeth accepted a scholarship to Alcorn University. By the grace of God and Liz's support, I also graduated. At any second during the commencement exercise I expected someone to tap me on the shoulder and say, "Get your butt off this stage."

To my surprise, I found myself enrolled at Southern University in Baton Rouge, Louisiana. Because things were beginning to boil over I had to get out of New Orleans. It was just a matter of time before Dan and I ended up in prison or Mount Olivet Cemetery. We had begun gambling, loaning money and drinking excessively.

Elizabeth was always in my corner. She'd write regularly and call frequently. I seldom returned her calls and never took the time to write. She wanted more attention from me than I was prepared to give. One day she called and asked if she could visit me in Baton Rouge. I had serious reservations but relented. I picked her up at the bus station on a Friday afternoon. I had made some money in New Orleans, so I was able to purchase a car and afford a room, kitchen, and bath off campus. I continued loaning money while in college at twenty-five cents on a dollar. Plus, I'd rent my room several times a month to couples that were too hot to cool down. I was the 'Joshua Hilton' of Southern University.

As Liz stepped off the bus, she looked as fresh and pure as the morning dew. It had been six months since I had seen her. She had gained about ten or fifteen pounds, and it complimented her thin frame. She no longer looked like a young girl. She was every bit a young woman. Her hair had grown out and now rested on her shoulders. Her skin was healthy, and she was beautiful. She had a chipped tooth that I always found attractive. It made her look young and innocent. While her face would light up when she smiled, sadness was always in her eyes.

I picked up some burgers and milk shakes, and we drove down by the river. It was one of those afternoons when everything moved in slow motion. It was an overcast day and the breeze blowing off the river was cool and refreshing. We talked about school, the girls, and what the guys were up to.

Having thought of something important, she exclaimed excitedly, "Joshua. Joshua, guess what?"

Without waiting for an answer, she blurred, "Rita is dating and I think it's serious! Can you believe that?"

I said casually, "Now that your butt is out of her house, she can begin spreading her wings. Tell her I said hello."

Sucking hard on the straw trying to get the milk shake to cooperate she arched her eyebrows and said, "When I told her I was coming to visit you, she was not happy."

"Maybe you should have listened." I offered. Grimacing she asked, "Are you sorry I'm here?"

"No, of course not. It's just that —", not wanting to spoil her mood I said, "Let's take in a movie."

Sitting there with Liz and watching the ships go by, I thought about New Orleans.

Dan and I had begun cheating at cards, and the money was coming in faster than we could count it. Because of my extra activities, I wasn't seeing much of Liz or the girls. I'd see them at school when I was there or not at all. Liz didn't take kindly to my absence, and in no uncertain terms let me know. She was aware of my drinking and missing school. It was no secret I was loaning money. What she didn't know was, I was loaning money to several of our teachers.

There are certain truths in life, such as, 'You shall reap what you sow.' 'Say hello to everyone you meet going up, because you'll meet the same people coming down.' 'The bigger they are the harder they fall.' All those adages could have applied to Bobby. The man I thought could never fall didn't only fall he never rose again.

A gang called High-Tech was beginning to make a name around the city. They were cruel, violent, and sadistic. When Dan and I received word, they wanted to meet with us, we knew we were in serious trouble.

We met with them in an old abandoned building on St. Roch Street. The leader of High-Tech was a hard nose ex-con called "Jaw Bone". He was stocky, and unsightly pimples dominated his face.

Sitting in a chair and using a wooden box for a desk he spoke to us as the other members hung the wall he said, "Thanks for coming Josh."

He didn't acknowledge Dan.

He lit a reefer with a cigarette and offered it to me. I took a short toot and handed it back.

After thanking me for all Bobby had done for him and his boys, he got to the reason we were there. Simply put, he wanted Dan, and I to finance a drug deal. All we had to do was put up the front money. This would be a one-time thing to get them started. From that point on, we would get a percentage of the profit. We didn't have to put our hands on anything. The return they quoted on our initial investment was unbelievable.

Dan and I had no intention whatsoever of getting involved in drugs.

In their world, their philosophy is "Either you are with us, or you're against us."

Dan and I had to tread lightly. We told them our money was spread out all over the place. We'd needed time to collect all the juice. To finalize the deal, we agreed to meet in a month then shook hands all around.

Dan and I didn't know what to do or which way to turn. I didn't want to ask Bobby for assistance. And Dan and I had a guy working for us named Harold, but he was no match for High-Tech. So, Dan decided to join the army, and I went to college.

The weekend was over much too soon and we found ourselves sitting in the bus station waiting for Liz's bus to depart.

Sipping a coke and holding my hand, she was happy. She made me promise a thousand times that I'd write, visit, and call. I promised on all counts.

With a broad smile, she asked, "You mean it Joshua?"

"Of course, I mean it." I uttered. "Why else would I say it?" She was bubbly and happy. She was the last to get on the bus. As she stepped aboard, her mood changed from glee to sadness.

Standing on the step of the bus she asked again, "Promise?"
I put my hand on my chest and said, "Cross my heart. I'll write, visit, and call. You have my word."

As the bus pulled out the terminal, I stood there lost in thought. I wondered what my life would have been like if I had never known her. She had touched my heart in such a way it would be impossible to forget her. She had helped to educate me on so many levels about so many things. Without her pushing me, pulling me and encouraging me, I would never have graduated from high school.

Elizabeth never saw or heard from me again. Not one of my promises was ever kept. Through the years, I heard pockets of her progress. Upon graduating from Alcorn, she took a job with the Agricultural Department in Jackson, Mississippi. She married a guy who worked in a savings and loan company.

The last letter I received from Elizabeth said in part, "You are cold, indifferent, and insensitive. No one can reach you. You've never had any respect for me or my feelings, something is eating at you, and until you come to terms with it, you'll never have peace. You've never had the decency to return my calls or answer any of my letters, so I don't expect to hear from you now. You have my deepest sympathy. Good luck, God bless, and goodbye. Love and regrets, Elizabeth."

Through the vestiges of time, I have heard Ivory Joe Hunter sing:

"The teardrops that you stepped on
As you danced across the floor
Were crushed like my poor heart was
When you walked out of my door."

CHAPTER 11

The year was 1957. I was seventeen and a senior in high school. Dan and I began hanging around Parks. Parks was located on Claiborne Avenue and Pauger. Parks sold hot dogs, burgers and packaged liquor. Drinking on the premises was not allowed.

Behind the store was a make shift patio. There were many rinky-dinky chairs, an old dilapidated bench and an old beat up table and beer cases. There was another table and chairs on the right side. Two large spotlights illuminated the left and right sides of the building. The back of the store was well lit.

Friday was payday for the men who worked on the riverfront. Parks would cash their checks, and behind the store the men would congregate to drink and gamble. One side of the patio was for the drinkers and checker players. The other side was for the hard-core gamblers. If you were not in the game, you could not hang around the tables. This rule was strictly enforced. The primary games were Poker and Tonk.

Youngsters were not allowed behind Parks. The old timers would run them off. But, Dan and I were the exception. They accepted us because we didn't engage in any horseplay. And of course, they never knew when they might need Bobby.

We became their runners. Whatever the gamblers needed, Dan and I would get it. They'd tip us generously. They called us Youngblood. 'Hey,

Youngblood, cop me a burger.' 'Youngblood, get me a pack of smokes.' 'Youngblood, get me a beer.' Whatever they wanted, we would get it. Dan and I began saving our tips for a special reason.

Being runners, we could hang around the tables. We learned a lot about gambling and even more about cheating. What we observed was during the game, someone always wanted a new deck of cards. Their reasoning was changing the cards would change their losing streak.

Someone would yell, "Youngblood, run up front and get a new deck of cards."

Sitting under a palm tree one afternoon, Dan handed me a hot deck of cards. A 'hot' deck is one that has been marked.

"Find the mark," Dan instructed. "We're in natural light. You shouldn't have a problem."

I looked at the cards from every angle. I could not find any marks. The purpose for the hot deck was one day they would allow one of us to sit in the game. We would slip in our marked deck and show them that luck really is nothing more than a residue of design.

These men were not fools. We were aware of the risk we were taking. As dangerous as cheating is, it didn't seem to bother the two of us. There was something about the excitement that pushed us onward.

We bought several decks of cards, slit the cellophane with a razor blade and easily took it off. Then, we took a stickpin dipped in black or red ink, depending on the color of the cards, and marked them. One dot indicated it was a face card. Numbers from two to nine were a small sign of some kind. After marking the cards, we took a hot iron and resealed the container. Once we were done, you could not tell the deck had been tampered with. Each one of us kept a marked deck with us always. We knew that one day they were going to let one of us in the game.

Every now and then, we'd ask if we could sit in. The answer was always the same. "Ya money's too light, Youngblood."

That meant they thought we didn't have enough. We didn't push or shove. When we got in, we wanted them to think it was their idea. We were patient. It was just a matter of time.

One Saturday about 1:30 a.m, things were jumping. The game was in high gear. Dan and I were running back and forth getting whatever was ordered. Guys were losing and dropping out of the game like flies. There was quite a bit of money in the game.

Hank Martinez, whom everyone called 'News', had lost again. He didn't know diddly about gambling. I think he was just addicted to the thrill of it all. They called him 'News' because he always brought bad news. He could tell you who died before it hit the paper, who got fired or laid off, whose wife left the nest, who got divorced, who was in the hospital, or whose daughter was in trouble. He couldn't pass a funeral without viewing the body, whether he knew the deceased or not. He was bad news walking.

News was broke again. He hung around the table with that sad expression a dog has when he is watching two other dogs sharing an intimate moment. He stood there drooling and wishing. He couldn't make a loan because he owed everybody at the table.

This was our opening. I asked loud enough for everyone to hear, "Mr. News, do ya need a little help? I can get ya out of the rain. How much do ya want?"

Everyone at the table was looking and listening. He twiddled his chin, cleared his throat, and gave the gamblers a knowing look.

He halfheartedly laughed and said, "Bout fiddy should do the trick."

Reaching into my pocket, I said, "No problem, Mr. News. I know ya good for it."

Taking the money and grinning, he was as happy as a kid on Christmas morn.

Dan and I had saved up three hundred dollars between us. We had five twenties and two hundred one-dollar bills. It looked like more than it was. We wanted them to think Dan had just as much.

That night, they made the mistake and allowed Dan to sit in. We slipped the marked cards into the game, and Dan won every dollar. The next night, eager to recoup their losses, Dan played again with the same result. Before long, they were borrowing money from us at twenty-five cents on the dollar.

The money began rolling in like a wheel going downhill.

Once we had capital enough, we stopped gambling. We never sat in another game. It was much too risky and no longer necessary.

The interest, or juice, on the money one guy owed, was fifty dollars. I knew he was struggling. He only had forty-three dollars.

I patted him on the back and said, "That's good. Don't worry about the rest."

Dan interrupted me demonstratively, yelling, "He owes fifty! He pays fifty!"

I pulled Dan off to the side and tried to explain that the old man had a rough go of things.

He said harshly, "If he were home with his family instead of out here gambling, he wouldn't owe anything."

"He has children home depending on him, and he is out here fuckin' round. He pays what he owes. Fuck him. You collect it, or I will."

And Dan did. Money would become Dan's master and he its humble servant.

Dan and I became full-time Hood Rats. Any time, day or night, you could find us rambling. We were making a name for ourselves, and that wasn't good. Rodney made sure Bobby was informed of all my activities, but by now, there was not much he could do with me. He broke me in many ways. But one thing he could not break, was my spirit. Many tears were shed because

of Bobby but he never saw me cry. I could not, and would not give him that satisfaction. Before you can do anything with a wild animal, you must first break his spirit. I was wild and not about to be broken.

All the guys in the group had quit school and were working various jobs riverfront, department stores and clothing factories. I was still going through the motions as far as school was concerned, but my chances of graduating were slim. I was hanging on by the skin of my teeth. If Elizabeth didn't do my assignments, it didn't get done. One thing I had on my side was the money I was loaning our teachers.

When I'd miss school, which was often, Liz would get word to me to call her. Sometimes, I did. Sometimes, it slipped my mind. The days I would go to school, she would corner me in an empty classroom and have a million questions. "Why are you doing this?" "Why that?" "You're sabotaging your future." "You need to stop running the streets." On and on, she'd go.

She'd say, "We need to talk after school." I'd sneak out early, failing to let her know.

There were times when she'd shove piles of papers in my chest, and angrily say, "I hope you have time to go over these assignments."

Before I could say thanks, she'd hold up her hand and say, "Save your breath."

I'd try again to speak, and she'd tell me to please go away. I would stay away only to receive a message asking if I were avoiding her..

CHAPTER 12

I knew Dan Brumfield longer than anyone in the group. We lived in the same neighborhood for as long as I can remember. Dan lived with his uncle Randolph Becker, whom everyone knew, respected and called Bro. Becker. He was Head Deacon at Pure Light Baptist Church. He was an honorable man with meager means. He had one double-breasted suit that he wore to service each week. Since putting on weight he could no longer button the coat. His shoes contained cardboard to cover the holes in the soles.

Bro. Becker and Dan lived in a one room, kitchen and bath. The house didn't have gas or electricity. Oil lamps were used for light, and a wood stove provided cooking and heat. Bro. Becker slept in the bed and Dan slept on an army cot. Bro. Becker was eligible for some kind of government assistance, but his pride would not allow him to accept any type of aid.

Dan's father died in a fishing accident when he was five years old. His mother Miss Ruthie, became chronically ill, and had to move in with her sister. Not having enough room for Dan, and thinking that she would be returning to work soon, allowed Dan to move in with her brother. Miss Ruthie never recovered and died in her sleep.

Soon thereafter, Dan became a common fixture on the street. Since he was small in stature and older than his years, the hustlers called him "Baby Red". He became educated. That is, he learned how to survive. We met early in life exactly when I can't recall. We were friends from the very start.

We saw the world through the same eyes and didn't like it. We both had an ax to grind, and grind it we did.

Dan was tall and skinny. He didn't weigh a hundred pounds with rocks in his pockets. He was a soft spoken, meek, and extremely friendly person. Because of his personality, now and then someone would think he was soft and weak. They'd learn the hard way just how deep still water runs.

We were playing stickball on the neutral ground. It was Dan's turn at bat. He had just stolen a pie from Capo's Grocery. He sat the pie on a tin can. Alfred Davidson, the bully of the neighborhood, decided to eat Dan's pie. He outweighed Dan by at least fifty pounds. Realizing Alfred had eaten his pie Dan didn't say a word. Without a warning, he began hitting Alfred with the bat. He was hitting him so fast Alfred didn't have time to rub the spots where it hurt.

When he tried to run, I tripped him thinking the fight was over. As he fell to the ground, Dan raised the stick. Had he hit him, Alfred would have been severely injured. Instead, I wrapped my arms around Dan warding off the attack.

All the while saying, "Ya made ya point. Ya made ya point."

Trying to free himself he kept repeating, "I'll kill him. I'll kill him."

Alfred may not have known, but Dan was capable killing him.

Dan and I were the original odd couple. He was too light to fight and I couldn't fight. We simply would hit you with anything we got our hands on.

Louis, Jerry, and Count moved into our old neighborhood just about the time we started high school. Count met Gladys Turner. Gladys introduced us to Elizabeth Jenkins, Barbara White, Cindy Hudson, and Gilda Hunter. And, as they say, the rest is history.

The interest, or juice on the money Dan and I were loaning was too good to be true. Some Fridays when we'd make our collections, we wouldn't have time to count the money. We'd put it on the side and count it later. Dan and I were not naïve when we began loaning money. We were aware of the risks and dangers it entailed. We had run in and out of the projects long enough and were well acquainted with that way of life. There are many laws in that subculture, but the one that must be maintained at all cost is respect, respect, and respect.

When you're loaning money, as we were doing you must collect what's owed. There are no ifs about it. You must not let a debt go unpaid. If you do, your reputation is shot. Get off the street. The word that you are cotton or soft, will spread like a leaf in a windstorm, and no one will pay.

We were wise enough to know that the respect that was shown us was limited. Our strength was due in part because of Bobby's power and influence. While his reputation aided us tremendously, it wasn't enough.

It was just a matter of time before someone said, 'fuck ya. And fuck the horse ya rode in on. I ain't paying. Now, git the fuck out of ma face.'

When that day came, and it was on the way, we had to be prepared. Dan and I were not gangsters nor did we pretend to be. Respect is fine, but the kind of people we were dealing with we needed them physically to fear us.

Three doors down from my parent's house lived Mrs. Viola Brooks, her daughter Elaine and her son Harold. Harold was eight, or nine years older than I was, and looked awful. Mrs. Brooks spent a great deal of time talking with Momma. They had a tremendous amount of respect for one another. My sister Gilda and Elaine sang in the church choir together. Harold was her only son, and he was nuttier than a fruitcake — two fruitcakes. I spoke to him only when it was absolutely, positively necessary.

Harold was born with a genetic disorder — some-kind-of muscular problem. It causes weakness of the muscles. There was no cure and drugs did not help. As a young child, Harold wore leg braces. By the time, he was school age he could walk independently, but he was unsteady and would have frequent falls.

When he became school age, Mrs. Brooks was advised that he would make faster progress in a mentoring program. She would not hear nor have anything to do with an isolated setting. She insisted on a traditional school. No one could persuade her to do otherwise. She would live to regret her decision.

From his first day in school, the kids were unmercifully cruel. They teased Harold constantly. They called him Crippy, DD, and other awful and degrading names. Passing him in the hall they'd give him a little nudge, causing him to lose his balance and fall. As soon as he'd regain his balance someone would push him and he'd fall again.

Harold withdrew and began to stutter when he'd try to speak. In the schoolyard, the kids would mock the way he walked and talked.
They would circle him and chant, "Harold can't walk. Harold can't talk. Harold is a dog, but Harold can't bark."

Someone would push him, and down he would go. They would laugh and high five each other.

Harold couldn't articulate his pain and feelings, so he suffered in silence. When he'd attempt to explain to the teachers what he was enduring he'd become nervous causing him to stammer and stutter worse.

Every day after school Harold would wait for all the students to leave before walking home. He would entertain himself by tossing horseshoes. This was the most peaceful time of his day. No one could see or hear him behind the schoolhouse. He'd pitch a shoe, laugh to himself and throw another. He was happy as a lark.

One evening Leroy Waters and Stanley Blaine had detention for a school violation. Upon being dismissed, instead of using the front exit, they left through the rear of the building. To their surprise they saw Harold, without saying a word as they passed Leroy pushed Harold causing him to fall face first into the sand. Leroy and Stanley walked off laughing.

Harold struggled to his feet, and without meaning to yelled, "Bi, Bi, Bi, Bitch!"

As they stopped in disbelief, Stanley said, "Leroy, Crippy called you a bitch."

Leroy dropped his books and ran as fast as he could back towards Harold. When he was in arms reach, Harold hit him with the horseshoe with all his might. By the time, Mr. Ray, the janitor, pulled Harold off Leroy, he was a bloody mess. His left eye was missing, nose and jaw broken, and he had several other facial fractures.

Stanley Blaine was hailed a hero for summoning the janitor and Harold made his first trip of many to the juvenile center. As he sat in the holding cell, he began laughing. He didn't have a clue as to why he was so happy. All he was conscious of was he felt good, and he couldn't stop laughing. Little did he know he would become addicted to that feeling.

As the Turnkey made his rounds, seeing Harold's strange and bizarre behavior, he paused and asked, "Something wrong, boy?"

Harold still smiling said, "Fu, Fu, Fuck ya.", and continued laughing.

The guard shook his head murmured something under his breath and went on his way.

Harold slid off the bunk and stood in the middle of the cell. He allowed himself to drop to the cement floor. He rose and fell again. He stood and repeated the act several times. Lying prostrate on the cement floor he was oblivious to the blood oozing from his arms where the skin had broken by falling on the concrete. Looking at the wounds on his arms he began laughing again. He was overjoyed. He had never felt so elated and happy. He was too young and immature to know, but he was beginning to learn the power of pain. All the days of his young life, pain had held him hostage, and it was pain that would set him free.

In the juvenile center and later in the house of detention, he would come to learn that prison is a dog-eat-dog society. He would learn that it matters not the size of the dog in the fight, but it comes down to the size of the fight that's in the dog. He would learn in that environment you are judged by the size of your heart. And if you have no heart then you'll just end up being another dog's bitch.

One look at Harold's size and physical limitations, and the way he walked, in jail, one might mistake him for a punk, queen, or faggot. The inmates soon would learn better. In time, everyone at the juvenile center, the house of detention, and the entire court system in New Orleans, collectively would refer to Harold Buford Brooks as, 'That crippled, crazy Motherfucker.'

His first evening at the center, while eating dinner, an inmate took two slices of bread off Harold's plate. The Inmate was a huge kid whose reputation in jail was right-on. Harold didn't say or do anything. Not even when the inmate whispered, "I'll be by ya cell tamarow night to tap dat ass."

The next day while mopping the hall the inmate passed by Harold and whispered something in his ear. As he walked away exaggerating the dip in his walk, Harold hit him on the right side of his head with the metal part of the mop, damaging his eardrum. He dropped to his knees. While trying to deal with the pain and the ringing in his head, Harold hit him with the metal bucket causing a concussion.

When the inmate was released from sickbay, Harold wasn't through with him. As he entered the tier, vision impaired, Harold saw him, but the inmate didn't see Harold. He put a bar of octagon soap in a sock. The weight of the soap stretched the sock beyond its normal length. Holding the sock by the leg portion, when the inmate was close enough Harold swung the sock as hard as he could, hitting him flush in the face, breaking his nose and forcing him to require emergency dental attention.

By the time Harold made it to the house of detention, which was a few years later, the boys had given Harold the nickname, 'Mr. Beam'. Jim Beam is a brand of whiskey. He was given that nickname because he walked as if he were intoxicated. Harold would learn to love his reputation, his nickname, and he loved inflicting pain.

He soon derived, not only satisfaction, but pleasure in being cruel and vicious. It gave him a feeling of superiority and control. He began to realize that when he was violent people didn't laugh or ridicule him. Through fear and intimidation, he gained self-worth. Harold's reputation for violence began to spread. After getting his hair cut, nick the barber extended his hand for payment.

He took nick's razor from the counter, held it above his head, and asked "wa, wa, what the fu, fu, fuck ya got yo, yo, ya hand out fo, mo, Mothafucker?" He kept the razor.

Seymour Bennet, a neighborhood thug, was showing off a gun he had stolen. He and his buddies were behind Johnnies' Sweetshop. He passed the revolver around for everyone to see. Trying to impress Harold, he gave it to him to examine. Harold checked out the weapon and asked if he could have it.

Seymour said indignantly, "Fuck no. Is ya outta ya fucken mind?" Just then, Harold made a move on the checkerboard and started laughing. The move landed him in the king's row. He had won the game. Still laughing and without much ado, he placed the gun against Seymour's thigh and pulled the trigger.

As Seymour rolled around on the ground in agony, standing over him, Harold said, "If yo, yo, you te, te, tell the po, po, police, I'll sh, sh, shoot yo, yo, Momma."

Mrs. Brooks was in and out of court with Harold, or visiting him in jail. It was always one thing after another. She sought Bobby's counsel often. Bobby would listen to her patiently, and he never failed to help Harold. It made little or no difference to Bobby how vicious an act Harold committed. He would still use his power and connections in support of him. He was instrumental in keeping Harold from doing hard time in the penitentiary. Despite Harold's physical limitations and his extensive criminal record, Bobby got him a job in the warehouse of Compono's Furniture Store.

Even the dogs and cats knew it wasn't prudent to walk on Harold's side of the street. Whenever they saw Harold they'd run. He had tormented them enough until they had learned to associate the sight of him with pain.

He would throw beer bottles or bricks at them regularly. And if he caught a dog he'd put a clothespin on its tail. The poor animal would go insane spinning around trying to remove it. Harold found that extremely funny, and amusing.

He didn't fear anything or anyone. While stumbling home early one morning, he was stopped by the police. They found the straight razor in his possession.

When they asked Harold what he was doing with it, he replied, "Ya kn, kn, know I ain't no, no, no, fuckin' Barber."

One night on my way to make a collection, I passed The Bucket Of Blood, that's what Ronald Picous' joint was referred to. It was so named because every weekend the Country Boys would gather there and a bucket of blood would be spilled. They raised max hell.

The doors were always wide open, and the music was loud and low down. The chairs and tables were as old as the buttons on Jacob's coat. To cover the spit and tobacco juice sawdust was generously spread on the floor. You'd never find my buddies or me in that joint. As I walked by, I saw Harold standing at the bar motioning for me to come in.

Hating myself for having been seen I wondered what in the world could this maniac want? If it had been anyone else I would have waved him off and kept walking, but for me to ignore Harold would have been an unforgivable sin. It would have been disrespectful. On the street that is inexcusable and unpardonable.

I took a deep breath, whispered a silent prayer and entered the devil's den. The last thing I wanted was to be in this moron's company. I tried to beg off explaining I had urgent business, but he wouldn't hear of it. Harold insisted that I have a drink with him. Having no choice, I poured the drink reluctantly and cursed myself again for coming that way.

Being this close to Harold, or "Mr. Beam", gave me the heebie-jeebies. He was cross-eyed, but one eye stayed focused on me.

He spat on the floor shoveled sawdust on the tobacco juice with his shoe and said, "I ne, ne, ne, need to ta, ta, talk to yo, yo, ya."

I thought to myself, "Then open up your mouth and speak. Stop all this stuttering and spitting so I can put some distance between you and me."

I hated myself for not having the nerve to say that. The way Harold looked and walked from a distance was frightening. Close-up he was terrifying. There were spaces between his teeth and they were brown from years of chewing tobacco.

He had potholes in his face and he drooled constantly, every few seconds he'd wipe his mouth with his hand. Standing this close to him I could feel the presence of evil, and depravity. He gave me the creeps — big time.

Harold took a drink, spilling some on the pocket of his shirt. Mrs. Brooks made sure when he left home he was presentable. Most of the time he wore starched white shirts, khakis, and house slippers. He was neat except for spills on his shirt and urine stains on his pants. He put his hand on my shoulder and began stammering and stuttering. He explained how happy he was that my sister Gilda cared about his sister Elaine. He was happy my mother cared about his mother, and he was happy Bobby cared about him. I was happy there was 'care' enough to go around.

Listening to this "yo-yo" talk I thought to myself. I really didn't give a rat's pee-pee about how much Lil' Red Riding Hood cared about her Grandma, or how much Jack cared about Jill, or how much that nasty old woman who lived in a shoe cared about all those ill-legitimate babies she had. The only thing I cared about was getting his hand off my shoulder, for him to stop spitting on me, and for him to allow me to go on my own way. I had enough of this clumsy, mumbling, bumbling, bastard.

He poured himself another drink and began mumbling, "I he, he, hear yo, yo, yo, you is lo, lo, loaning mo, money?"

My heart fell into my stomach, and for a moment I felt dizzy.

My world was about to fall-down around my knees. I had no idea as to how to deal with this nut. I gulped down my drink and hurriedly poured another one. Fear was running away with me. I had no idea as to what to do. I'm sure everyone in the joint could see I was trembling. What he said next was music to my ears.

Patting me on my shoulder he said, "If dem niggers, fu, fu, fucks wi, wi, wit ya money, le, le, let me, me know and I'll fu, fu, fuck'em up."

Looking at this psycho for a moment I thought he was going to cry.

With a crack in his voice said, "Yo, yo, ya is ma, ma, ma br, bro, brorder"

I felt like jumping for joy. I felt like singing and screaming, "Thank you Harold. Thank you. Thank you. Thank you."

Dan and I would not have any problems collecting our money with

Harold on our side. I was overjoyed and wanted to do something for Harold to show my appreciation. I took two ten-dollar bills out of my pocket and slid them along the bar to him.

"Take this," I said, "snatch those two pretty ladies sitting near the jukebox and have some fun."

He looked at the money on the bar and with a sad expression on his face pushed the money back to me. With sincerity that is seldom heard on the street said, "I don, don, don't want yo, yo, ya mo, mo, money. I to, to, told ya, yo, yo, ya is my brorder. I me, me, meen it."

No longer in a hurry to leave I ordered more to drink. He explained that I had better watch my back because the word was some unsavory characters had their eyes on Dan and me. I was too excited to be concerned about that now. Harold was not a man to be taken lightly. I gave him the respect he deserved. I was no different from anyone else. I feared him.

Every Friday, when payday rolled around, we'd collect our money in full. Harold was always present. We never had a problem. He made more money working one day for us then he made two weeks at the warehouse.

I learned to like Harold. There were times when I truly enjoyed his company. Now and then, we'd go fishing on the lake. Sometimes we'd sit under a palm tree and drink beers. The funny thing was you couldn't tell when he was sober or intoxicated by the manner-in-which he walked.

I know in my heart he truly enjoyed being in my circle. He gave me a piece of his crippled heart. In return, I gave him money. It may have been a lot, but it wasn't a part of me. It was just money. I could not allow him to get too close.

When dealing with Harold I kept a song I had heard in mind called, 'The Snake'.

A young woman was walking home from work and saw a half dead frozen snake in the snow.

The snake cried out, "Please help me. I'm sick, and I'm cold. Please. Please help me."

The young woman picked up the snake and held it close to her bosom then took him home.

Feeding him milk and honey she nursed him back to health. Then one night, while stroking his beautiful skin, he gave her a vicious bite.

As she lay dying, she shouted, "Your bite is poisonous, now I'm going to die. How could you be so cruel?"

The reptile laughingly replied, "Shut up stupid woman. You knew I was a snake when you took me in."

I gave Harold all I could. No more, no less — be it right or be it wrong. The way I saw it, Harold was a snake. I knew that the day I took him in.

The unsavory characters Harold spoke of contacted us. They were a violent gang called High-Tech.

CHAPTER 13

My father Robert Anthony Lange was born and raised in the 7th Ward. The 7th Ward is the largest of the seventeen wards in the city of New Orleans; located there are Dillard University, the Fair Grounds Race Track, and the St. Louis Cemetery.

Most people of color, who possessed a trade it seemed, resided in the 7th ward. They referred to themselves as Creoles. They were known for music, business and building. Bobby's Father and Grandfather were carpenters.

Bobby, his mother and two Sisters resided on Pauger and Galvez St. They struggled to make ends meet. Many days his Mother had to rob Peter to pay Paul. Bobby's Mother, whose name was Corina often would say, "I'd rather my children be poor and healthy than rich and sick."

His father, Jasper Lange, was a carpenter and a barber.

He built the three-bedroom house they lived in with the spacious backyard. In the corner, where the fence formed a right angle, stood a massive old oak tree. It provided an abundant amount of shade during the summers and as a youngster Bobby spent many hours playing and relaxing under it. From one of its huge branches hung a metal swing. His mother loved that old swing and many days she'd rock her cares away.

Jasper died when Bobby was eight years old. He succumbed to a chronic stomach illness. He was known to raise a glass or two and alcohol was a major contributing factor in his demise.

Debbie and Inez, Bobby's two older sisters, married and left home. Debbie married a butcher and moved to Lake Charles, Louisiana. Inez married a boy she had dated since high school. Upon graduating they married and moved to San Diego, California.

Bobby's mother did domestic work for the affluent white folk over in Metairie, Louisiana. She didn't relish the idea of the long bus ride in the mornings, nor the return trip at night. Many nights she'd come home dog tired, every muscle in her body crying out for relief. Many nights she'd fall asleep while soaking her feet.

Bobby attended A. P. Walker Sr. High. He was an average student who enjoyed school and running track. Because of his flexibility, speed, strength, and coordination, he excelled in the hurdles and relay events. He was very competitive and hated losing. He had hoped to be a math teacher, like Mr. Nicholas. He was impressed with Mr. Nicholas because unlike his other teachers, Mr. Nicholas took the time to explain every problem until the entire class understood.

At the end of the class, he would always ask the same question, "Young people, do you understand? Speak up."

He'd shout. "Don't sit there like dimwits, and don't you ever believe ignorance is bliss. For if it were, according to its author, 'It's folly to be wise'. If there are no questions... Class dismissed."

Bobby's mother suffered from rheumatoid arthritis and was in constant pain. The middle of his junior year, her discomfort became unbearable, and the pain was unmanageable. The stiffness and swelling made it impossible for her to perform simple tasks. She became bedridden. Bobby had to drop out of school and find work. Debbie and Inez would send what money they could afford monthly. It wasn't much, but it helped.

Pounding the pavement looking for work, Bobby submitted applications in all the major department stores. He tried the riverfront only to be told he was too young. He sought employment at Flint Goodrich Hospital, Charity Hospital, Pouatoni's Supermarket, Fredrick's Lumber Company, Sherman's Discount Tire Center, and Peamount's Supply House. There was no steady work to be found for a teenager. In the meantime, he earned money selling scrap iron, copper, aluminum, and shining shoes.

Tony's Grocery and Fish Market was located on Claiborne and Pauger. Many evenings the kids in the neighborhood would gather around the pinball machine. The store paid a nickel for every game won if lucky, a few dollars could be made. Bobby seldom played. When the kids didn't have any money to operate the machine they'd idle their time away hanging out on the corner.

One morning, after job hunting and finding nothing, Bobby, on his way home, stopped to admire the truck the pinball man drove. It was a metallic blue late model Ford whose sleek body made it appear as if it were moving while motionless. The white wall tires made it look even more impressive and stylish. It was highly polished and spotless. The painted sign on the door panel read, "Cerberus, Inc." In small print was written, "Where Business Is Always Business." Bobby wondered what that meant. They must build and service pinball machines, he concluded.

While standing and admiring the truck, from over his shoulder he heard, "You like that, kid?"

"Sure do, sir. I sure do." Bobby said smiling. Shaking his head in appreciation he sighed and uttered, "It's a beaut. Yes, sir, it's a beaut."
Bobby tapped on the window as the pinball man stepped into his truck. As the window rolled down the gentleman asked, "Something wrong, kid?"

Now that he had his attention Bobby was confused as to what he should say next. Without thinking the words fell out of his mouth excitedly. "Mister, I need a job. I really need a job. Can you help me?"

"A job?" The man exclaimed. "Why aren't you in school?"

Bobby rushed through the circumstances that had brought him to this moment in time. He began a self-promotion pitch.

"I'm a good worker. I'm dependable, and I really do need a job." He pronounced.

Not knowing why, he blurted, "And I mind my own business."
Maybe the last remark was made because the pinball man looked a lot like the gangsters in the movies. Or maybe the gun in his waistband triggered the response.

Whatever the reason Bobby said again, "Yes, sir. I mind my own business."

The pinball man's name was Allen Adamo. Little did Bobby know, but in time, to grant favors, pull strings and open certain doors he'd depend on Adamo. In years to come, certain events that were foreign to Bobby's nature would bond them together for life. It has been said, and Bobby would learn that power kept not in check is apt to corrupt the minds of those who possess it.

Allen Adamo was a muscularly built man who was the epitome of health. He started lifting weights while in prison and now it was a part of his weekly exercise routine. In the middle of a meeting, if the urge hit him, he'd drop to the floor and do a hundred push-ups. Adamo found it difficult to pass a mirror without admiring himself. His associates called him "The Batman" because he kept a solid oak bat in his truck and, when necessary, would use it to stress a point. Whoever was the focus of the point being stressed would carry the pain of that memory to his grave.

Adamo started in the business working for Francis Francino. He controlled the gambling in Jefferson Parish, as well as the illegal gambling in New Orleans. Adamo's job was to collect the "Take" from the lottery vendors in the Parishes.

Every so often a book would be short by such a margin that stealing or scheming was indicated. When this occurred, the accused's hand would be placed in a vice and Adamo would pulverize it with his bat. If the offense was egregious enough, he offender's head was afforded the same attention, but with a different weapon.

Adamo never knew his parents. As far back as he could remember he was a ward of the state. He was in one foster home after another. Entering his teens he had enough of the system. To survive he turned to crime and violence. Soon he became a known felon.

While serving a sentence for what the state called attempted manslaughter he met and became friends with Benny Petina, the brother-in-law of Mr. Frank. Upon his release, Frank gave him a job running numbers. Then he became a driver, and he gradually moved up to his present position, which was third in command of Cerberus, Inc. His job consisted of collecting the money from the pinball machines, jukeboxes, and all the other mechanical games. When the company financed new businesses, it was his responsibility to get them running. Restaurant owners needed refrigerators, freezers, stoves, tables, and chairs. Bar owners required different equipment, and it was Adamo who got these businesses open and operating as efficiently and expeditiously as possible.

He was also responsible for seeing to it that payments on all loans were made regularly and in a timely manner. Failure to do so was never an option.

If Cerberus had a product they wanted to sell, the proprietors of the restaurant or bar had no say in the matter. They were at the mercy of the lenders — and the lenders showed no mercy.

In spite of how unfairly they were treated, and excessive the interest rates were, there were colored men and women in the City of New Orleans who succeeded in the world of business, and commerce.

Adamo was a very perceptive and intelligent man. Had he channeled his energy in another direction he could have been a member of the Mensa Society. He'd do crossword puzzles with an ink pen, and seldom made a mistake. He was well versed in finance, business, politics, and literature and was a master of non- verbal communication. He spent his life studying a man's body language and reading his eyes. His safety and longevity depended on his accuracy. He knew that the eyes spoke volumes. They said what words could never express. Within a few seconds of meeting a man, he could tell if he were weak, timid, faint-hearted, lying, untrustworthy, or honest.

Having studied Bobby for a minute, he concluded the kid had heart, cold maybe, but heart never the less. He had desire and ambition. He possessed attitude and a drive that would take him far. There was something special and different about this kid. Bobby piqued Adamo's interest causing him to study him very closely. He zeroed in on Bobby's movements, gestures, and facial expressions. For he knew he'd obtain more information by observing him than listening to the words he was uttering.

When he made eye contact with Adamo, Bobby didn't blink excessively. Adamo read that as truthfulness. He spoke quickly. The truth, unlike a lie, doesn't require a pause. He was convinced Bobby wasn't peddling some kind of con or hard luck story. As he talked his hands were in his pocket, and he stood straight. This indicated he was confident and comfortable in sharing his problems. There was no doubt in Adamo's mind the kid had strength. And where there's strength there's character.

When Bobby said, "...and I mind my own business." The way Adamo saw it that was not a slip of the lip. Bobby was reading him also and reading him well. He was impressed with the kid. He'd give him a break. Not once during the conversation had Bobby shifted his weight from one foot to the other. Adamo smiled for that told him he was fearless.

He opened the door of the truck and said, "Get in."

Before getting in the truck, Bobby thought about the name "Cerberus, Inc." He figured Mr. Cerberus must be the boss. As they rode along the aroma of rich cologne filled Bobby's senses. It didn't smell at all like the rubbing alcohol the old men in the neighborhood used for after-shave lotion. It was obvious to Bobby the pinball man had never picked cotton. He admired the alligator loafers, the cut of his trousers, the silk shirt, the diamond ring and gold watch. He concluded the gentleman was a man of means.

The truck pulled into one of the private parking spaces behind Eve's Garden. Eve's Garden was a private key club and exclusive restaurant. It was located on the corner of Tulane and Villire. There were two luxurious cars parked in a private space behind the restaurant. Bobby had passed this club many Sunday evenings coming from the Palace Theater. He wondered if all the stories the old men told around the city about this place were true. One story circulating was that powerful white men openly escorted beautiful women of color to Eve's Garden. It was said that many of these men had two sets of families — one with white children and one with colored children. The mothers of the colored kids were set up in homes somewhere in the city, and the kids were educated and provided for.

In time, Bobby would learn that the men who frequented the club lived in a World within a World. A world where the rich, powerful and wise took the first six months of every year attending to their own business affairs, and utilized the next six months leaving the next man's business alone. Adamo turned off the key and lit a cigarette. He rolled down the window and spoke in a firm voice.

"I'm Mr. Allen Adamo pay attention. I will say this only once."

His tone made Bobby uneasy.

"Working here you'll see and hear a lot of things. Those things are to remain here. As you said kid, mind your own business."

Taking a drag on the cigarette, and letting the smoke escape from his nostrils said, "The job is yours if you want it. If not the bus stop is on the corner."

He hadn't mentioned anything as to what the job consisted of or what was expected. As Bobby pondered his options one thing rang clear, he needed a job in the worst way.

Adamo asked impatiently, "Well, do you want the job or not?"

Bobby sang out his answer excitedly, "Yes, Sir. I want the job. Thanks."

Adamo opened his briefcase and fished out a five-dollar bill.

As he gave it to Bobby said, "This should hold you until pay day."

Bobby couldn't believe his good fortune. He felt rich and cried out with glee.

"Thanks, thanks. Thank you very much."

Stepping out of the truck Adamo retrieved his briefcase and said, "Come on I'll introduce you to your boss — Momma Mae Thomson."

Eve's Garden was a magnificent piece of architecture. Bobby thought how out of place it looked compared to the other buildings in the area. It had many large arches on the first level and small ones on the second tier. An extravagant use of marble donned the exterior walls. Four large columns, which were both decorative and functional, supported the extended roof. The overhanging eaves were complimented by Cornish wood design. The windows were decorated with wrought iron. Twelve-foot long steps with eight-inch risings were set between two columns. The doors had come from Florence, Italy. They were constructed of colored glass encased in brass so well balanced they could be opened with a gentle touch.

On the step to the left of the entrance was a statue of Cerberus. In mythology, Cerberus was a three-headed dog with a serpent's tail. Each head was said to represent the past, the present, and the time yet to come. Cerberus is said to have guarded the gates of hell. The spirits could enter, but not allowed to leave. On the north side of the building was the employees' entrance. The area was sufficient enough for delivery trucks to be loaded and unloaded. The help was not permitted to use the front entrance at any time. Off street parking spaces for customers were provided.

From the service entrance, Bobby and Adamo entered a receiving room where two guys were putting in and taking food out of a walk-in freezer.

Upon seeing Adamo, they said in unison, "How ya doing Mr. Adamo."

He said something concerning the work schedule but did not stop. Bobby followed Adamo down a long hall, past an office, a restroom, and a supply room into a gigantic kitchen. Several employees, all dressed in white, were busy performing food related duties. They all glanced over at Bobby and Adamo but said nothing. They were unusually quiet.

Sitting in a high chair looking as old as Methuselah, was an elderly, commanding colored woman. She was well past retirement age and was loud and demanding. Her complexion was the color of caramel candy. She had a head full of hair that resembled London fog, and a disposition a junk yard dog would envy. Her face was wrinkled as a dried prune. In her hand at all time was a custom- made ivory walking cane with a silver handle. She would poke anyone with it who seemed a bit slow at his assignment.

"Momma Mae, I found you some help." Adamo said laughing. Hugging her he asked, "How are you doing today?"

"Why do you want to know? Are you writing a book?" She questioned pretending anger.

Turning her attention to Bobby she looked at him as if inspecting a side of beef. "Where in the hell did you find this pitiful looking child?"

Seeing smoke coming from a frying pan yelled, "Dominic, don't let that rue burn. Then added, "Don't you dare call yourself a cook. I'm sick and tired of telling you the same damn thing every day. I have a good mind to fire your ass."

Dominic did not look in her direction or respond.

Adamo smiled and said, "I'm glad to see you're in a good mood."

Putting his hand on Bobby's shoulder he announced, "You wanted a youngster to help out, well, here he is."

She grunted and gloomily stated, "I hope he's not like that simpleton Ivan hired."

She laughed and then said, "The poor child didn't know the difference between a head of lettuce and a head of cabbage. He was one for the books."

Looking at his watch and walking away said over his shoulder, "He's all yours. When you finish the paperwork on him see that Angela gets it in personnel."

Stepping down from her perch she barked, "Dam it to hell. Look lively people. We'll be opening soon, and we still have a lot to do. Dominic, I won't tell you again, check that rue."

Poking Bobby with her cane she directed him to follow her to her office. She wobbled down the hall with Bobby trailing behind.

Passing an employee, she instructed him to inspect the produce carefully when the truck arrived, and shouted, "This time use both eyes."

She mumbled something under her breath and entered her office.

Momma Mae's office was state of the art. Dominating the room was a marble fireplace. On the mantel was a vase of cedar chips, giving the room a sweet odor. The floor was marble, set diagonally, matching the fireplace. Off to the right was her private bathroom, which no one was ever allowed to use. A huge sofa occupied the wall near the door. It looked as new as it did the day it arrived.

On her mahogany desk were piles of papers, neatly stacked in an orderly fashion and a photograph of two young white girls with their arms around Momma Mae. Bobby's first inclination was to inquire as to whom the girls were but decided against it. They had to be twins, he thought.

A plant that had outgrown the room stood prominently along the wall near the large picture window. Behind the desk was a high back maroon leather chair, fit for a queen. In the corner sat a huge rock, with the words, "I am stone" carved into it.

On the wall behind her desk was a picture that had obviously been enlarged. It was a colored woman. The frame Bobby thought must have cost a mint. The woman in the picture was sitting on a rundown porch in a rocking chair. The house was in dire need of repair. Next to the chair was a large dog. She had a sun hat on her head and a bandanna around her neck. Starring at the photo he wondered why her eyes were so lifeless that they seem to reflect years of misery, heartache, and pain. At the bottom of the image, in the right-hand corner, was scribbled, "ta ma babi wit luv mutha deer."

Momma Mae flopped her large frame into the large high back chair all the while talking to herself. Wheezing as she breathed, she pulled out one drawer then another. Finding what she was looking for, she tapped two fingers on her tongue and separated several sheets of paper. Giving the papers to Bobby she said, "Fill these out on your own time and return them tomorrow."

Repositioning herself in the chair, she shoved some papers to the side and clasped her hands before her. She thought for a second, and in a motherly sort of way she spoke, "There are only four colored people working here: Me, Claude, the doorman, Sammy, the maintenance man and now you. There are more colored folks working for Mr. Frank at his other businesses around the city."

Raising her voice a bit said, "If you work here long enough you'll find that Mr. Frank is a fair man. He treats all of us very well and pays us very well. I've been with him for many years. Because of him I own property all over the city. I work because I want to not because I have to."

Changing her tone and turning her attention back to Bobby said sharply, "You are expected to be on time, do what you're told, and be regular in attendance. And remember this, Mr. Adamo may have hired you, but I can fire you. If there are no questions… get your ass to work."

In time, Bobby would learn that Mabel Ann Thomson had total control over "Her" kitchen, and those under her charge.

As a young girl, Mabel Ann Thomson was born in Clarksdale, Mississippi. Clarksdale has developed and produced many blues artists: Muddy Waters, Howlin' Wolf, Sam Cooke, Ike Turner, and John Lee Hooker to name a few. Bessie Smith, who was known as the 'Empress Of The Blues', had a mega hit with the song, "Nobody knows You When You're Down And Out." A refrain from the song says:

"If I ever get my hands on
A dollar again I'm going
To hold on until the eagle Grins.
'Cause I found out beyond
A doubt nobody knows you
When you're down and out."

Rumor has it that Bessie Smith was in a car accident driving through Clarksdale and bled to death because a Mississippi hospital would not admit her.

Mabel, her Mother, Tilly and her father, Zack, lived on a small unproductive farm in the rural section of Mississippi. At night, it was so dark you could count the stars.

The night and the darkness were not friends to Mabel. When the sun went down, she'd become depressed. The only things worse than the darkness were the awful sounds of the night. Sleep never came easy to Mabel and in the years to come sleeping at night became almost impossible.

As a teenager, she was unhappy and found comfort in food. Because of her caloric intake, she was overweight. On the way to and from school, she would be seen munching on jellybeans, which she seemed to be unable to live without, Mabel was a terrible student. Her homework assignments were never adequately prepared nor was she. The teachers liked her and would often counsel Mable about her lack of attention and class participation.

Mr. Pitts, her favorite teacher, would often say, "Mabel, you have a brilliant mind, but it's housed in a very lazy body. I know you can do better, and I expect you to do so."

She disliked going to school because her friends were few. She was withdrawn and not very sociable. Her home life was always worse than the day before. Whenever Zack was home, which was all the time, peace and serenity would find a place to hide. It was up to her and her mother, Tilly to work the farm and maintain the dilapidated house. Her father Zack slept all day and when he wasn't sleeping he was drinking and cussing.

Zack Thomson was a lead singer for the Delta Bad Boys, a small six-piece band known locally around Memphis and Clarksdale. Even though his family was living hand-to-mouth he held onto his dream that one day he'd be a star. He refused to find steady work and when Tilly would suggest he seek regular employment she'd become the recipient of a fat lip. Each night after the band's sessions would end he'd hang around the club drinking most of his earnings away with some barfly. In his mind, Zack thought he was "Hot Shit". In the minds of the barflies, Zack was just shit.

About two o'clock, each morning, unable to sleep, Mabel would hear his old beat up truck on the gravel driveway. She would listen as he stumbled into the house, usually drunk. Being well familiar with the routine, she'd cover her face and ears with a pillow.

The pillow was never enough to drown out her mother's protestations.

"No, please stop. Don't make me do that Zack. You're hurting me. Please stop."

Mabel hated herself for not having the courage to rush into the room and stop him from hurting her mother. But, like her mother, she too was terrified of Zack. He slapped her around more times than she could remember. When he did, the pain would last for days.

So, as she held the pillow tightly over her ears trying to muffle her mother's cries, Mabel suffered along with her. The sounds of those nights would haunt her forever.

She had been taught to believe in God, and she did. Each night she'd kneel by the side of her bed and pray. Her prayer seldom changed. It was simple and to the point.

She'd pray, 'Dear God, please hear my prayer. Don't let Zack come home tonight. Let him have a fatal accident. Have someone shoot and kill him. Let lightning strike him. Let him just drop dead. Amen.'

Zack was very bitter. He felt that he wasn't getting his fair piece of the apple pie of life. Everyone he knew in the music business was getting a hit record, a contract and moving on up.

In his mind, Tilly and Mabel were holding him back. Not accepting responsibility for his own shortcomings, he struck out at them in anger on a daily basis. He'd slap Tilly for so much as forgetting to butter his toast.

Mabel would beg and plead to her mother to report him to social services or to whatever agency that could help them.

Holding Mabel's hand and weeping she'd say, "Babi gurl ya jist don't undostan. What is I ta do? If he puts me out where is I gon go? One day ya gon undostan. Babi gurl some thins a woman is jist gots to take. Dat's jist the ways tis. Ya gon see."

Mabel walked on eggshells around Zack. In her heart, she knew his treatment of them wasn't right or healthy. She couldn't understand how there were laws protecting animals but not human beings. Over the door hung a sign that said, "Home Sweet Home".

She laughed and said to herself, "Ain't that a joke. A cruel joke, but a joke nonetheless."

Trevor Metcalf was a very nice and congenial boy. He was extremely friendly but self-conscious. He had a mild case of teenage acne and was shy around girls. He lived down the road a piece from Mabel; they boarded the school bus each morning, and sat together on the last seat.

Most of the boys paid little attention to Mabel. It was really a two way street because she didn't care about them either. Because she was a bit heavy and had a short fuse, the boys as well as the girls didn't rattle her. Trevor was different she thought. He was nice to Mabel; he would go out of his way to be friendly. He truly liked her, and she liked him. So, if allowing him to rub up against her in the lunch line, or feel her legs on the bus made him happy, so be it.

One day he begged her to skip class and meet him in the basement. The basement was off limits except for dressing and undressing for Physical Education. She had no idea why he made such a request, but she agreed to meet him. Once there she couldn't understand why he was so glad to see her since he had just seen her a few minutes ago. He began kissing and rubbing his body against hers. She stood there like a statue not knowing what to do or what he was doing. Refusing to allow him to pull her panties down he pleaded with her just to hold him between her thighs.

Seeing a penis for the first time she giggled. It looked like a broomstick with veins. As Trevor thrust his body against hers, Mabel could not understand why he was so excited, talked funny, and was so messy. For a moment, she thought he had a heart attack... or something.

A few months after graduation Trevor and Mabel were married. Soon after the wedding she found herself residing in the city of a thousand eyes, New Orleans, Louisiana. Once the union was consummated, Mabel found the act to be uncomfortable and unpleasant. She found sex to be overrated, a waste of energy, and the positions down right embarrassing.

Within a few months, they were living apart. The following year they were divorced. They realized it was a mistake and would never work.

Her parting words to Trevor were, "Tre", her name for him, "I've never known anyone as kind and nice as you. The problem is with me. I don't fault you for anything. I hope and pray you find someone deserving of you. Heaven knows I care about you and I thank you. God bless." She never saw or heard from Trevor again.

A few days before they graduated, having lunch together, Trevor informed Mabel that following the commencement exercise he'd be leaving for the Army. He promised he'd write because he wanted to stay in touch.

After graduation and Trevor away in the Army, Mabel was miserable. When she was in school, at least she was away from Zack for a few hours. Between his cruelty and the backbreaking work of farming, she didn't know which was worse. She concluded it was Zack.

On Sundays, she'd go to the Ritz Theater. It didn't matter what was showing. It was a joy just to be away from the house. Afterward, she'd browse the department store or pass by the bowling alley. She observed but never bowled. She didn't know she could miss anyone as much as she missed Trevor. He had been gone for over two months. While she had received two letters from him, she gave up any hope of ever seeing him again. She knew that most of the boys who left Clarksdale seldom ever returned. After all, she thought, what was there to return to?

Daydreaming while ironing Zack's shirt she burned a hole in it. The shirt was the one he wore with his band uniform. Seeing the ruined shirt, without warning, he screamed several expletives, and hit Mabel violently across her face with a boot he was about to put on. The blow caused a concussion. He had cussed and hit Mabel in the past but never like this. It took a while for her head to clear and for her to return to her senses. In the years to come, she'd have frequent headaches.

Tilly prepared an ice pack for her to hold beside her face. The pain in her ear and head would not subside. Sitting on the back porch and crying she wondered if all fathers were mean and ornery as Zack. She couldn't understand why he treated, Sandman, the family dog with more respect and kindness than he did them.

One morning Zack stumbled into the kitchen still drunk from the night before. He ordered Tilly to fix him some Grits, Eggs, and Bacon.

When she informed him they were out of Grits, he yelled, "What? No Grits."

Pushing her out the door he screamed, "Git yo simple ass down to da genal sto and git some."

As she half walked, half ran down the dusty road she heard him yell, "Ya ass bit not be gon all day. I'm hungry."

Slamming the screen door, he stormed back into the house. Mabel was sitting in the corner trembling, afraid to look in his direction.

Seeing Mabel, he said in a rough voice, "If ya ain't got nothin' ta do, git yo fat ass out dare an milk da cow."

He went into his room and fell across the bed.

In a few seconds, she heard him snoring. An idea entered her head that could not be ignored. Trying to disregard the thought, a force, much stronger than she, compelled her to listen and obey. The force motivating her was an emotion so strong it required action. It's called hate.

Mabel walked slowly to the kitchen and filled the large gumbo pot with water. She sat it on the stove and waited. She had heard that a watched pot never boils. She waited for what seemed an eternity for the water to reach the desired temperature. As the water began to dance and sing she allowed it to boil a few extra minutes for good measure.

The water was ready and so was she. She could not believe how calm and unconcerned she was. She felt giddy. As if she were about to ride on the Ferris Wheel. She couldn't wait. With two face towels, she picked up the pot by its handles.

She said out loud, "Never again will you put your hands on me or my Mother."

"You will spend the rest of your days looking like a big boiled ham." She uttered as she started walking towards his room.

Just as she was about to kick open his door with her foot someone on the porch called out, "Is anybody home?"

She hurriedly placed the pot back on the stove and rushed to the door. She couldn't believe her eyes. It was Trevor. He had lost a few pounds, and his skin had begun to clear up. He explained he had finished his basic training and his duty station would be Camp Leroy Johnson in New Orleans.

After a lot of small talk Trevor asked nervously, "Mabel, will you marry me?"

Mabel was speechless. This was too good to be true. This was her ticket out of Clarksdale and away from Zack. While she didn't love Trevor or even know what love was, for that matter, she liked him, and he was kind. The way she saw it two out of three wasn't bad. Before the pot of boiling water on the stove had cooled, Mabel was married and living in the city that care forgot... the Crescent City, the Big Easy, the Party Capital of the World, New Orleans, Louisiana.

At the age of nineteen, Mabel had married and divorced and was alone. She was not only alone, but lonely. She wondered through life with a broken spirit. It was as if she had a huge hole in her soul, and she was powerless to mend it. For the next twenty-two years, Mabel worked in every bar and grill in New Orleans. While she was surrounded by people of the night: pimps, prostitutes, gamblers, and hustlers of every kind, she had no personal or social contact with them. She knew people but had no close friends. Once her shift was over, and she entered her apartment, emptiness would envelope her and cause periods of great distress. Like her shadow loneliness followed her.

Sleep was foreign to her. She could not fall to sleep until she saw daylight peeping through the blinds. For reasons, too complex and complicated for her to understand, she was terrified of the darkness. At night, every light in the apartment had to remain on. To pass the time she tried reading and listening to music but couldn't concentrate. She tried alcohol. It burned her stomach and made her sick. She tried drugs they made her paranoid. Night after night she suffered until dawn. Many times, she'd turn out the light just before daybreak to see if things would be different. If it were dark she'd have an uninvited guest, and they would frighten her beyond words.

Mabel was an intelligent woman. She knew her fears were irrational, and her sensory experiences were distorted. She was aware something in her brain was misfiring, and what she experienced in the darkness was not, and could not be real. She was determined to face her fears head on. Tonight, she would try once again to remain in bed with the lights off.

When it was bedtime, she stood trembling by the light switch on the wall. She put her hand on the switch and held it there.

Telling herself, "Think positive thoughts. Everything is going to be all right. It's just my mind playing tricks."

She took a deep breath, quickly hit the switch to off and rushed to her bed. All the while telling herself, "There's nothing to be afraid of. Think happy thoughts. Happy, happy thoughts."

She kept repeating, "Think happy thoughts."

Lying in the darkness with her throat dry, her head throbbing, and feeling the stillness in the room, she was convinced that this time and this night she'd be fine. After all, she thought, while drumming her fingers nervously on her stomach, "I'm a strong-minded woman."

Inhaling the silence of the darkness, she felt a soft breeze pass over her body. Weeping softly and her heart palpitating she knew they had arrived. Crying now and unable to move, trying to hold her heart in her chest, and having lost her ability to speak, Mabel managed to mumble, "Please, please go away." She was paralyzed with fear — by now her mouth was dry as the desert. She could not utter a sound.

It would begin like it always did. The bed would begin to move slowly, then the bedsprings would begin to squeak, and

lying in bed next to her would be her mother and Zack. She'd hear her mother once again pleading: Please stop Zack. — No, Zack — and there was nothing she could do to drown out those sounds emanating from him like those of a wild animal. Then he'd reach out with his sweaty hand and push Mabel out of bed. She'd hit the floor with a loud thud.

Screaming and terror stricken, she would begin scurrying around the floor as if lost in a maze. The fear was so intense until she thought she was going to die. Disoriented and too weak to stand, she'd scramble around on her knees trying to find the wall with the light switch. After what seemed like an eternity, she'd find it. Sitting on the floor with her back against the wall, and breathing heavily, trying to hold herself together she'd survey the room. With the light on everything was in order. She could make no sense of it. She'd cry until dawn then fall asleep.

Mabel soon learned that when someone was in bed with her she had no trouble with the darkness. She'd sleep like a baby. Armed with that knowledge, Mabel allowed more men to pass through her apartment than through Grand Central Station on a holiday: men of all colors, shapes, and sizes; some were charming, some were witty, some were boring, some were exciting and interesting.

And there were those who wanted a long-term relationship. She'd make it exceedingly clear to these love-struck gents that was an impossibility, and they never received a second invitation. While she detested sexual intimacy, she mastered the art of pretending. As a woman, Mabel's self-image, and concept of herself was totally opposite from the perception many men had of her. In her eyes, she was unattractive and overweight. Men saw a large shapely woman who was engaging, and alluring. She had a pure, alien, yet unexplored innocence, they found irresistible.

Each night, about an hour or so before her shift ended, she'd scan the bar, she'd zero in on a gentleman who appeared available, approachable, and non-threatening. Bringing him a drink he hadn't ordered, set the drink before him, pull out a chair and ask, "Mind if I take a load off?" "Not at all."

Pointing to the drink, the stranger would ask, "What have I done to deserve this treat?"

With smiling eyes, she'd reply, "I need a ride home." Having been around the block a time or two, giving Mable the once over, the stranger asked, "How much is this ride going to cost me?

Reaching over and holding one of his fingers tightly in her hand she whispered, "The same as the drink. The ride is on the house."

Rising from the chair added, "I'll be off in forty-five minutes. I've got to get back to work."

With a smile and a wink, he uttered, "It's going to be one long, hard wait."

It was obvious to most men who entered Mabel's apartment she was not a common whore. Her place was neat and orderly; clean towels in the bathroom, fresh linen on the bed. Her apartment was immaculate. They found Mabel to be a contradiction. They were confused. When they'd ask, 'What gives? How come ya don't have a steady man?'

Her answer was always the same. Not wishing to divulge her fears of the night or her panic attacks, she'd give them all the same story. Sitting on the side of the bed, removing her stockings, she'd pause and ask, "What did you say your name was?"

The gentleman would respond, and she'd continue.

"The answer is quite simple. I don't want a man around all the time dictating what I can, and cannot do. I won't allow myself to be controlled. I work every day. I don't have to ask a man for a dime. After we've shared a moment or two, he can go his way, and I'll go mine, no strings attached."

Then in a voice of years gone by and a memory as clear as her last heartbeat she added, "Some men can be so cruel, and I can't handle that."
Feeling the pain of her childhood stated, "Because of their inability to face their own problems and frustrations, they abuse women, either verbally, emotionally, or physically."

She stated bitterly, "With some low life sons-of-bitches, it's a combination of all three."

The stranger a bit surprised by the conversation asked, "Why do you suppose that is?"

Slipping into bed she'd give a slight grunt and reply, "Because they're weak, cowardly, and unsure of their masculinity. They misplace their aggression. They don't have the balls to stand up to their boss at the workplace: or fight the guy who disrespected them at the bar. So, what do they do? To feel manly, they knock their woman around."

"If you ask me," she offered coldly, "that's a piss poor way to judge a man."

Easing his body close to hers and feeling her warmth, the stranger asked, "And just how do ya judge a man?"

Fondling him and seeing his erection, she murmured, "I judge a man by the size of his heart."

Realizing he was proud as a rooster in a hen house, she rolled over on top of him. In a voice, as warm as a summer breeze, yet as strong as the rock of Gibraltar, said, "I don't need you to lie to me. I know my limitations. I don't need you to say I'm beautiful. I don't need you to say I'm fine. And I don't need to hear I'm the greatest piece of ass you ever had."

Receiving him, with a heavy sigh she winced, and uttered, "Save the bullshit for those who need it."

Not knowing how to respond the stranger asked meekly, "Just what do you need... friend?"

Hiding her face in the pillow next to his shoulder so he wouldn't see her tears, and holding onto him for dear life she whispered, "All I need is for you to be kind, and promise you won't leave before the rooster crows."

The older Mabel got the more frequent the headaches became. This was from Zack hitting her with his boot. At times, she didn't know what hurt the most; her ear, head, or the loneliness. The doctor advised her that the problem was due to a mild case of depression, aggravated by being alone and the loud noises associated with working in bars for so many years. He wanted to prescribe a tranquilizer, but she declined. The side effects were worse than the aches and pains. The doctor then strongly suggested Mabel find other employment.

Mabel was now forty-two years old. Finding a new job would not be easy. She checked the want ads daily. When something interesting would catch her eye, her spirits would drop when she'd read the line that said, "Experience Required."

Just when she was about to give up, one morning while drinking coffee, an ad caught her attention. It simply said, "Housekeeper needed immediately." She smiled thinking she had a chance because the ad did not mention experience as a requirement. She called the number listed and to her surprise the lady was extremely polite and pleasant. Mabel was asked to come in for an interview the next morning at 10 a.m. She was given the address and told to have a nice day.

Mabel was excited but had no idea what was expected or what to wear. For the last twenty years, she had worked taverns and restaurants. This job had something to do with housework and to her that was a brand-new ball game. Not knowing what to wear, she went to a medical supply house and bought a white nurses uniform. She thought dressing in white wouldn't make her look so whorish. She wanted to look pure and Saintly. She smiled at the thought.

Mabel arrived at the impressive looking house with the manicured lawn and beautiful landscape at 9:55 a.m. She walked up the long walkway and standing on the porch nervously rang the doorbell. She took a deep breath and waited.

A young woman about twenty-two opened the door smiling brightly, said, "You must be Mabel. My name's Adela, please, come in."

On the coffee table was a pitcher of iced tea. Pouring Mabel a glass and handing it to her with a napkin said, "I'm so glad you came." In the same breath added, "I need help, and I need help now. I've been interviewing people for over a month."

Listening to her talk Mabel couldn't get over how beautiful and neat the interior of the house was. The furniture must have cost a fortune.

Shifting her weight and sipping her tea, Mabel said, "Don't you think you should tell me what the job entails?"

Crossing her legs and clasping her hands together Adela said, "My husband is out of town at the moment, and I need help with the twins. They are three years old. I need help with preparing meals and maintaining the house".

"Oh, she exclaimed, I almost forgot. You must live on the premises. There's an apartment in the rear that I'm sure will meet your approval. Before you accept or reject the position, allow me to say this. You have a presence about you Mabel that tells me you're perfect for the job. But, with all due respect, I have a few questions I must ask."

Leaning back on the sofa she asked somewhat cautiously, "Since you'll be spending a considerable amount of time with the twins, what is your philosophy when it comes to children?"

Mabel was puzzled by the question because she had no experience dealing with children. While gathering her thoughts, she asked if she could have another glass of tea. She cleared her throat and not knowing what to say said, "Well, when I say no. I mean, no. When I say stop, I mean immediately."

Seeing a bit of agreement in Adela's eyes she gained confidence and continued.

"I think it's important to be consistent with children but fair." Sipping her tea and remembering her childhood the sincerity in her voice permeated the room.

Closing her eyes and seeing Zack, she lamented, "I don't think hitting or spanking a child is ever warranted. I believe in warning a child for the first offense and taking certain privileges away thereafter."

Thinking how she had turned out, said, "Physical abuse and that is what hitting and spanking is doesn't teach good behavior."

Adela was certain Mabel would be perfect for her family. She couldn't wait to inform her husband she had found the right person.

The salary was unbelievable, and she'd be living on the grounds. She was overjoyed for that meant there would be people close-by, and she'd be able to sleep without panic attacks. How would she get along with the twins she wondered? If they were too difficult to manage, she'd quit.

It was a mutual admiration society from the start. The girls, as Mabel referred to the twins, adored her. And she in-turn loved them. Mabel didn't know she had so much love to give or so much love could be received. She treated them as her own. She was present for every major event in their lives, birthdays, school plays, communion, graduations, and the pains of puberty. They grew up calling Mabel, Momma Mae. And taking their lead from the children, Adela and Francis Francino did likewise.

When Mabel began working for the Francino's, Frank was in prison. Adela had said he was away on business. After she had worked awhile, Adela told her the truth. When Frank was released, he took to Mabel like a fish takes to water. He never interfered with how she ran the house, or her method of dealing with his children. He knew the twins loved her, and to him, nothing else mattered. When Frank opened Eve's Garden, the twins had grown up and were away at college. Mabel was financially well off by this time in her life. Frank had seen to that. But once again she was alone and lonely.

One evening at supper, Frank was explaining to Adela that the restaurant would be opening soon, and he had to find a manager to run the kitchen.

Hearing that Mabel blurted out, "Mr. Frank, I want the job. I need something to do."

He thought for a second and said, "What the hell. The kitchen is yours." Hugging him tightly and smiling she said, "And don't you forget it."

From day one, Mabel ran the kitchen, her 'kitchen' as she referred to it, like a drill sergeant. Every meal leaving "Her kitchen", had to be perfectly prepared, or there was hell to pay — big time.

Fingernails had to be clipped and cleaned; haircuts were mandatory and the entire staff had to be clean-shaven. Mabel would raise holy hell for the least infraction of her kitchen rules. The cooks, bartenders, and waiters could not understand how a colored woman could have so much power. The waiters were not permitted to socialize in her kitchen. Loud talking, laughing, and joking were strictly prohibited.

She often would shout, 'People, this ain't your house or some other nasty place. I want this kitchen spotless. I won't say it again.'

When the help would complain to Adamo about something Mabel may have said or done, he would not entertain their concerns.

He simply would hunch his shoulders, smile and say, "I would love to sit up with you, but I am sick myself".

He knew it was senseless to say anything to Frank about Mable that wasn't positive.

The customers were always sending generous tips to the kitchen staff along with compliments. If Mabel suggested someone be terminated, Frank took her request very seriously.

Down through the years when Mabel would hear or read something negative about Frank's illegal activities, she'd turn a deaf ear. To her they were all vicious lies, and nothing but lies. To Mable, Frank was the salt of the earth and could do no wrong.

CHAPTER 14

Bobby was eighteen when he began working at Eve's Garden. He would remain there for thirty-seven years and then go into business for himself. When he began working his mother gave him advice he utilized all his life.

Her admonition was, "When ya round white folk keep ya mouth shut and ya eyes open. It's not prudent to let ya right hand know what ya left hand is doing."

Weekdays, Bobby worked in the kitchen from 3 p.m., until midnight; Saturdays and Sundays 3 p.m., until closing; which was always about 4 a.m. He worked the dining room on the weekends busing tables. His salary was twelve dollars a week plus ten percent of what each waiter made in tips. While he had no way of knowing what the waiters made, he was never disappointed with what they put in the can for him. In little or no time, Bobby was earning as much as men working on the waterfront.

After Momma Mae introduced Bobby to the cooks she gave him a green jacket, two white shirts, and a green bow tie. She explained that was for working the dining room.

Throwing him an apron said, "That's for working the kitchen."

She then gave Bobby a tour of the lounge. Bobby couldn't believe his eyes. It was a palace. The china and silverware on the tables sparkled. The dining facility was extremely spacious. It easily could sit two hundred people in the eating area and another one hundred and twenty in the lounge. There were four chairs to each table. The chairs were super plush and different in color. One set of four chairs was lime green another set burgundy, another set yellow, and another set tangerine then the colors would repeat. It put a rainbow to shame. There was a long mahogany bar with high back chairs with armrests. The bar was stocked with every kind of liquor known to man. The mirror behind the bottles of alcohol ran the entire length of the bar. You could see your reflection wherever you were sitting.

The dark multicolored carpet ran from one end of the room to the other. You couldn't hear yourself walking. The drapes hung from the ceiling to the floor and complimented the interior of the club. Overhead, beams were exposed from which hung a colossal bohemian crystal chandelier. The lights could be made to flicker giving the effect of candles. All the fixtures were gold, giving the facility a sense of harmony. With the push of a button, the stage would extend outward towards the customers creating an atmosphere of intimacy. Eve's Garden was magnificent, prompting Bobby to think how nice it must be to be rich.

Carlos the headwaiter spoke with a heavy Italian accent. He was an elderly man who was extremely friendly and took Bobby under his wing immediately.

On Bobby's first day, he said to him, "Wen in doult alrays smile."

He instructed him to hold the door open when a couple was leaving, providing the doorman was on break. "Pleasantly say goodnight and don't ever look at the gentleman's lady. Boobvi," he'd say, "dis vill gurantee a vig tip."

"What if the gentleman is alone?" Bobby asked. "Do I still open the door?"

Carlos thought for a second and said, "In dat case, fuck him, let him open his own door."

Bobby began to prove his worth in leaps and bounds as an employee. He was dependable, efficient and respected by all. Frank said little to any of the employees, but he had a mental file on each one. He saw Bobby as a decent, hard working kid. Plus, all the reports on Bobby were positive. Momma Mae spoke very highly of him and with Frank that went a mighty long way.

In time, Bobby learned his way around the kitchen. He soon got used to

Momma Mae's poking him with her cane and ranting. Before you could say: Who would have thought it? Bobby could make any salad served; dessert, green bean, pasta, vegetables, and his favorite layered salad. He became knowledgeable of beef since it was a mainstay at Eve's Garden.

Momma Mae taught him that beef is muscle tissue. The more it is used the longer it had to cook. It required slow moist heat. While the tender cuts, which were generally served, were sautéed, and grilled, roasted or broiled. He had no way of knowing but one day that information would pay huge dividends.

Eve's Garden was not for the common man; you could not walk in off the street. It was an exclusive and private key club that catered to the rich, affluent, and powerful — State Officials,

Corporate Executives, Actors, Actresses, Bank Presidents, Realtors, and those with exceptional means. They came not only for the food, shows, and atmosphere, but to be among the movers and shakers of the City of New Orleans, and to remain close to Francis Anthony Francino. They never knew when they might need him.

CHAPTER 15

A Greek by the name of Alexander Aniketos, along with his wife Sophie, operated a candy store. They worked long hours trying to obtain the American Dream. They had one child, a son, named Brandon.

The day Brandon graduated from college, Alex, holding his hat in his hand, dropped to his knees and cried out, "Lord Almighty, thank you very much!"

Alex and his wife arrived in America with the clothes on their backs and a dream in their hearts. They took a simple candy called Turkish Paste, or Lokum, and turned it into a productive business. They were happy, healthy, and self-sufficient. Their son, Brandon, married his college sweetheart and had given them three beautiful grandchildren, named Alice, Victoria, and Brandon Jr.

In Alex's heart of hearts, he felt tremendously blessed. He had a wife who truly loved him. She stuck by him through the highs and lows of life, and the joys and heartaches of the candy business. He had a son who didn't abandon him and never brought any shame to the family name. Alex was a proud man. He did what the Lord instructed listened, obeyed, and believed.

Despite their good fortune, Alex and Sophie were getting up in age, and longed to see their old friends and home. Home was Delphi, Greece, once considered the center of the known World. Delphi was one place they longed to be. After months of soul searching and praying they made their decision — they were going home. They would sell the inventory and property to Brandon and return to the savory taste of Zealotry, Dolmen's, Daisy Cheese and the smell of Wheat and Barley.

As Brandon stood in the airport watching the plane take-off he shed a tear of thanks and gratitude. Everything he was he owed in part to his parents. He would repay them the only way he knew how and that was by being the very best he could be. Brandon always knew that one day the candy store would be his. That day had arrived. He felt prepared and confident. In college, he majored in Business and Accounting and along the way his father taught him, when he was knee high to a duck, the three things that were necessary in Business: a product, a need, and an audience.

The Candy Shack employed sixteen people, plus Brandon and his secretary. In the beginning, only a few flavors of candy were sold. In later years, cakes, pies, cookies, ice cream, jams, jellies, marmalades and novelties were added to the inventory. Several years had passed since Brandon had taken over the operations of the candy store. Under his supervision and attention and with the help of dedicated workers, the business had grown by leaps and bounds. The increase in the number of customers was due in part to extended operating hours, attention to detail, added inventory, advertising and dedication.

Late one evening, as Brandon examined orders, invoices, and receipts, Lala, his secretary, informed him that a gentleman was in the outer office and requested to meet with him. His first thought was to turn him away when his secretary strongly suggested that he should reconsider. Entering his office, the gentleman projected an air of importance. He was not a large man, but he had a presence that filled the entire office. He could not be ignored. He wore a dark pin-striped blue suit, red silk tie, black wing tipped shoes and sported an eight-inch Cuban cigar. Brandon could feel and smell the vile, sordid, debased, corruption of the animal standing before him.

Standing erect, with a sly grin the animal extended his hand and said politely, "Good evening, Sir. I thank you for taking the time to see me. My name is Francis Francino. I know you're a busy man so I'll be brief."

CHAPTER 16

Francis Anthony Francino was born and grew up in the Third Ward. The Third Ward houses the seat of city government: City Hall, the Court House, Charity Hospital and the Orleans Parish Prison. The great jazz musician Louis Armstrong was also born in the Third Ward. Francis resided with his parents on Bolivar and Perdido Street. His folks were poor Italian immigrants who were eating shit with the chickens trying to hold body and soul together. His mother had her hands full trying to manage Francis, his three sisters, and maintain the house. His Father, Aldo, caught a few days a week on the waterfront. All the slots were filled with White men first, if other bodies were needed, then and only then, were Italian and Negroes hired.

The work was hard, degrading, humiliating, and dehumanizing. The last hired were always the first fired. They were constantly accused of not pulling their weight and loafing, and when it was necessary to address them the remarks were always racially insensitive.

Tulane Avenue was the Mason Dixon line that separated the whites from the Italians and Negroes. Under no circumstances were 'Grease-Balls' or 'Jig-A-Boos', as they were referred to, allowed on the downtown side of Tulane Avenue after dark. To survive, the Italian and Negro kids had to join forces to fight the Zits. The Zits was the name given to the white kids who lived on the downtown side of Tulane Avenue. They were big, strong, and considered void of all intelligence. They hated Italians, Jews, Negroes, and Irishmen. They hated them with a passion. They were called Zits for obvious reasons.

Many nights, having nothing better to do, the Zits would come across Tulane Avenue looking for the Italians and Negroes. Most of the time they could be found on the corner shooting dice, or just hanging out. The Zits would jump out of their cars swinging bats and chains. Sometimes the police were notified sometimes they didn't respond.

Francis' gang was called Wop's, to the State Department those letters stood for 'Without Papers'. To Frank's gang they meant 'Without Pity'. Francis was vicious. He introduced guns to his gang, and they didn't hesitate to use them. He soon became a force to be reckoned with on both sides of Tulane Avenue. He became a neighborhood terror. His reputation for violence began to spread faster than a runaway train. In a very short time, the Zits and all the other boys began to fear and respect Francis Anthony Francino.

A block from Aldo and Eva Francino lived Joseph Black and his family: Sarah, his wife, daughter Naomi, and son Samson, whom they called Sam. They were a very religious family who never missed Church. Joseph Black, who the neighbors called Joe, was a proud, Negro man. As a youngster, he picked cotton from sun up to sundown in the cotton belt of Tennessee. He was well acquainted with hard work long before moving his family to New Orleans.

His son Sam began having problems in school. First, he started missing school; then his grades began to deteriorate. He became withdrawn and wanted to quit school all together. Feeling a change would brighten his spirits the family decided to move to New Orleans.

Arriving in New Orleans and unable to find work, Joseph Black bought a pick-up truck and began selling fruit and vegetables.

Every so often he'd stop his truck, get out and yell, "I've — got — watermelon, — Lady, — Red — to — the — rind."

Hearing him, the women would rush out to his truck to buy what they needed for the days' meal: greens, tomatoes, garlic, potatoes, and cabbage.

Joe bought his produce from the French Market. He'd always be the first to arrive but the last one whose order was taken. All the White vendors received attention first. The way Joe operated he preferred it that way.

The French Market has endured over two hundred years. It began as a trading post on the river. It's one of the oldest public markets in the world. The vendors or peddlers, as they were known, would purchase their fruit, vegetables, and grocery goods all during the week. The market was open and busy twenty-four hours a day. Once their trucks were loaded, the merchants would peddle their fruit and vegetables products; a common site around the City of New Orleans.

After the white peddlers had loaded and departed, then attention was directed to Joseph. As if seeing Joseph for the first time that morning, the insensitive and cruel retailers while smiling, would slap him on his back, and ask in a loud voice, "What ya want t'day Black Joe?"

Joseph would endure this vile and disrespectful treatment as-a-means to an end. For no matter, what the merchant would charge for the mustard greens, turnips, fruit, or whatever he ordered, Joseph would haggle about each and, every price.

He'd grin and say, "Ya gotta give po Joe a betor price den dat, boss."

The retailer would argue and complain, but Joseph always would win out. Everything Joseph bought was reduced. Joseph never, ever paid full price for anything ordered.

When he would prepare to pay for his load the merchant, by now, totally disgusted with haggling with Joseph, would snatch the money from his hand and shout, "Don't come here next week wit dat po' mout shit."

Of course, next week there was more of the same.

There was always some fruit and vegetables that couldn't be sold because they were beginning to spoil.

Joseph would say, "I'm gon take dat rotten stuff and git rid of it for ya, boss." He'd go through it once on his route, and a lot of it was salvageable.

He'd purchase enough fruit and vegetables to last a week. This was done every Monday, on Friday, he'd return to the market for his fish. When the fish would arrive at the stall, the Catfish, Redfish, Trout, Drum, and Flounders would all be mixed with the outlaws. The outlaws were the inferior fish that the supermarkets didn't want — Mullets, Hardhead Cat, small fish, and other rejects.

The owners, not wishing to pay someone to separate salable fish from the rejects, would allow Joseph to do it. In return, they gave most of the rejects to him. Most Fridays he'd end up with three number two tubs of fish. Before leaving, to save a few more pennies, he'd use their ice to pack down the fish.

If a penny saved, is a penny earned, by underpaying for his produce and getting over a hundred pounds of fish for free, before pulling away from the dock Joe had made a week's pay before making a sale. Of course, it broke his heart the way the merchants talked to him at times, but he'd smile, swallow hard, and remember he had a family to feed.

He'd often think to himself, "Pride might be a profound virtue, but it ain't gon put no beans and rice on da table." He would not allow pride to get in the way of bargaining, and haggling.

Before driving off, Joseph would look at his load with satisfaction. He'd laugh knowing he had beaten the retailers out of quite a few dollars. As he drove off, and still laughing about how he got over on the merchants, he'd cuss them under his breath for being so racist and insensitive.

In the next breath, he'd say, "Lord, please forgive me for I have sinned."

When he'd arrive home on Friday evenings, whatever fish he hadn't sold he'd give to the neighbors. On Saturdays, after finishing for the day, he'd give the fruit and vegetables away, providing he had not sold out. He then would wash the bed of his truck out and get ready for Monday. Sundays were set-aside for the Lord.

Eva Francino, her family, and the other neighbors would be the recipients of Joseph's generous nature. Many weeks, her husband Aldo, would only catch a day or two on the Waterfront. At those times, they'd be thankful to Joe that they had fish and potato salad to last a few days. Plus, whatever mixed greens he had given them. The Francino's didn't see Joseph as just a neighbor, but a very dear friend.

As a youngster, Francis could not comprehend how a poor man like Mr. Joe as he had been taught to call him, could be so kind and generous. The way he saw it, the poor man, didn't have a pot to piss in or a window to throw it out of, yet, he was free hearted. It was an impression that Francis forever would remember.

Naomi and Samson, Joseph's two children, were members of the Youth Choir and other church related organizations. By fifteen, Samson wandered away from the church and began just to drift. The Reverend and his parents tried counseling him but to no avail. He began to stray without direction or purpose.

Samson was different from other boys. He didn't like sports or rough housing. He spoke in a soft voice, was extremely quiet, and reserved. He kept to himself. He was aware of how the boys standing on the corner would stare at him as he walked by. How they laughed at his mannerisms behind his back and the awful and degrading names they'd whisper among themselves. As fragile and delicate as Samson appeared, there was something about his demeanor that forced the other boys not to disrespect him directly. Samson may have been unlike them, but the thing they didn't know was, he had the heart of a lion. And soon, very soon, the laughing and whispering would come to a screeching halt.

Sam would talk with Francis when his parents would send him to see if Joseph had any leftovers. Francis was cordial, but like the other boys in the neighborhood, he too kept his distance. Samson was not the type of person he'd want for a friend.

One Friday, when Francis came to see if Joseph had any fish to give to his family, Samson asked if he could get a moment of his time. Reluctantly, Francis agreed to speak to him briefly. At night, Joseph would park his truck in the yard. He had two German shepherd dogs he kept chained up during the day and released at night. This was necessary in order to keep the kids from jumping the fence and stealing his fruit. Sam and Francis walked to the rear of the huge yard and stood by the doghouse. The dogs were secured on the south side of the yard during the day.

Trembling as he spoke Samson said without hesitating, "I want to join the WOPS."

Francis had to control himself to keep from laughing. He allowed Sam to continue.

With a slight quiver in his tone, he said, "I want the name calling and laughing to stop. And I want it to stop now. If I were a member of your gang I'd be respected, maybe even feared."

Then giving it some thought added, "Of course, being feared is not important to me. That's not important at all."

Samson, pouring his heart out to Francis stated, "All I want is to be treated like a human being."

As if talking to himself he patted his chest and shouted, "I have feelings, ability, value, and purpose."

Taking a deep breath and becoming more forceful, said, "I'm not a fool. I realize I can't make people like me. All I want is for them to behave in a civil and decent manner."

Almost on the brink of tears he said pleadingly, "Is that too much to ask?"

Having listened to Samson as if he were the most repugnant and despicable person he'd ever met, Francis said, "Are ya fucken kidding me?"

He was unable to conceal the disdain he felt for Samson. "On the streets", he scornfully sneered, "our reputation depends on fear and intimidation."

Waving his arm as if disregarding Samson altogether said contemptuously, "Ain't nobody scared of no fag, queen, punk, or whatever the fuck ya — "

Before he could complete the insult Samson hit him high on the side of his head. He fell backwards over an empty apple crate. Before he could rise or clear his head, Samson had straddled him.

A few weeks earlier having formalized a plan, Samson went into the project and bought a gun. He never held a pistol before and found the experience frightening and intimidating. It took several days for him to feel comfortable with having a revolver around. Sitting on top of Francis with the muzzle of the weapon pressed hard against his forehead, he could not contain his pain and humiliation.

Spitting out words through clenched teeth he yelled, "Apologize or I swear my dogs will have your brains for super."

The WOPS were the most vicious and dangerous gang in the city. Members were well acquainted with the justice system, especially Francis. He was cold, deadly, and ruthless. As a teenager the syndicate, or mob, watched him closely for they knew they'd have use for him in the future.

Before he was seventeen, he was charged with two cases of manslaughter. One case was dismissed because the witness could not be located. The second charge the witness recanted his testimony. Before he was twenty-five, he married had two children, and was on his way to becoming a figure to be reckoned with in the criminal underworld.

Feeling the cold metal on his forehead and looking into Sam's eyes, Francis saw the eyes of death. This evening he was prepared for a lot of things, but he wasn't ready to shake hands with the devil. Swallowing hard and trying to think, he knew Samson was serious — deadly so. He had been on the block and in and out of the Juvenile Center enough times to know when a man was just wolfing and when he was prepared to take his convictions to the limit.

Not recognizing the sound of his own voice, he mumbled, "Can, can, can we talk, talk this over?"

Pressing the revolver into Frank's forehead and loosing patients with each breath, pulling the trigger back, Samson screamed, "Apologize! Now!"

With his heart beating faster than a hooker can lie, Francis nervously and quickly said, "I opal — pol, apologize. I'm sorr — sorry — I didn't —"

"Shut the fuck up." Samson ordered. Not one to express himself with the use of such language he was surprised at how powerful he felt.

Leaning over he whispered in Francis' ear, "I'm going to look into your eyes and if I don't see the truth, to this world, you'll be just a memory."

Slowly, very slowly and with great difficulty Francis met Sam's gaze. What Sam saw he understood. He saw pain, cruelty, violence and savagery. What he didn't understand were the tears running down the side of Francis' face.

Sam stood and extended his hand to help Francis to his feet. He sat the gun on the roof of the doghouse. Pointing to the revolver he instructed Francis to take it.

Then added, "If I can't join your gang, one night when I least expect it, use the gun to take me out, make it as painless as possible."

Francis stood there confused, not knowing what to say or do. He had no response for such a request. He had never met anyone as fearless as Samson.

As Samson was walking away, he paused and said, "You've got seven days to decide. If I see the sun rise on the eighth day and I haven't heard from you, I promise, you won't see it set. I'll kill you."

Francis could convince the gang to accept Samson by selling them a bill-of-goods.

"We can use him as a decoy, or patsy." Francis explained shrewdly.

"No one would ever expect him of anything. He don't act, talk, or look threatening. Besides that, he's green as grass. If something goes down wrong he'll take the fall."

Reluctantly, they agreed to give him a try. The only charges they had against Samson was he had delicate features, spoke softly, took short steps when walking, and appeared extremely fragile. In spite of his so-called liabilities, there was something about him that held them at bay.

Francis and Tyree, while incarcerated, had seen many guys running wild on the street but in the house of detention they were somebody's old ladies. Some were turned into common whores and were passed around like the sport's pages of the newspaper. They were commonly referred to as "Pancakes", meaning they'd flip in a heartbeat.

Tyree hated punks, queens, and homosexuals. In prison, those not having someone to protect them were afraid of the other inmates; but where Tyree Mayo was concerned they were horrified. He was cruelly unmerciful to them. He'd call them unthinkable names, and subject them to unbearable pain and humiliation.

Tyree wasn't present when Francis met the gang to discuss admitting Samson. He was violently opposed to Samson being accepted.

Seething he yelled, "Fuck no. I ain't runnin' da street with no queen bee. It ain't gon' happen."

Walking off angrily, he asked, "What in the world is fucken wrong with ya Frank?"

Standing by the doghouse in Samson's yard Francis gave him the bad news. He informed him that a unanimous vote was required to become a member of the gang, and one guy was opposed to his joining.

"What's his name?" Samson asked.

"Tyree Mayo." Francis replied, "Do ya know him?"

Shaking his head in the affirmative, Samson said, "Yes, every time I see him he spits as if the mere sight of me repulses him."

"Well," Francis added, "I just want ya to know it's not likely he's going to change his mind."

Picking pebbles off the ground and tossing them, without emotion Samson said, "That's unfortunate Francis. Be that as it may there'll be no amendment to our agreement."

Disappointed and mortified by Samson's attitude, raising his voice Francis asked angrily, "What the fuck do ya want me to do? I'm trying my best to help ya. Ya getting on my fucken nerves. Do ya know who the fuck ya talking to? If ya was anyone else I'd blow your fucken brains out here and now."

Pointing his finger in Samson's face said savagely, "Shut the fuck up and stop pushing on an open door. And I mean now. Do you fucken understand me? I won't tell ya again."

Unfazed by Francis' show of temper, Samson softly said, "You've got two days left. You know the agreement.", then began walking away.

With urgency in his voice Francis nervously yelled, "Wait. Wait a minute. Tonight, we have a meeting behind Monroe's pool hall. Be there at nine."

"What for?" Samson asked.

"Maybe you can convince Tyree to change his vote." Samson shrugged, smiled and said, "Maybe I can."

Looking at Samson with eyes as cold as steel Francis said ominously, "If you can't, I suggest you go down to Broadmoor's funeral home and pick out ya casket."

The WOPS would gather behind Monroe's Pool Hall on Perdido and Romain. That was their headquarters. Monroe was the owner of the billiard parlor and the adjoining tavern. The shed was used to store empty beer cases and used chairs and tables.

It had electricity, heat, an old sofa, and a broken jukebox, paint cans, a ladder, and a wheel barrel. Monroe knew the WOPS were responsible for most of the criminal activity in and around the Third Ward. Allowing them to congregate in the shed was a form of insurance. He was a firm believer in the old saying: Keep your friends close, but your enemies closer.

Samson had passed Monroe's pool hall many days. He knew he would not be welcome, so he stayed away. Secretly, he thought he'd be good at pool. Walking down the dimly lit alley on the side of the pool hall Samson was not nervous or afraid. He had come to terms with his decision and was prepared to let the chips fall where they may. As he neared the shed, he could hear loud laughing and talking. Not knowing what to expect, he adjusted the pistol in his back pocket, took a deep breath, opened the door and entered.

At the sight of Samson, a hush fell over the room. It appeared as though time had ceased. No one moved or uttered a sound. There were about twenty-five boys present. He had seen most of them around the neighborhood. He had gone to school with three of the five colored kids present. Two of them would pass him in the hallway at school, and on the street as if he were invisible.

Some of the gang members were sitting on the sofa, some were leaning against the broken jukebox, and others were sitting on the floor with their backs against the wall. They were smoking, drinking, and pretending to be busy while doing absolutely nothing. They generated nervous energy. They all had the same expression — anger, disgust, contempt, indignation, annoyance, and resentment. Francis sat at his desk refusing to acknowledge Samson.

Samson stood in the middle of the room allowing them to become acclimated to his presence. He was about to make his introduction when Tyree Mayo broke the silence.

Tauntingly he laughed and said, "Well, well, well if it ain't my fair lady."

The gang looked at one another and broke the stillness in the room by laughing and guffawing. Samson was unnerved and did not respond.
Wearing a red bandanna tied around his head, a dingy undershirt, jeans and boots, Tyree spoke again.

"If ya want yo butt plugged ya come to the wrong place. Dis ain't no meat packin' company, and it sure ain't fairy land."

The way the gang was laughing and clapping you would think they were at an all-star comedy show.

Still, Samson gave no discernible signs that he was uncomfortable that Tyree could decipher. Smiling and displaying smoke stained yellowed teeth he continued.

"Tell us something sweet Georgia Brown, is it better to give or receive?"
Francis wanted to say something on Samson's behalf, but he knew the rules. Every tub must stand on its own bottom. A man must show he's worthy of help by helping first himself. At that moment, Samson wasn't doing anything to support his cause.

Samson, not worth Tyree's attention, spat at Samson's feet, turned and began looking out the window.

Samson, in a very composed and constrained manner asked, "What are you afraid of Tyree? That is your name, isn't it?"

Not appreciating the insinuation Tyree turned, pointed his finger, and screamed, "I'm not afraid of nothin' ya little fruitcake mothafucker — not even death."

Samson nodded and without blinking said, "I apologize. I meant no disrespect. For after all, death is only a new beginning and the man who doesn't fear death truly knows what it is to be free."

"Whatever." Tyree uttered and resumed looking out the window.

Without saying a word, Samson reached in his back pocket and retrieved the pistol he'd been hiding. At the sight of the gun, a collective sigh fell over the group.

A stocky colored kid, called Moose, was sitting on the floor with his back against the wall. He had done a few months in the correctional center with Francis and Tyree. He had also gone to school one year with Samson before dropping out. While he didn't socialize with him, he spoke when passing and gave him some semblance of respect.

He didn't agree with the other guys' assessment of Samson. He simply found him to be different — nothing more, nothing less.

Not knowing what Samson intended to do with the gun

Moose said authoritatively, "Slow ya roll Sam. Ya in way over ya head. Dis ain't da schoolyard. Ya can't say, oops, I'm sorry, and all is forgiven."

Samson completely ignored him. He was concerned with Tyree, and Tyree only. At the sound of the word gun, Tyree turned to see the weapon in Samson's hand. This was not the first-time Tyree had a weapon pointed at him. It was always the same. Someone would be jaw-jacking, bragging, or showboating, trying to impress other gang members. Nothing ever materialized. It was one of the hazards of being in a gang. He had faced gang bangers with guns before, so he certainly wasn't afraid of Samson — yet. But, in a moment he'd be terrified and his life would never be the same.

Leaning against the window with his arms stretched out along the sill, he began laughing.

He sneered and mockingly inquired, "What is ya gonna do Lil' Liza Jane, shoot me?"

Grabbing his crotch, he snorted, "It takes balls ta shoot a man. And I don't think ya got any. So, while ya here snowflakes tell us, how long do yo period last?"

The gang members still concerned about the gun in Samson's hand gave a halfhearted laugh.

Not at all disturbed by this banter, Samson repeated, "Shoot you?"

Then asked in a very placid manner, "What good would that do? By your own admission, you don't fear the great unknown. No, Tyree, I'm not here to harm you."

Then added, "Violence only begets violence."

Upon hearing that Tyree relaxed a bit, comfortable in knowing he had made his play in front of the boys.

Gaining confidence, he asked mockingly, "If ya not gonna shoot me, what do ya intend to do with dat gun, shove it up ya ass?"

Samson didn't acknowledge the insult. The revolver was a six-shooter. He removed the bullets from the barrel. He placed five on the table where Francis was sitting. All eyes were riveted on Samson. They looked at each other wondering what he was up too. Holding one bullet for everyone to see he inserted it into the chamber.

With the gun at his side, Samson said serenely, "Since you and I agree that death is nothing to fear, let's demonstrate the extent of our convictions. I'll go first."

Samson spun the barrel of the pistol. He had no way of knowing which chamber the live round was in. He held the revolver to his right temple.

He said without much ado, "If It's time for me to make my exit, give my regards to my family." Without hesitating, he pulled the trigger.

The click of the gun was as loud as a sonic boom. The anxiety, and concern in the shed was intense. A stillness accompanied with total disbelief infiltrated the alcove behind Monroe's pool hall. It was if they had been privileged to something sacred and did not know how to respond.

After a period of deathlike silence, and tension, someone whispered, "Dis motha fucker is crazy. He's outta his fucken mind."

Samson stood spinning the gun barrel in a relaxed and unconcerned manner. With the pistol in his right hand, he walked over and stood directly in front of Tyree. He could see the terror in Tyree's eyes and smelled the fear.

Tyree's brain was racing a million miles a minute, yet he couldn't think. His thoughts were jangled and distorted. His confidence had been replaced with dread, horror, timidity, and cowardice. To keep from falling he had to hold onto the windowsill. As beads of sweat trickled down his armpits, he found it difficult to breathe.

"Take the gun." Samson said reassuringly, "Show the boys that death is just a word and nothing to fear."

He looked into Tyree's eyes and then down at the barrel of the revolver. He repeated this several times. Tyree followed Samson's eyes and realized he was pointing to the chamber with a finger of his left hand indicating that the first two chambers were empty. He could pull the trigger without fear.

Tyree stood there in a fog of confusion. He was bombarded with a series of emotions. This experience was worse than death. Wanting it to be over he snatched the weapon from Samson's hand. In one rapid motion, he raised the gun to his head and pulled the trigger.

It was eerily quiet for a few seconds as if everyone's perception had been put on a five second delay. Then the gang jumped to their feet and began chanting and applauding. They were high-fiving while yelling, "Ya da man, Ty. Ya da man. Ty Ya got balls, and nerves of steel."

Amid the congratulatory remarks and praises Tyree stood motionless. Still trembling and breathing shallowly he couldn't take his eyes off Samson. He wondered where Samson's courage originated and how he could be so forgiving.

Placing his hand on Samson's shoulder he gently pushed him aside and dropped the revolver to the floor. He was afraid to make eye contact with anyone for fear they would see through his transparent nature. He was certain they could see him for who and what he really was. Dispiritedly he walked slowly from the shed. The gang never saw or heard from Tyree again.

Tyree sat on the side of his bed. His lips were painted blood red with lipstick. He had on women silk underwear, high heel shoes, a long wig and a padded bra. He was confused and bewildered. He couldn't get Samson off his mind. When he asked, "What are you afraid of?" He was saying, continue the life of a lie and merely exist, or face your truth and live. Tyree had fought against his personal thoughts, desires, and fantasies since childhood. His macho image, the gang, his vicious and cruel behavior towards homosexuals, were smoke screens, used to direct attention from what he really was. The time had come to bury the lie, the deceit, and the masquerade — forever. He had to man-up — he had to find the strength and integrity to admit to himself, "He was what he hated." Placing his hand inside the silk lacy panties, and feeling what he perceived as Nature's monumental mistake he began sobbing and sobbing... violently sobbing.

The next morning, to his Mother's delight, he boarded a bus to Sunflower, Alabama to go work at his brother Nathan's construction company.

When his Mother learned of his decision, she began praying and weeping. A few years later, when Francis Anthony Francino was making headlines as public enemy number one, Tyree Bertrand Mayo had joined Church and was singing in the choir. His favorite hymn was "Amazing Grace." The song had special meaning for him, especially the part that says, "I once was lost but now I'm found, was blind but now I see."

It has been said beware of what you want most you just might get it. Samson was not only accepted into the gang, but in a very short time became one of the acknowledged leaders. He received the approval that he had wanted for so long. When he talked even though his voice had a high pitch and sounded feminine, no one laughed. His gestures, while gentle, no one stared or made negative or insensitive comments. Samson hated and detested violence. It was foreign to his sensibilities. Be that as it may, one thing he could not deny, he was content. He was at peace, and he was happy with the favorable treatment, respect, and recognition the gang bestowed upon him.

Because he sang with such feeling and emotion, when he quit the choir and started running the street, Samson was surely missed. The church collectively prayed he'd return. His Father tried to show him the error of his ways, but his efforts were all in vain. Early one morning he was summoned to the morgue to identify Samson's body. He was shot and killed in a gang related incident.

A gang known as the "Eight Balls", so named because each member wore a chain with a small eight ball attached to the end of it, had been feuding with the WOPS. Seeing Francis' car cruising their territory, they fired upon it thinking Francis was driving. Samson had borrowed the car. In a few months, three members of the Eight Balls met a fate the same as Samson's. Francis and his gang were questioned and released due to a lack of evidence.

A year later, Francis walked into a jewelry store and bought an expensive gold bracelet. After completing the transaction, he reached in his pocket and gave the jeweler an ornament to attach to the bracelet. It was a small eight ball. Francis was never, ever, seen without that bracelet.

Francis became powerful in the underworld, and before long he and his associates had become strong enough to overthrow Henry "Boot-mouth" Gaspari. That gave him control of all legal gambling in Jefferson Parish, as well as illegal gambling in New Orleans. In time, he oversaw all work concerning the waterfront. He received compensation for everything that was imported and exported. Cerberus, Inc., of which Francis Anthony Francino was the C.E.O., held major contracts with the sanitation department.

It was common knowledge that Gaspari's soldiers gathered every day at Benny's for breakfast. It was an outdoor Café located on Carrollton Ave. Two men on bicycles, coming from opposite directions, shot and killed the six members of his crew one morning.

They stepped into an approaching car and were gone. Frank allowed Gaspari to think he had escaped, but his business and whereabouts were closely monitored. Frank continued to negotiate with Gaspari's corrupt politicians and dirty cops. He placed his brothers-in-arms in official positions, in Jefferson and Orleans Parishes. He soon held the Key to the City of New Orleans in the palm of his hand.

Francis was a very wealthy man. He wined and dined with the elite of the business world. Yet one thing he wanted and didn't have was respectability. The words 'Dago', 'Grease-ball', and
'Wop', were forever ringing in his ears. His parents hadn't lived
long enough to gain respect in America and he would not allow that to be his fate. He became obsessed with the idea of respect. He knew he had power, and men feared him. He was conscious of the fact that might didn't make right. So, he sat out to purchase the respectability he longed for... and to accomplish his goal he would open a private, exclusive, key club and restaurant.

Francis' Mother, whom he loved dearly, was named Eva, but everyone called her Eve. There was nothing she enjoyed more than working in her backyard garden. She'd spend hours adequately preparing the soil. She was well schooled on when to plant Annuals, Biennial, Perennials, and how to maintain the proper balance between the clay, sand and silt. She derived great pleasure out of watching her plants grow and mature. Since his mother loved her garden so dearly, in her memory, he would name his supper club, "Eve's Garden".

After combing the city for months, seeking an ideal location to erect his dream, he decided on the corner of Tulane and Villirie. To own and operate a business on the very street that he was forbidden access to as a kid would be quite an achievement. There was one major obstacle standing in the path of Frank's vision. On the corner of Tulane and Villirie was a very productive and booming enterprise called, "Anketoes, House Of Fine Candy".

CHAPTER 17

As Brandon rose to shake Frank's hand his heart rate increased. He wasn't sure his legs would support him. He had seen Frank's picture on the front page of the newspaper many times. He was always in trouble with the State Department for one reason or another. He was linked to every crime known to man: gambling, drugs, prostitution, racketeering, fraud, obstruction of justice, and murder.

Brandon said nervously, "Have a seat. What can I do for you?"

Leaning back in his chair, crossing his legs and twiddling the tiny 8-ball on his bracelet, Francis smiled and said, "Today is your lucky day, Mr. Anketoes. Did I pronounce your name correctly, Sir?"

Brandon nodded.

As if brushing lint off his trousers, Frank continued in a very nonchalant, yet definite manner, "I would like to purchase this building. Name your price and we can seal the deal."

Brandon was caught totally off guard. This was a complete surprise and utterly ridiculous. The last thing he'd ever do would sell; to do so would be retailing a portion of his parent's heart, not to mention the dishonor it would bring to his Father's legacy. Such an act would anger the Gods. What in the world gave this gangster such an idea, he wondered.

After playing cat and mouse with Brandon, Frank realized it was going to take persuasion of a different kind to convince him to cooperate.

As Frank rose to leave he handed Brandon several sheets of paper and said casually, "If you change your mind, call Mr. Adam Christopher at the National Bank. A check has been deposited in your name for the inventory and the current appraisal value of the property."

Then with a deep sigh of disappointment said, "Good day, Mr. Anketoes."

Brandon began to tremble as he examined the sheets of papers Frank had given him. Listed was his financial history; current assets, receivables, inventory, fixed assets, liabilities, stocks, investments, his entire net worth, and the company's financial performance.

In detailed printouts were the Balance Sheets, Income Statements and Cash Flow Statements. Brandon couldn't believe what was happening. He sat in his office at a lost as to what to do next. If he called the police what would he say, an offer was made to buy his property? That's no crime. As far as his financial reports were concerned a lot of that information is public record. The only thing Brandon was sure of was under no circumstances would he nor could he sell the property.

Before Brandon had time to think, odd incidents began to occur. First, the inspectors from the board of health began levying undo fines for unfounded health infractions. Then, out of the blue, his supplies were discontinued without warning. There was no response to his many phone calls. He'd wait for hours at City Hall to speak to an official but, to no avail. Soon, the bottom fell out, his water was cut off. He received orders from the Board of Health to dispense conducting all business with the public until further notice. Mr. Adam Christopher, at the bank would call regularly informing him that a check was awaiting his signature should he decide to sell, and of course foreclosure proceedings were eminent.

Brandon sat in the dark office alone. He had no one to turn to for help. The beautiful, and productive world that had been built for him had tumbled and fell apart on his watch. Why? Why? Why? The questions were constant, with no answer forthcoming. There was no water, electricity, or supplies. His employees, loyal to the end had no choice but to seek employment elsewhere. When the problems related to the business began, not knowing what to expect from day to day, he asked his wife to take the children and move to Greece with his parents. She protested in vain.

The place had an eerie silence. Six months had passed since his meeting with Frank. The inventory had been depleted. The display cases that once housed, cakes, pies, and pastries, were now empty. The ice cream machine that hummed the same continuous song was now quiet as a Church on a Monday morning. The chitter- chatter of customers entering and exiting the store was now a distant memory. The metal racks that were once dressed with bags of chips, pretzels, and cheese bits, now stood naked as a Jay bird.

The anxiety and despair Brandon had experienced for months was overwhelming, and inundating. His troubles, disappointments, and miseries were compounded daily. He began to lose weight and was unable to sleep. The words "failure, failure," kept reverberating in his brain, followed by, "shame, shame, shame." His thoughts were thunderous. He had to escape the turbulent and sonorous sounds in his head. The pounding was endless and grew more intense with each passing day.

The alcohol and drugs he had begun using to medicate himself and help him sleep and concentrate were no longer effective. Not able to visualize an end to this horrific predicament, all his thoughts were turned inward. The tearful morose and sullen episodes he had begun experiencing increased. The constant drumming in his brain would not cease.

He kissed the picture of his parents. It was taken the first day the doors opened for business. They were standing in front of the candy store, filled with love, hope, and happiness. Two portraits of his daughters hung on the wall. Love flooded his heart as he recalled all the joy they had brought into his life. He took a long lingering look at the photograph on his desk. It was his wife and Brandon Jr. leaving the hospital.

It had been a very difficult birth. She had been in labor many hours. The drugs used to aid in delivery were too strong resulting in Brandon Jr. having seizures the first 5 years of his life. He welled up with tears when told his son would suffer no long-term affect from the ordeal... but the Doctor's couldn't be sure, only time would tell.

Through eyes filled with gloom, anguish, and hopelessness, he saw Peace, Serenity, and Comfort standing in the doorway. With arms extended, they invited him to join them. Suddenly, a sea of calm, which he hadn't experienced in months, enveloped him. He was happy, free, and void of all cares and woes. The contentment and joy could not be ignored. It felt wonderful, so very wonderful, to smile again.

Peace, Serenity, and Comfort spoke again saying, "Come. You're welcome to join us."

He brushed the tears from his eyes and slowly opened the desk drawer.

Like a dedicated sentinel, he could hear the heartbeat of the Grandfather clock in the corner of the office. The sad face of the clock seemed to know what fate awaited him. He took one last look around the office, and without hesitating he picked up the revolver.

When he was found, he was slumped over his desk with a bullet wound to his temple. The note nearby simply said:

> My Darling Wife and Parents,
> Please forgive me for being such a coward. I cannot go on. I'm sorry. My Love, take the proceeds from the sale of the property and move our children to Greece, far away from this God forsaken City.
>
> I love you all, Brandon.

Months later after extensive remodeling and reconstruction, Eve's Garden opened with little or no fanfare. Frank wanted everything low key. He ordered the opening to be omitted from the Society page of the newspaper. Admittance was by invitation only. Everyone invited was screened and evaluated by Ivan "Nubby" Ettore.

Eve's Garden was a hit with the Power Brokers of the City of New Orleans. It became the ideal setting for networking. On the second floor was a huge conference room. Many major deals were conceived and finalized there.

Ivan "Nubby" Ettore was second in charge at the supper club, then Allen Adamo, rounding out the chain-of-command. Ivan was responsible for the band, showgirls, visiting entertainers, and the upstairs luxury suites; only a privileged few were allowed those accommodations. Frank or Ivan could grant only a key, and no one could remain in a suite after closing time.

CHAPTER 18

Ivan Ettore was a physically strong man. He had a receding hairline and a ruddy complexion. His eyes were cold as water flowing from the Antarctica, and so was he. He had no time for small talk, and the most hardened criminals in the underworld feared him. Once an assignment was completed, regardless of how brutal, violent, or deadly, Ivan never gave it a second thought.

As the saying goes, he walked softly and didn't give a damn. He was addicted to salted peanuts and Coco-Colas. Every so often he'd remind Momma Mae to add a case to her supply list. He had a wife and four daughters, and while beautiful showgirls surrounded him, he didn't mix business with pleasure. He believed in the slogan, "Business Is Our Only Business". Ivan was called "Nubby" because, as a youngster, he lost a finger on his left hand in a hunting accident while, in jail, he lost another one.

He was born into a world that had no love for him. Upon being told she had a son, his mother began crying. She begged and pleaded with the midwife to give the boy away. He grew up being unloved, abused, and neglected. When Ivan was about four, or five years old. His mother sold him to a neighbor for fifty dollars. She was a very elderly woman who had been childless.

While her heart was in the right place, she was unable to provide the time and attention a young child requires. At the age of twelve, he had

taken up residence in the street. The older homeless kids taught him how to survive. He learned how to steal, beg, shoplift, pickpockets, and do whatever was necessary to exist. Consequently, he was always in trouble with the law. By the age of twenty-one, he was a professional criminal whose gun was for hire. Before reaching thirty-five, he had become a legend as a "Hit Man" for the mob. He was known as a man of few words, who showed
no mercy, and did whatever he was contracted to do. No questions asked.

Ivan was older than Francis, and his reputation preceded him. When they met, he had eleven months remaining on a seven- year sentence for manslaughter. Francis had been transferred from another facility, and had only a short time left to serve.

Those associated with the world of crime, both in and out of the prison, were aware that Francis was on his way to becoming one of the youngest crime bosses in the South. It was just a matter of time.

When incarcerated Ivan, realizing how important Francis would be to his future, began sharing valuable information with him. He knew the inner workings of Henry Gaspari's gambling operations, and how he controlled the entire State of Louisiana. While Ivan had accepted contracts from many sources, he never worked for Gaspari. What a man did for a living meant very little to Ivan, but knowing that Gaspari engaged in slave trafficking, turned his stomach. Owing no allegiance to him, and having no respect for him, he aided Francis in taking over his business enterprises.

By the time, Ivan was released from prison, Francis was beginning to make his presence known. He had successfully overthrown Gaspari and had taken over all gambling in Jefferson Parish, and illegal gambling in New Orleans. Ivan would play a significant role in Frank's rise to power. To give the appearance of legitimate businessmen, Ivan suggested Cerberus, Inc. be established. Years later, the exclusive restaurant and supper club, Eve' s Garden, would open its doors, and Ivan Isadore Ettore, would be second in command.

When Francis was released from jail, word had reached Gaspari of his plans. Gaspari flexed his muscle by having two of his underlings in prison, lean on Ivan. They cut his finger off. After Ivan had been mauled, a message was sent to Frank simply stating, "Back off, or Nubby's head will be next." When Frank overthrew the Gaspari regime it would have been a simple matter to eliminate Gaspari, but because Ivan asked Frank to spare him, he was allowed to flee to Waco, Texas thinking he was safe.

Upon being released from prison with Frank's blessing, Ivan's first stop was Waco, Texas. With a bogus tip concerning some young girls Gaspari could use in his sex industry, Henry Gaspari was lured to a remote location, near the railroad yard. Upon arriving, Ivan shot and killed his bodyguard instantly. He forced Gaspari, pleading and begging, into the trunk of his automobile, then set the vehicle on fire.

As the agonizing and excruciating screams resonated from the car, Ivan stood eating peanuts. After the automobile exploded Ivan continued his trip to New Orleans. Four years later, an inmate who was involved in severing Ivan's finger made parole. Walking out of the prison gate he inhaled the fresh air of freedom. A car and three men were waiting.

He casually asked. "And who are you gents?" "Friends, just friends.," was the reply.

Taking the reefer offered, he lit it, and allowed the smoke to infiltrate his lungs. How rewarding and gratifying he thought, after fifteen years, the boys had not forgotten him. As they drove along, sipping Bollinger Blanc, a dark and very expensive champagne made from Pinot Noir grapes, he talked about all the things he wanted to do. The weed and wine had him feeling better than he had in years.

"The first thing I want," he said vulgarly, "is for some whore to fuck me from sun up to sun down — every which way — like there ain't no tomorrow."

An hour and forty-five minutes later, they arrived at and abandoned building. Woozy from alcohol and reefer, he imagined a welcome home celebration had been planned. As the door opened, he saw Ivan Ettore and an array of tools present, including a chain saw. He dropped to his knees and began crying and vomiting.

Without saying a word, Ivan had him strapped to a table. Starting with his fingers, he was dismembered. Before the ordeal was over, he had gone insane. Upon hearing the news, his partner who assisted in assaulting Ivan in jail, jumped from the third tier of the cellblock. A shovel had to be used to remove his remains.

CHAPTER 19

Part of Bobby's responsibilities was to keep the area surrounding the club spotless and litter free. When he'd come on duty, his first order of the day was to sweep and hose down the sidewalk and gutters. Because of his attention, the corner of Tulane and Villirie had a clinical and sanitary appearance.

Mr. Claude, the doorman, would often say, "Boy, dat sidewalk is clean, 'nuff to sup off."

One evening as Bobby performed his chores, a young girl, standing at the bus stop, was staring at him. He waved hello, and she smiled. His first impression of her was that she was too tall and lanky and needed some sun.

For several days, he'd say hi, and she'd smile. One afternoon while hosing the sidewalk he held the hose high allowing the water to sprinkle on her.

As she squealed and stepped away, he exclaimed, "Oh, I'm so sorry. How careless of me. I — "

Before he could complete his apology, laughing and shaking the drops of water from her shoes the young girl said, "You did that deliberately."

With a smile that would shame the sun, he said, "I'm guilty as charged. My name is Robert Lange. What's yours?"

With eyes as bright as a moon on a summer's night, she smiled and replied, "My name is Mira Gardner."

Now that Bobby was standing next to her she didn't seem tall or lanky. She and her complexion were perfect. He had never seen anyone with eyes like hers. They seemed to reach out invitingly. They were green or grey or both. He wasn't sure. He only knew they were beautiful, piercing and penetrating. Because of her eyes, in the early years of their relationship, his pet name
for her was "Cat". Bobby's heart was dancing. He thought Mira was gorgeous. She had freckles that bunched up around her nose. Her hair was long, beautiful, and soft to the touch. She was tall and shapely with a fair complexion.

Mira worked as an orderly at Charity Hospital. She enjoyed her work immensely — especially interacting with the patients. She was very religious, and many times, instead of requesting a priest or preacher, patients would ask Mira to pray with them.
She was immediately smitten with Bobby. Asked in later years what attracted her to him, she said, "Besides being beautiful, he had a pure and simple honesty about him. He was so real and genuine I was mesmerized. He was unblemished and unsoiled." , she explained.

"He was so happy, carefree, and considerate. He made me proud. He was not tall, but he stood erect and exuded a magnetic confidence that was hard to come by."

With a nervous smile and a slight quiver in her voice, she'd say, "He was dark, strong, and had a charm about him that could melt the glaziers in Central Asia and more than anything in this world I know he loved me. He loved me dearly."

Then with sadness in her voice, and tears in her eyes, she'd hang her head. Hardly above a whisper she uttered, "Something happened to change him. Something took my husband away — far away. Whatever it was, he couldn't bring himself to share it with me. Then, one day, without warning, I became a stranger in his heart. He shut me out of his life completely. Why? I've never known."

Sobbing, she'd conclude, "I hope he knows how much I love and need him. He's my life."

My mother and Bobby married after a short courtship. They wasted no time in starting a family. First, they had Rodney. A few years passed then Gilda was born and later, Melanie came along, eighteen years elapsed, then I made my grand entrance... surprise, surprise, surprise.

Mira was an only child. Her father was a Baptist Minister, and her mother was a housewife. When Mira was born, she had the prettiest greenish-grey eyes her parents or the neighbors had ever seen. Five years after Mira was born her mother was diagnosed with a cardiovascular disease. She died sitting on the back porch with Mira on her lap. When her husband found Mrs. Gardner, Mira was staring into space. She stopped talking. Now and then she'd make a gesture but would not speak.

Days turned into weeks, weeks into months, Mira would not utter a word. Her father had her evaluated by a medical specialist for communication, language, motor skills, speech and thinking abilities. The Behavioral Pathologist concluded that there wasn't any speech disorder — that was the good news because as the report stated, a speech disorder cannot be outgrown. Mira had what they referred to as an articulation delay and given time it would pass.

With her greenish-grey eyes, Mira had an uncanny way of looking directly at whoever was communicating with her. As a young child, her eyes were keen and sharp and as she grew older they became piercing and penetrating. In time, very few people could hold her gaze. Many were afraid to be near her and thought she was possessed but by what they didn't know.

Almost a year to the day of her Mother's passing, there was a violent electrical storm. The lighting flashed and skipped about as if celebrating. The thunder roared and rumbled causing the windows to shake and rattle. Suddenly, a streak of lightning lit up Mira's room followed by the sonic boom of thunder. Startled and panic-stricken, Mira ran down the hall to her Father's room screaming, "Momma! Momma! Momma!"

Her Father scooped her up in his arms and trying to calm her down kept repeating, "Momma is alright sweetheart. Momma is alright." That was the first time she had spoken since her Mother's death.

Mira developed into a beautiful, intelligent and perceptive young lady. In social situations, she never forgot the basics: she observed and listened. Her eyes never left whomever she was speaking with. Because of her eyes, her friends nicknamed her "Peepers".

Mira was peculiar and different, there was no doubt about that, but she did not possess any divine knowledge, nor was she gifted or paranormal. Nothing could be further from the truth. But her friends could not be convinced otherwise.

When Mira stated that if Rayfield Windon didn't stop riding his motorbike so recklessly he wouldn't live to graduate. Two months later he was killed at a railroad crossing. She said very casually, that Bert Tucker had better stop smoking those funny cigarettes and hanging out with that rowdy crowd on St. Bernard Avenue and Miro. A week later he was arrested in a liquor store robbery. She politely advised Anna Parker to stop being so liberal with her body, or she'd end up in trouble. When Anna became pregnant and had to drop out of school, she blamed Mira for jinxing her.

There were many such incidents that occurred that only added to the belief that Mira Gardner possessed a body of knowledge foreign to her spiritual or academic level.

No, Mira was not gifted in a supernatural way. She was simply an intelligent, perceptive, and observant individual. What Mira saw a blind man could see. A person's behavior is a good indicator as to what is waiting to greet him around the bend. If changes are not made, disaster will win out.

When she graduated from high school, she immediately took a job as an orderly at Charity Hospital. Riding the bus home one evening, the bus stopped at the corner of Tulane and Villire. She noticed a handsome young man hosing the sidewalk. Every day, at the same time, she saw the young man busy at work. He appeared to be carefree and interesting. So, instead of boarding the bus across from the hospital, Mira decided to walk to Tulane and Villirie. Standing there at the bus stop one day the young man noticed her. And one day he sprinkled water on her.

As Mira grew older, her reputation as one guided by a divine source only became stronger. Coupled with the fact that she had strange eyes, studied the Bible daily, could recite a verse for any and, all situations, and because many of the things she said came to pass, she was a mystery.

CHAPTER 20

By the time I was born, Bobby was forty-eight years old, and earning more than most men — white or colored. He had met and greeted the elite of society, shook hands with Mayors, Governors, and other Dignitaries. Because of his association with Francis Francino, my Father was known and respected throughout the city of New Orleans. He had the ear of many powerful people.

When Momma Mae became ill and realized the end was near she sent for one of Frank's legal representatives. Not having anyone to leave her wealth to, she requested that Trevor, her ex-husband, be located. He had retired from the military, and he and his family were residing in Macon, Georgia.

Along with the documents, making him the sole heir to all her worldly possessions was a hand-written note. It said:

> Dear Tre',
> You are the nicest, kindest, man God ever died for. It is so regrettable, but it has taken me a lifetime to realize how much I truly love you. My last thoughts will be of you. Thanks for being so kind and loving. Till we meet again.
> Mabel

Mabel died a few years after Bobby was employed. Mr. Claude, the doorman, retired right after her death.

He would laugh and say, "I wanna spend some of dis money Mr. Frank done pay'd me."

Mr. Sammy, the janitor, retired about the same time. He moved to Gonzalez, Louisiana, to do what he said he was born to do — fish.

Bobby stood at his post, the end of the bar, observing the waiters and busboys serving the customers. Every seat in the club was occupied as usual. Frank would stop by a table or two, exchange a few pleasantries and move on. Most of his time was spent in his office, doing whatever it was he did.

In his many years at Eve's Garden, Bobby had witnessed many things. He had seen men of authority reduced to shame and disgrace and lesser men elevated to positions of power. There had been laughter, pain, and tears, unbelievable joy, happiness and death. Bobby had come a long way, a mighty long way, and had seen more than he bargained for.

The year was 1940. I was a year old. I often wondered what Bobby thought when told he had another son. I would like to think that once in my life I made him smile, and I hope he said, 'Attaboy."

By this time in his life, Bobby's income was substantial. He could have moved out of his Mother's house years ago. Instead, after her death he bought his sister's share and added several rooms to the existing property. Bobby Lange's house and, everyone knew it was his house, was one of the finest residents in the 7th Ward

It has been said that we gravitate towards our own. If that's true, then Bobby was with his own. His association with Frank and Frank's business partners had a profound effect on him. He gradually became detached, self-absorbed, and cold.

Many times, Mira said, "You're not the man I married."

He'd give her one of his patterned stares but said nothing. Mira would never know what caused such a change in the man she thought she knew.

For reasons known only to Frank, Ivan Ettore, and Allen Adamo, Bobby was promoted to Associate Manager of Eve's Garden. This was an unheard-of position at the time for a person of color. He assisted in the daily operations of the club. He was primarily responsible for the bartenders, waiters and busboys.

Standing at the end of the bar in his black tuxedo that he, Ivan, and Adamo were required to wear, Bobby was overcome with memories of his promotion. When Frank informed him of his advancement he was petrified — scared beyond words. He had never been in a situation where he gave men orders — especially white men. Adamo worked side by side with him for six weeks.

Then one night he patted Bobby on the back and said, "It's your show now, Bobby. Either shit or get off the pot."

Many of the customers didn't know what to make of Bobby's position, but they didn't question it out loud. They all knew in time they would need Frank for one reason or other. If he saw fit to place a colored person in charge of white men, so be it. The way they saw it, Frank was skinning the cat, and if they just held onto the tail, they'd get one of the kittens.

The waiters and bartenders resented Bobby and tried to undermine his orders at every turn. They'd mumble and grumble among themselves regularly. Alfred Lucas was their leader and was very vocal.

When Bobby would give him an order he'd say, "Fuck you. Go make yourself a watermelon salad."

Regardless of the insults, Bobby saw that his orders were carried out.

There was a section of the dining area set aside with a velvet rope exclusively for the dignitaries of the highest order. It was common knowledge that the higher tips were generated there, and the same waiters worked that area all the time. Bobby thought that was unfair. At one of the Monday morning meetings, Bobby said he thought the waiters should rotate the V.I.P. section.

Frank agreed, saying, "That's a damn good idea. It's long overdue. See that it's implemented."

Bobby was conscious of the fact that the other employees disapproved of his position but didn't openly and brazenly disrespect him the way Alfred Lucas did. Bobby spent many hours and a tremendous amount of energy trying to come up with a way to bring Lucas around. He decided that, since Alfred was so outspoken and demonstrative, he'd use that against him. After all, Bobby thought, Lucas operated off emotion not intellect, so he'd open the door and let the fool walk in.

The rotation of the waiters was the trap Bobby was counting on. Alfred Lucas was one of the waiters who enjoyed the privilege of working the V.I.P. area.

When the new schedule was posted three waiters would approve because they would have an opportunity to earn larger tips. The three regular waiters would disapprove for obvious reasons. It was a simple matter of divide and conquer.

Bobby was certain as to how Lucas would respond. Without hesitation, Bobby posted the new work schedule on the bulletin board, poured himself a cup of coffee and sat down in his office to read the newspaper. From his vantage point, he had a clear view. The club would be opening in an hour. The fireworks soon would begin.

As the waiters arrived, they entered the locker room to change into their green jackets and bow ties. The conversation seldom changed. They talked about family, sports, and women. They said very little to Bobby. It was as if he didn't exist. It was twenty minutes before the club opened, and no one had read the board.

Carlos was one of the waiters who had always liked Bobby. Through the transition, he had remained civil and would benefit from the rotation.

As he passed Bobby's office, he stuck his head in the door and said, "Hello, Bob. How ya doing?"

Without looking up from the newspaper Bobby whispered, "Check the bulletin board."

As the six waiters gathered around the bulletin board, three were thankful and appreciative, and three were angry and disappointed.

Alfred Lucas, unable to contain himself shouted, "Son-of-a-motherfucking bitch. That dumb fucken Nigger has lost his fucken mind."

Showing Bobby no respect, he bypassed him and stormed into Adamo's office. Bobby gave a slight grunt and continued reading the newspaper. Just as sure as there is ice in Greenland, he knew if he gave Lucas enough rope, he'd hang himself.

Forgetting he was in a work environment, Lucas entered Adamo's office without knocking.

Nervous, agitated and screaming, "What the fuck is that nigger doing changing the work schedule! Has he lost his fucken mind?"

If he had thought it through, he would have known Bobby could do nothing without management's approval. Throughout the club, he could be heard ranting and raging. Frank heard every word but would not interfere. There were three managers on duty, he thought, one of them had better handle this matter, and quickly.

"What is the world coming to," he screamed angrily, "When a white man has to take orders from a jig-a-boo?"

Breathing heavily and completely out of control he shouted, "I'll die and go to hell before I take orders from that jungle bunny."

Adamo had made a mental file on every employee at the club. No one had been omitted. He had a good read on their strengths and weaknesses. Adamo had only thought Lucas was delicate, frail, and shallow, but this display of contempt and disrespect removed all doubt. He read Lucas as a social bully. As a kid in the schoolyard, he'd fight if he had help, but get him alone, and he'd tuck his head and run like a scared rabbit. Adamo had seen his hold card — Lucas was weak.

Adamo was sitting behind his desk eating a ham and cheese sandwich; the mayo was on the corner of his mouth. Wiping his mouth and hand with a napkin said, "Calm down, Lucas"

"Fuck calming down." He roared. "I don't have to take that shit off of that 'coon."

He began pacing back and forth with his hands on his hips, and heaving.

Arguing was not Adamo's strong point. If someone disagreed with him, he'd simply take his bat and bust their heads open. And if need be, Adamo would simply remove a person from the rolls of humanity. Adamo was known to act not argue. He once shot a man in the face for cussing him over a parking space.

Looking at the mean-spirited coward standing before him, Adamo shook his head and said, "You're right, Lucas you don't have to take orders from a nigger, 'coon, or jigger-boo."

Lucas hinted a smile of victory until he heard, "Go to personnel and tell Angela you quit."

The blood left Lucas' face. He became as white as quick mix flour.

"What?" Lucas managed to utter. "What do you mean, quit? Is this the thanks I get for all the years I've been here?" Adamo did not respond.

After a few awkward moments, he asked pitifully, "What am I to do? I come to you for help, and you spit in my face." Having had enough, Adamo stood abruptly and said forcefully, "Lucas, go to personnel or get back to work."

"Now!" Raising his voice said, "In the future take your concerns to Bobby. He's your supervisor."

As Lucas returned to the workroom floor, he was ghostly pale. He appeared as if he might faint any second. He was unsteady. He was a picture of dread, horror, and fear. He could not believe nor comprehend what had taken place. Confused, embarrassed, and ashamed, he silently approached his new assignment with short steps, eyes downcast, and head bowed.

In time, the waiters and bartenders came to respect Bobby's authority. They couldn't understand why he was given such a prestigious job at Eve's Garden or why he was such a hit with the customers. To one and all it remained a puzzle.

That was eight years ago, and now as he stood at the end of the bar watching the customers enjoy themselves, it all seemed like yesterday. One day a diamond, one day a stone, he thought. He had money, property, prestige, and power. He wished his mother could have lived to see all he had accomplished. While glorifying in his success and the many rivers he had crossed, one thing was always constant on his mind — that awful night years ago, the night that changed his life forever.

From his vantage point at the bar Bobby saw a tall dark woman, the color of midnight with a diamond necklace that could pay off the national debt. From the corner booth, she rose followed by a stockbroker from Oklahoma. Bobby knew they had been granted access to one of the upstairs suites. This was just another way Frank had of keeping important people indebted to him. Watching this scene unfold, Bobby recalled that awful night years ago. The memory was etched in his mind forever. Shortly after that eventful night, Frank, called him into his office, present were Allen Adamo and Ivan Ettore.

Without much ado, Frank simply said, "Bobby, Adamo will be grooming you for your new assignment. Congratulations, you are now an Associate Manager. You will oversee the bartenders and waiters. Address all your concerns to Adamo. That will be all. Get back to work."

When Bobby was a busboy part of his job entailed maintaining the upstairs suites. He would strip the beds and replace them with fresh Linen, clean the bathrooms and vacuum. This was always done after closing. Before entering a room, Bobby was instructed to knock. If anything were out of the ordinary or if a gentleman was drunk, which often happened, Bobby would report to Ivan, and he'd summon a cab.

It was a Monday morning, about four a.m., maintenance had been performed on the lounge and dining room, and the kitchen had been cleaned and sanitized. While Adamo let the employees out the freight entrance, Ivan checked the daily receipts. The band members, having packed their instruments, were the last to leave. The singer Ivan had booked for two weeks was named Dame

Wright. Her hit single, "Ain't No Salt In My Tears", was making waves in Louisiana. All the luxury suites had been cleaned and inspected, except the yellow room. Pushing the wagon down the hall containing the linen, towels, and toiletries, Bobby knocked on the door. After a few taps without a response he opened it.

Bobby stood frozen in the doorway with his mouth agape. The sight that greeted him was frightening. Miss Dame Wright was lying on her back half out of the bed. She was completely nude with her eyes and mouth open.

Sitting on the floor with his back against the bed was James Pinta, a well-known City Attorney. Drug paraphernalia littered the floor. Bobby knew in a heartbeat they were dead.

Bobby ran breathlessly down the stairs into the club. He hastily explained to Adamo and Ivan the scene in the yellow suite. The three of them returned to the room. Adamo and Ivan looked at the scene as if they couldn't believe their eyes, all the while cussing.

Not wishing to be there any longer than necessary, Bobby nervously asked, "May I leave Mr. Adamo?"

"Not yet." He responded, "Go to the bar and pour yourself a drink."

Ivan yelled, "Remain there until we tell you what to do." Bobby wanted to remove himself as far away from this situation as possible, but knew he had to do what he was told.

Pouring a glass of wine with trembling hands he could hear

Adamo talking on the phone probably with Mr. Frank.

Ivan entered the lounge and said to Bobby, "Take these keys and bring the gentleman's Buick around back. It's right out front."

Bobby was so frightened he could hardly walk.

When Bobby returned the two bodies had been brought down and wrapped in two-drop clothes the painters used. They were then placed in the trunk of the Attorney's car. Adamo drove the lawyer's automobile, Ivan followed. They drove slowly down Tulane to Johnson Street. They turned left at Johnson and continued to Poydras. Running along Poydras was a canal. This was the heart of the colored section of the city. They parked the Attorney's car on the side of the canal, removed all valuables and identification from the couple and then set the vehicle on fire.

Before leaving to dispose of the bodies, Bobby was instructed to wait at the club for Mr. Frank. In the meantime, he was told to retrieve some disinfectant from the supply room, strip the room and scrub the walls and floors. Before heading for the supply room, he poured another drink. Ivan and Adamo returned soon after Mr. Frank arrived. The three men inspected the room again, all the while talking in Italian. Bobby was glad he didn't know what they were saying.

Not knowing how to interrupt, Bobby gingerly said, "Excuse me Mr. Frank, may I leave?"

Realizing how upset Bobby was Frank calmly said, "No. I need to have a few words with you."

Seeing the bottle of wine on the table he said, "Pour yourself another drink."

Under different circumstances, Bobby could enjoy sitting in the lounge. There was a break room for the help but, they were not permitted to sit in the lounge or dining area at any time. The chairs were extremely comfortable. The tables were so arranged until no matter where one was seated there was a good view of the stage. He took a sip of wine and wished he could go home. The three men stood by the bandstand talking. They looked in Bobby's direction every few seconds. It was obvious he was the cause of their concern. Saying good night to Frank they did something Bobby had never seen. The two men kissed Frank's hand, said something in Italian and were gone.

Locking the bolt on the freight door, Frank walked slowly to the bar. He selected a glass, said a few choice words to himself and joined Bobby at the table; refilled Bobby's glass then his. He was in deep thought. He appeared to be standing at the fork in the road contemplating which direction to take.

With a sigh, he took a deep breath and asked, "How's Rodney doing with the fruit stand?"

Caught off guard by the question, Bobby stammered and replied, "He's doing well, Mr. Frank. Very well. He's thankful you allowed him to use the corner and he's prepared to pay whatever rent you request."

"Rent?" Frank bellowed, "There will be no such thing. That downtown property is vacant. Rodney can keep an eye on things for us. That piece of property is more trouble than it's worth. In a month or two we're going to put it up for sale."

Needing a shave, Frank rubbed his chin and casually asked, "How long have you been with me Bobby?"

Having no idea where the question was going, Bobby awkwardly responded, "I've been working here almost thirty years."

He wished he could go home to Mira and forget this night ever happened.

Frank leaned back in the plush chair, shook his head and with a smile said, "In all those years Bobby I've never received a negative report concerning you. You've been an excellent employee, it hasn't, and it won't go unrewarded."

Changing the subject, Frank raised his voice slightly and lamented, "This has been a traumatic experience for you Bobby, and I'm sorry. I'm so sorry that you are now a part of this sordid and regrettable affair. None of this was of your choosing and Bobby if I could change it for you I would."

Bobby was not naive. He knew very well who Mr. Frank was and what he was capable of doing. He had heard grown men cry like little girls in his office. Frank was always in the news, and it was never good. Frank was a criminal, bar none. Everyone in the City of New Orleans knew he was a menace to society. Sitting across from Mr. Frank on this Monday morning listening to him talk, Bobby was moved. For in spite of all he knew about Mr. Frank as he spoke this day, Bobby knew he was sincere. It was obvious Frank cared about him. He had observed through the years how Mr. Frank looked after Momma Mae, Mr. Sammy, and Mr. Claude. He saw to it their money was well invested and that they didn't want for anything. What his motivation was, and why he treated them as he did, Bobby had no way of knowing.

Light could be seen through the drapes daybreak was dawning. Frank walked to the massive window and slightly drew them open.

Returning to the table he stated with conviction, "Drugs are destroying this country. It's everywhere, and it's pure poison. If any of my people are caught using or distributing it, I'll terminate them. I give no second chances."

Frank paused, and then said, "What happened to those two-young people last night is most unfortunate."

Hitting the table for emphasis, he said, "But that's not my problem.

People overdose all the time. They have no way of knowing how pure or strong that shit is. They are fools, Bobby. Why else would they put a foreign substance into their bodies, purchased from a stranger on the street?"

Disgustedly he pointed his finger and said, "I'm a businessman Bobby. Business is my only business. Many people count on me for their livelihood, and I will not allow a few self- indulgent dope addicts to draw my associates and me into something that does not concern us. Eve's Garden does not need or deserve the negative fallout that this accident can generate. It could cause irreparable harm."

Sipping from his glass and adjusting his eyeglasses, Frank continued to express himself. Bobby had never seen this side of him. He never said much to his employees. Most of his time was spent in his office; Adamo and Ivan attended to the daily operations of the club. He explained that what happened had to be kept from the newspaper.

He was talking more for his benefit then Bobby's. "The people who frequent the supper club would be hesitant to patronize here if it were embroiled in a scandal."

Then he added, "I have people on the paper, that can hold our involvement to a minimum."

As if trying to figure out how to phrase his next question, Frank leaned forward and asked, "Bobby, do you know what fate is?"

Scratching his head, Bobby responded weakly, "I think its destiny Mr. Frank?"

"Not quite Bobby. There is a school of thought that says we design our own destiny by the choices we make throughout life. Without it we'd flounder like a ship at sea without a rudder."

Gaining momentum with his speech, Frank struck the table for emphasis and stated, "Fate, on the other hand, shows no mercy. If we speed down the highway of life, with little or no regard for the rules and regulations, fate stops us. You know how Bobby?"

Without waiting for a reply, he said, "It kicks the living shit out of us and doesn't look back to say I'm sorry. Fate is cruel, very cruel."

Taking a deep breath, and sighing heavily, he took a sip of wine and said, "Whatever circumstances have brought you to this point in your life Bobby is your destiny. Your fate is how you negotiate through these unfortunate events. One is a choice, Bobby; the other is inevitable."

Pushing back from the table to cross his legs, Frank placed his elbow on the table and stated forcefully, "Because of tonight Bobby your life will never be the same. Do you understand what I'm talking about?"

Bobby stammered, "Yes, Sir. I think so".

The wine had settled his nerves a bit but listening to Mr. Frank ramble and not having a clue as to where it was leading caused his heart to begin pounding again. He poured wine into his glass, spilling it as he did. The only thing Bobby knew for sure was Mr. Frank, his associates, and the people who patronized the club were cut from the same cloth. They were powerful, well connected, and extremely dangerous.

Frank slid his glass aside and said, "Four people know what took place here tonight. Unfortunately, Bobby, you're one of them. Under no circumstances are you ever to mention this incident to anyone. For all intents and purposes, it never happened. Do I make myself clear?"

Bobby, afraid to speak, nodded in the affirmative.

Frank reached in his pocket and placed a revolver on the table. The sight of the gun caused Bobby's heart to race. His mouth became dry. He cursed himself for being so afraid then gulped down the glass of wine.

Looking at him with the eyes of the devil he was, Frank slid he gun towards Bobby and definitively said, "Bobby, if you ever speak a word of what took place here tonight, the pain you'll endure will cause the dead to mourn, and stones to weep. If, for some reason, you can't lock this memory away and keep it to yourself, there's the gun take the easy way out."

Sensing the fear in Bobby and knowing he was between a rock and a hard place, Frank pondered his next move. After a few seconds, he concluded no further action was necessary.

Retrieving the revolver, he took a sip of wine with a deep sound of sadness he despairingly uttered, "With heartfelt regret, Bobby, welcome to my world."

Without drinking the rest of his glass of wine, Frank rose slowly and said, "It's daybreak, Bobby, go home to your family."

Walking to the door with his hand on Bobby's shoulder he reassuringly said, "In a week or two, this will all be a distant memory."

CHAPTER 21

When the car was found, the bodies were burned beyond all recognition. The newscaster reported that according to the medical examiner, it would take a few days to a week to make a positive identification. The preliminary investigation stated that it was a late model automobile and the motive suggested it was murder and robbery.

A few days later, a collective hush was heard around the city when it was reported that one of the victims was none other than Mr. James Pinta. Mr. Pinta, the article stated, was a partner with the law firm of Wagner, Dunn, and Pinta. It chronicled his career from college to the present making a point to stress his liberal contributions to the community, his pro bono services to the unfortunate, his many charities, and his distinguished service in the armed forces. A loving husband and father survived by his wife of seventeen years, Nina, and their three children, Jamaal, Patricia, and Lurlene. Service Monday, December 15, 1940, Dunbar Chapel. The interment will take place at the St. Louis Cemetery.

Underway was an all-out investigation. Every man of color walking the street was stopped, searched and questioned. Many were arrested and held for further interrogation. The citizens were in an uproar and demanded the culprit or culprits be apprehended. Two days later in "Section B" of the paper, the public was informed that the female passenger in the car with Mr. James Pinta was a colored singer from Lafayette, Louisiana. Her name was Dame Wright. Mr. Pinta, it stated in elaborate detail, was helping her with her struggling career.

Near the end of the article it said, "Miss. Wright had been appearing at a local dinner club here in the city." The name of the club was not mentioned.

The Lafayette News reported that Miss. Cecilia Larsen, whose professional name was Dame Wright, departed this world to be with her Lord and Savior Jesus Christ. She was a blessing to us all, a loving daughter of Mr. and Mrs. Jague Larsen, a Sister to Joyce Larsen-Cameron and aunt to two nieces. A grave-side service will be held December 13, 1940 one o'clock p.m., New Hope Memorial Park, Rev. Patrick Seymour, Jr. Officiating.

In two weeks, the investigation found its way to Eve's Garden. Because Frank had people on the newspaper, the press had not broken the association with the singer and the supper club. To divert attention, it was decided that the last person to see the vocalist alive would be the busboy, Bobby Lange. Adamo spent days briefing Bobby. He was told not to volunteer any information, answer yes or no. If it became necessary to explain anything, be brief, make eye contact, take deep breaths, speak slowly, allow yourself time to think and stand upright.

The employees at the club knew that the singer had been appearing there but had no idea what had caused her demise. The colored band members were in a state of total disbelief. Everyone thought it was just routine the day the detectives arrived. The buzz as to what was going on commenced when Bobby was summoned to Frank's office.

Thinking of this moment had kept Bobby awake several nights. As he paced the floor Mira would say repeatedly, "Robert, come to bed. What in the world is troubling you?"

He did not have an appetite as his nerves were on edge. He dreaded what he might be asked and how he'd respond. When told to report to Mr. Frank's office, he rushed to the restroom. He was scared.

In Frank's office were Adamo, Ivan and two detectives from the Third Precinct. Mr. Frank was sitting at his desk doodling on a sheet of paper. Adamo was near the window. He seemed composed and collected. Ivan was sitting on the sofa with one of the officers. He was secretly eating peanuts. Bobby caught Adamo's eye and held his gaze a few seconds. He couldn't understand why no one appeared concerned or worried.

"You sent for me, Mr. Frank?" Bobby asked nervously.

Frank stood, as he walked to greet him said pleasantly, "Come in Bobby. Come in. These gentlemen have a few questions to ask you." Frank nodded to the detectives and returned to his desk.

The Investigator looked Bobby up and down then at his worn and tattered note pad in his chubby hand, touched two fingers to his tongue and turned several pages. He was short and stubby. His face was the color of a red apple. He looked as if all his blood had decided to accumulate in his butterball face. His shirt was unbuttoned at the neck, and his tie was loose and dangling. His suit hadn't been to the cleaners in a while and his shoes had seen better days. It was obvious by his laborious breathing and wheezing he had eaten too many glazed donuts.

With a quick glance at the note pad and with a voice that originated somewhere near the coastline of Mississippi and traveled through his nostrils, asked, "What's your name, boy?"

"Robert Lange, Sir." Bobby answered in a strong voice. Bobby was surprised at his confidence. He lost sleep agonizing over this moment and now that it was here the fear and apprehension was minimal.

"How long have you worked here?" Bobby answered as instructed. After all the basic questions were asked: What time did Mr. Pinta leave? Was he alone? What time was it? Did the girl leave with him? Are you sure he left alone?

Dick Tracy closed his note pad and growled, "That will be all boy."

Mr. Frank waved his arm and said, "Thanks Bobby. Return to work."

The waiters were questioned briefly but had nothing to offer.

While being interrogated, Bobby was conscious of the eyes on him. Mr. Frank, Adamo, and Ivan watched his every move like a hawk. They were impressed with his poise and confidence. They knew he was lying yet he came across as sincere and honest as a Mother's prayer. Adamo smiled knowing that he had read the kid right — he had courage.

After a few weeks, Bobby began to relax. He realized that the incident was unfortunate and in truth no one could blame Mr. Frank for not wanting the supper club implicated. After all, he reasoned, it would serve no worthwhile purpose. What's done is done. Let sleeping dogs lie.

The investigation became extremely intense. A police dragnet was set up around the city. The usual suspects were apprehended, questioned, and released. The police relied heavily on their anonymously paid informants for leads concerning crimes that were committed or were being planned, but in this case, no one knew anything. The regular citizens in the community were also questioned — taxi drivers, restaurant and bar owners, motel operators, vendors, and street people. No information was available. Meanwhile, the public was demanding a resolution to this terrible and horrific crime.

The District Attorney's Office became irate when they discovered that the club Miss. Dame Wright had been performing at was Eve's Garden. They demanded to know why that information had been withheld. Since, there were no leads, and all the informants were mute, the District Attorney thought it was a good time to take another look at Frank Francino and the other mobsters operating in and around Louisiana.

CHAPTER 22

Wilfred Duford was a very manipulative human being. He was unusually frail, and his clothes always seemed to be one size too large. It gave him the appearance of being underfed and malnourished, almost gaunt and famished. His chest was sunken, and his hands were exceptionally small. His behavior, on the other hand, was risky and perilous. Wilfred Duford's self-esteem was null, and his self-respect was void. He was a compulsive gambler. The high he derived from gambling was greater and more intense than sex, alcohol, drugs, or any other experience. He was a well-known regular at the Horne of Plenty, one of Francis Francino's gambling parlors, in Jefferson Parish. He was indebted to the house, but Frank carried him because he was useful.

Wilfred was deathly afraid of Allen Adamo and rightfully so. He had witnessed Adamo's method of dealing with cheaters and lagers. Adamo informed him, on more than one occasion, that if it weren't for Frank he'd break his fucking neck. Whenever he was in Adamo's presence, he had an urge to use the restroom.

Wilfred Duford was a staff lawyer in the District Attorney's Office. He was responsible for assisting Judges in researching documents for civil litigation and other legal proceedings. He was privileged to vital and useful information. He had provided essential and indispensable documents to Frank many times in the past.

Speaking on the phone in a voice that could easily be mistaken for a woman, Wilfred said with urgency, "Mr. Adamo, it's imperative that I meet with Mr. Frank. Something is brewing, and I can't talk on the phone. Can you be at the club at noon?"

"We'll be there." Adamo responded tersely. Then added, "This had better be good you little runt son-of-a-bitch. It better be good."

Wilfred arrived at the club a few minutes before noon. He looked overly concerned and smelled of nicotine and cheap cologne. He was escorted to Mr. Frank's office and told to have a seat. Frank was on the phone and gestured with his hand indicating he'd be with him in a second. A few minutes later he hung up and asked Adamo "What's the emergency?"

Adamo pointed to Wilfred and said, "The floor is yours, smuck."

Wilfred cleared his throat and with trembling hands lit a cigarette. He slowly began to speak choosing his words carefully. He explained that Mr. Pinta's law firm was putting pressure on the District Attorney's Office to solve this horrendous murder. Also, the D.A.'s Office is being bombarded with complaints from the public concerning the crime rate in the city.

He took a drag off the cigarette and said nervously, "To divert attention from the City Attorney's Office, the Public Prosecutor is seeking an indictment from the Grand Jury on filing a charging document directly with the court. They are asking, once again that members of organized crime be investigated. The district attorney was a drowning man grabbing at a pointed sword. He'll use anything to get the heat off."

Hesitantly, Wilfred rose and walked to Mr. Frank's desk. Handing Frank several sheets of paper saying apologetically, "There are four names in these papers that the Prosecutor is concerned with, and your name is first on the list, Mr. Francino." He then explained what that all meant.

Wilfred, shaking his head said dubiously, "If the Judge sides with the Grand Jury and finds probable cause that could be embarrassing as well as time consuming. It comes down to this Mr. Francino, all your vital information will be scrutinized."

He looked at Adamo and knowing he was treading on thin ice wiped the perspiration from his face and continued. "Such as any criminal or racketeering history."

He qualified his statement by saying, "That is if a history exists. Your private, personal, federal, state, and all other records will be re-examined."

He sat back down, crossed his legs and being sympathetic to

Mr. Frank's position stated, "All business transactions, real estate, tax and corporate filings will be fodder for public consumption. No stone, Mr. Francino, will be left unturned."

After completing his report, Wilfred closed his briefcase and lit another cigarette. As an afterthought he uttered, "I don't know when this indictment will be presented to the Grand Jury, but it will be soon."

Frank's policy had always been to avoid publicity at all cost — positive or negative — especially negative. He didn't like the idea of his affairs being splashed all over the front page. Nor did he believe in bringing undue attention to himself. The last thing Frank needed were reporters hounding him at every turn, parked outside the club night and day, asking idiotic questions. His associates frowned on front-page news, and in the past, they let their feelings be known. For as powerful as Frank was, he too had those to whom he had to answer. Simply put, his associates were not going to go down with the ship, and Frank knew it.

Frank, becoming a bit uneasy upon hearing this information, rose from his chair and sat on the edge of his desk. He folded his arms and with grave concern seeping into his voice asked, "What can I do to ward off this legal assault?"

Wilfred shook his head and cautiously replied, "I don't know, Mr. Francino. It doesn't look good."

He looked at Adamo for support and said spiritlessly, "If someone isn't apprehended and soon, the arraignment will be a foregone conclusion."

Beginning to feel uncomfortable for being the bearer of bad news and not having anything more to add, Wilfred rose to leave. He extended his hand to Mr. Frank, and said, "I'm sorry Mr. Francino. I wish I could have been helpful to you." Not wishing to meet Adamo's gaze, he ignored him completely.

Mr. Frank held the door open for him and reminded him to stay in touch. Happy this ordeal was behind him he reassured Frank that he could be depended on and if anything, important materialized he would notify Mr. Adamo.

Deep in thought Frank sat in his chair. Neither he nor Adamo said a word for what seemed like an eternity. It was as if each one was processing the information that had been imparted and couldn't believe the problems they were confronted with. If the gavel fell, it wouldn't fall just on Frank, but the entire Cerberus Corporation. It was no secret Frank was jealous of his privacy. He was wise enough to know that the Politicians and City Officials that he had on his payroll would run, the cowards that they were, should he be indicted. The business at the club would dry up like the Sahara Desert.

With a major idea coming to mind, he said excitedly, "Adamo, get Ivan over here immediately. I have something for the two of you to do."

CHAPTER 23

The headline of the daily newspaper declared: "Let There Be Heat" in large print, followed in small print with "And there was heat — lots and lots of heat.

Heat reported illnesses, such as cramps, strokes, and heat exhaustion dominated the news. Parents were cautioned to keep a close eye on children, the elderly, and pets. The homeless were cautioned to seek shelter. The Goodwill Organization gave out electric fans to the needy.

The heat refused to have any mercy on the masses. Those individuals who were forced to be on the street that afternoon were paying penance for some past transgression. The sidewalk and street were cement and asphalt. There was no place for the sun's rays to penetrate causing the heat to intensify. Ivan pulled into the parking lot. It was located a block and a half from the Greyhound Bus Station. The area consisted of a conglomerate of businesses: restaurants, department stores, taxi stands, and vendors selling novelties.

Putting on the wig and cheap hat followed by the fake mustache, Adamo asked, "How do I look?"

Ivan laughed and replied, "Father Angelo or Sister Alma wouldn't recognize you and they practically raised you."

To complete his disguise, Adamo was dressed in an inexpensive and lamentable seersucker suit, bow tie, and black and white shoes. He took a mouthful of the wine he bought, swished it around in his mouth and spit it out. He never drank alcohol. He then dabbed the wine on his fingertips and rubbed it behind his ears and along his neck. Stepping out of the vehicle, he put on a pair of round rim glasses. He told Ivan to wait in the tavern across the street, gave him the thumbs up sign, and began walking towards the bus station.

He hadn't walked twenty yards when a woman chewing gum and looking as if life had forsaken her asked, "Would you like some company friend? I'll blow all your troubles away."

Adamo made eye contact but said nothing. Some things never change, he thought. In every major city near a bus or train station, you'll find pimps, hustlers, prostitutes, and con artists of every kind. Adamo knew exactly what he was looking for.

On the side of the bus station was an alley that the sanitation department used to pick up the refuge and garbage. It was a haven for unlawful activity.

As Adamo walked by he heard Harvey Brinks sing out, "Find the lady in red."

Harvey threw three cards to the delight of the few people who had gathered at the end of the alley.

"Somebody, please, please find the lady in red." He threw the cards again.

Harvey Brinks had been afforded every opportunity in life to succeed. His Father was a Brick Mason for the city's maintenance department, and his Mother was a Music Teacher. At an early age, it was discovered that Harvey had an exceptional talent for the piano. By the age of twelve, he was playing the Hammond Organ in Church. By the time he entered High School, every University of color had an eye on him. The consensus was he played the piano with an emotion and passion far beyond his years. He had a musical gift that was divinely inspired said the elders of the church.

Everyone agreed Harvey Brinks would go far, and he did. He went very far... far into the world of crime, violence, and deceit. He went from the honor roll, to a usual suspect. Instead of becoming a classical pianist, Harvey became an astute con artist... a common street hustler, and drug addict.

Instead of practicing the piano he found himself doing card tricks in jail. Because of his dependency on drugs he dropped out of High School in his junior year. By eighteen, he was well known to Law Enforcement and the State as a two-bit con-man who would do anything to maintain his habit. His family could not understand why Harvey chose to trade-in his God given gifts for a life of crime, degradation, and drugs.

Throwing the three cards, Harvey cried out again,

"Somebody, please. Please, find the lady in red."

A bystander put ten dollars on top of the makeshift table. He pointed to a card. Harvey congratulated the patron on winning once again and paid him. Adamo was-well-aware that the dealer and the "shill", the guy winning were working together. The object is to make an onlooker believe easy money can be made. All one has-to-do is find the red card out of the three that are shuffled. As skilled as Harvey was, the red card was found when only he meant for it to be found.

The third "shill", who was also part of the con, began working on Adamo.

With his arms folded, he confidentially whispered, "Dat mothafucka is either dumb, stupid, or both. I wish I had some money. I can spot the red card every time. I'd bust his ass."

Playing into the con, Adamo gave a senseless grin, adjusted the inane looking eyeglasses and mumbled, "I think I'll take a chance."

The shill rubbing his chin with a sly as a fox like look said, "I don't blame ya boss. I don't blame ya at all."

When Adamo stepped up looking like a country turnip green, Harvey Brinks couldn't believe his good fortune because, now, standing before him was the perfect mark, he began grinning. The hat, ridiculous suit, and simple looking glasses were a dead giveaway. This country bumpkin was made to order, was all Harvey could think.

Throwing the cards several times without trying to conceal the red one, Harvey exclaimed, "This is your lucky day Mr. Charlie."

He hardly could contain himself thinking what an easy take this would be. Besides taking his money, Harvey wanted the two gold rings, and the diamond watch country boy was sporting.

He called out with glee, "Find the lady in red. Find the lonely lady. She's all dressed up in red."

Before you could say the lady looks good in red Adamo had lost two hundred dollars, the two rings and the watch. Adamo stood before Harvey with his hat in his hands begging for money enough to buy a bus ticket.

Walking away with his buddies and laughing, Harvey said flippantly, "Today ain't Christmas, Mr. Charlie and I sure ain't Santa Claus."

As soon as Harvey Brinks and his two cronies were out of sight, Adamo used the public pay phone on the side of the bus station and lit a cigarette when the operator said, "May I help you?"

Taking a drag he blew a puff of smoke and said, "Please connect me with the police department."

It was Sunday morning. Saturday night at the club had been unusually busy. The cattle industry convention was held in the City. The conventioneers were a rough, loud, rowdy group dealing with issues from policy, trade shows, networking and of course beef.

The minimum waiting time for a table was an hour and a half. Each member was allowed three guests; which meant there were as many people as the fire code would allow.

Bobby locked the freight door behind the kitchen staff. Feeling pretty good, he began humming the last tune the band played. As he went about finishing up some odds and ends, he spoke to Ivan and Adamo about the need for another busboy.

"Sounds good." Adamo said, "We'll run it by Frank Monday morning."

It was about 7:45 a.m. when Bobby pulled into his driveway. The sun began to rise, stretch, and show its shiny face. He turned off the ignition and sat in his station wagon. He wasn't tired but sluggish, which he attributed to that second piece of cheesecake he had with his coffee about three that morning. He picked up the newspaper from the lawn, waved at a neighbor, and entered the house. Trying not to awaken Mira, he took off his tuxedo and hung it in the closet. He put his shirt, socks, and underwear on a chair, to be placed in the clothes bin. He put on his silk robe and returned to the kitchen. He poured a large cup of black coffee, grabbed the newspaper and headed for the backyard swing — all the while humming.

Next to the swing was a large overturned flowerpot that he used to set his coffee on. It was one of those rare mornings when his well-being was at an all-time high. He took a sip of Java and separated the sports page from the Sunday paper. The Cincinnati Reds and the Detroit Tigers were in the baseball world series. The Reds won the championship in 7 games.

Joe Louis was the heavyweight champion. Once a month he fought. His opponents earned the tag, "Bum of the Month". One fighter said his plan of attack would be to stick and run. To which, Joe Louis replied, "He can run, but he can't hide."

Finishing with the sports section, Bobby set it aside and picked up the front page. As he read the headlines, his heart dropped into his stomach and began pounding. His breathing became laborious, sweat broke out on his brow and he began trembling uncontrollably. Unable to believe what he had read he stared at the headlines for several minutes. In bold print was written: Three Negroes apprehended and have confessed to the murders of Mr. James Pinta, a well-known Attorney, and a singer from Lafayette, Louisiana. The prosecutor said the arrests were due to diligent police work and is seeking the death penalty.

The article stated, among other things that Harvey "Shinny Ball" Brinks and David "Two-Lip" Bonds, two well-known criminals were arrested late Friday night, near the vicinity of the crime. A gold watch and two rings belonging to Mr. Pinta was found in the suspects' possession. A third suspect, Richard "Red Man" Olson, a witness for the state was allowed to plead guilty to a lesser charge for testifying against the codefendants. He confessed to robbing the victims but had nothing to do with killing them. Because of the confessions, the public defender will ask for mercy. The many violations of the three were noted and a statement from Mr. Pinta's law firm was cited.

Unable to concentrate, the newspaper slid from Bobby's hand onto the dewy grass. He sat there in a daze. This was unbelievable. This was an experience unlike any he had ever known. He had no frame of reference from which to draw. He was emotionally empty, and his thoughts were jangled and incoherent. He could not rid his brain of the pain, torture, and brutality those poor souls must have been subjected to for them to confess to first-degree murder — especially one they had not committed.

He sat on the backyard swing staring into space. He searched his mind trying to make some sense of it all. One thing that kept reverberating around his brain was two innocent men were going to be electrocuted, and he didn't have the power to intervene.

He tried rationalizing by saying, "They were criminals. It was just a matter of time before their luck ran out. They were doomed anyway. That's the penalty for living as they did."

There was no way Bobby could justify his silence. But silent he knew he had to remain. Bobby was numb. This couldn't be real. It was all a bad dream, and at any moment he would awaken. That was only wishful thinking for he could not deny the reality of the nightmare that was unfolding.

Sunday evening found Bobby still sitting in the backyard. He couldn't move. He knew that somehow, someway Frank had the lawyer's jewelry planted on those young boys. Knowing those young boys were going to die would affect Bobby's disposition, and personality the rest of his life. He would be forever changed.

Mira walked from the house and said, "Hello, Robert. How long are you going to sit out here?"

He didn't respond. Sitting down next to him, she tried making small talk to no avail. Feeling the negative vibrations radiating from him it was obvious he was troubled.

"Is there something you'd like to talk about Robert?" She asked caringly.

Without looking in her direction, he grunted, "Go away woman and leave me be."

Whatever was disturbing him, she knew it originated on Tulane Avenue.

She had said a million times or more, "Robert that place is a den of iniquity. The devil and his accomplices reside there."

No matter what angle he analyzed the situation the answer came back the same — there was nothing he could do to change the course of events. To interfere in any way would bring irreparable harm to himself and his family. With that thought in mind, he decided to channel his energy in trying to live with himself.

The awful fate of those three unfortunate young men was never mentioned in Bobby's presence. At the club, you'd never know anything out of the ordinary had taken place — it was business as usual. Looking at Frank, Ivan, and Adamo, one would never know how violent, heartless, cruel, and unmerciful they were.

Several months later Bobby was summoned to Frank's office. Present was Ivan and Adamo, Frank said without fanfare, "Bobby, you're being promoted to Associate Manager. Adamo will work with you until you get accustomed to your new assignment. Congratulations. That'll be all."

Bobby stood by the end of the bar, the perfect picture of a proud

Mandingo, lost in solitary thought; caught up in the revenue of the years that had come and gone. His dream was broken by a tug on his sleeve.

Ray, one of the bartenders said, "Bobby I'll be a few hours late tomorrow. I have a dental appointment."

Bobby replied, "Put it in the book, Ray. I'll sign it."

During one of the Monday morning meetings, Frank announced that the dry goods store on St. Bernard Avenue was being put on the market for sale. It had been vacant for a while, and vandalism was a major concern. When Bobby voiced an interest in opening a restaurant at that location he was taken by surprise.

To his astonishment he was offered, not only the dry goods store, but also the entire corner, property included. More unbelievable then that was the price. The total cost would be forty-nine thousand dollars. Bobby immediately retired from Eve's Garden. For an added ten thousand, Bobby had the buildings revamped and remodeled. In four months, he opened Bobby's Café, Barbershop, Pool Hall, Fish Market, Rooms-For-Rent, and later Bobby's Cleaners was added.

From day one, the corner was a gold mind. Bobby had learned a lot about business and cooking working all those years at Eve's Garden. If truth were told, Bobby was a genius when it came to business. He may have fallen short with me but not in his business affairs. He felt blessed to get away from the club.

The stress and tension was beginning to take a serious toll on his health. He was easily annoyed and agitated. He began cussing and screaming for no apparent reasons. For health-related issues, he began taking several pills a day.

When the doors opened for business, Bobby was fifty-seven years old. I'll never forget that day. I was nine years old and just out of short pants. Rodney was King of the Hill. Unlike Bobby, he didn't quite have the knack. By no extension of charity could he be called an entrepreneur. He didn't possess the knowledge, vision, experience, nor know how. It didn't matter, he was second in command, and he marveled at his position.

In little or no time, who Bobby was and to whom he was connected became public knowledge. He found jobs for those who were out of work. Those who needed aid from the city were told whom to see. The Ministers who, from time to time, would have trouble-obtaining permits for their Church suppers had only to notify Bobby. And of course, he assisted those needing legal aid. Bobby, or Mr. Bobby, as he was called, was the most powerful colored man in the City of New Orleans.

Whatever the problem, more than likely, Bobby could have it resolved. All the good he did for the community was overshadowed by the aid and comfort he gave criminals. For the love of God, the Ministers and other leaders in the area could not comprehend why he'd use his power and influence to help those who were a blemish on the face of society. They couldn't fathom why he used his time and energy assisting pimps, prostitutes, drug dealers, and criminals of every kind. No one in our family could understand it either. Momma begged him to discontinue such practices to no avail.

Bobby was an extremely complex man with complicated issues. To understand him, they would have had to reside in his world and walk in his shoes. By offering a helping hand to the 'bottom feeders' of society, that's what they were called, was Bobby's way of seeking atonement and redemption for allowing two innocent men to be electrocuted. It was a type of Moses complex. To free himself from guilt, he felt he'd use his power to free those who were in bondage; prison, right or wrong, guilty or innocent was no concern to Bobby.

The death of those two young men and the incarceration of the third one behind bars for life affected every phase of Bobby's existence. It's said that a brave man dies but once. Bobby died daily. He was not a religious man, and I'm not sure if he believed in anyone or anything, but when he was alone he'd pray to whomever or whatever he perceived his God to be. He'd beg for forgiveness, for peace, for deliverance, and for that psychological mortgage he owed to be paid in full. Bobby's troubles were many, but little did he know, darker days were yet to come.

For Momma said to him many years ago, "Robert, write these words on your heart. Just as sure as the eagle rules the sky and the rooster crows at dawn you will pay dearly for what you are doing to Rodney." For reasons known only to him, he wouldn't listen.

CHAPTER 24

It was a breezy Tuesday morning, slightly overcast and cool, nothing unusual for an October day. People made their way to work, from work, or to find work.

The peanut vendor on the corner yelled to passers-by, "I've got hot nuts; peanuts; 5 cents a bag. Get your hot nuts here."

The handsome young blonde haired man with eyes as blue as the sky stood before the bench. As a woman standing at the bus stop sneezed, he quickly covered his nose and mouth with a handkerchief, even though she was several yards away. Before sitting he took a section out of the newspaper and spread it on the bench. Not satisfied, he unfolded the paper and re-folded it again, making sure the corners were perfectly square.

He took a seat not allowing his hands to contact any part of the bench. The young man had an abnormal and deep-seated respect for germs and contaminants. Every day he spent an excessive amount of time cleaning and re-cleaning. Checking the stove and doors repeatedly, everything in his house had to be in place and in order. His shoes had to be lined up like soldiers. The hangers in his closet had to all face the same direction. All the canned goods in the pantry were exceptionally neat and organized. His bathroom was so sanitized; surgery could be performed in it. Under no circumstances could he touch the lever to flush the toilet, and he would be willing to face a firing squad before using a public restroom.

Long before adulthood he had tried medication to relieve his compulsions. It did nothing to alleviate the problem. He then joined a support group. His anxieties seemed to increase. He could find no comfort, and as he grew older his compulsions worsened. Once a thought was conceived, if strong enough, it would fester and magnify until acted upon. It would become a full-blown obsession. And so it was with Francis Francino he had become one of the young man's mental impressions that could not be ignored.

He was in his early teens when he first began reading stories about the man who would take up residence in his brain. He kept and maintained a scrapbook on all of Frank's activities: how he rose to power in the world of crime, his control of the labor unions, his racketeering, his gambling joints, his involvement in murders and of course his ownership of the exclusive and private supper club, Eve's Garden.

He had an emotional reaction to photos and stories concerning Frank that were so intense that he would set the pictures on fire and marvel at the flames. He'd pin the newspaper, with Frank's picture printed within, on the door and throw darts at it. There were times when doing so would cause him to involuntarily ejaculate in his pants. He knew his feelings were irrational and knew what he had to do to free himself.

Francis Francino had become the young man's mission in life. And just as sure as he washed his hands several times an hour and performed simple tasks over and over, like a carousel, Frank revolved around his brain. The intrusive and unwanted thoughts of Frank grew stronger, more powerful and potent than the day before. For him to know any semblance of peace, his mission had to be completed.

On the last day of his life, Francis Anthony Francino rose at 6 a.m., turned off the alarm and turned on the radio. His music of choice was classical. He was intelligent enough to engage in conversations regarding some of the great composers Chopin, Haydn, Beethoven, and Tchaikovsky, his favorite being Wolfgang Amadeus Mozart.

When he'd tell his associates that Mozart wrote, "Twinkle Twinkle Little Star" at the age of 5, played the violin, was a master of symphonic chamber piano, operatic, and choral music.

Disinterested they'd snarl and say, "Who gives a fuck?"

Puffing on his cigar, Francis would smile and with an attempted aristocratic air, state, "I do. You ignorant bastards." When he began moving up in the underworld, he knew it wasn't prudent to be a creature of habit. It made it easy for his enemies to keep tabs on him. As he grew older, he began to relax and felt one bodyguard was enough. Failing to heed the advice of others, he dismissed the services of the other three. He then committed the cardinal sin of falling into a routine.

Before getting out of bed, he'd reach for the prayer beads that hung faithfully on the bedpost. Kissing the beads, he asked the Virgin Mary to look after his wife Adela. Soon after she died, which was a few years ago, he sold his house. Without Adela, he couldn't bare residing there alone. His daughters persuaded him to move into an assisted living apartment. It provided high standard services with beautiful surroundings and he didn't have to worry about maintenance, housekeeping, or security issues.

Sitting on the side of the bed, he stretched his arms above his head while yawning. He took several deep breaths and picked up the small bag containing his medications. Also, on the night stand with his medicines was a covered glass of water. The water was his reminder — otherwise he'd forget.

He adjusted his thick-rimmed eyeglasses, swallowed a handful of pills, and with the help of his walking cane, rose very slowly from the bed. Entering the bathroom, he left the door opened, allowing the music to join him.

After showering and shaving, his breakfast was sent up with the newspaper. His breakfast, like his routine, had become a habit. Each morning was the same: oatmeal with cream, lightly buttered, one slice of toast with jelly, a small glass of pineapple juice, a large cup of coffee, and a pitcher of slightly chilled water.

At 9 a.m., he picked up the phone and called his daughters. He talked to each one for about five minutes. Where his grandchildren were concerned, if there were functions that he needed to attend, he'd write them on the calendar and have his secretary record it. If he forgot, he'd have hell to pay.

He put on a beige suit, brown tie, and white shirt. In his lapel pocket, he placed a chocolate colored silk handkerchief. Stepping into a pair of expensive tan loafers he imitated the music — Rumber-bum-bum. Rumber-bum-bum. The last thing he put on was the gold bracelet with the tiny 8-

ball. Time had not diminished his affection for the little ornament or Samson.

Walking through the lobby, he passed the handsome blonde haired, blue-eyed young man. The young man looked at his watch, smiled and said, "Morning, Sir."

Frank nodded thoughtlessly and waved for his driver who was flirting with one of the apartment's representatives. At 10 a.m., he'd be sitting in his favorite pew in St. Paul's Catholic Church.

Frank enjoyed sitting in the Sanctuary alone during the week. It provided him an opportunity to collect and organize his thoughts regarding his life, business, and future. His religion was purely a cultural matter. It had to fit into his circumstances at the moment and was subject to change in the blink of an eye. He felt no remorse or guilt concerning the things he had done or might do. The solutions to the problems he had to resolve in his business affairs were always justified. After all, he reasoned, any God who was omnipotent would surely understand that everything he had done was due to cause and effect.

His rationalization was simple; the world didn't give a damn about him or his kind and heaven help those poor souls with the wrong paint job. It was a pathetic dog that didn't wag its own tail was his philosophy.

Francis would talk to the lifelike statues as if they could understand his every thought.

There were days when he pleaded, "Didn't I do the things I was supposed to do, didn't I? I'm a man. What kind of God respects a coward? I provided for my wife and children the only way I knew how. If that's a crime, then I'm guilty as hell."

Conversing with the marble figures in this Holy Place Of Refuge, he'd share with them how his Father had to bow his head and kiss ass to get along.

He'd ask, "What good did bowing down do for him. What good at all? They'd spit on him, push him aside, and call him disparaging names. He was a man. It broke my heart to see how he was treated. Why did they treat him that way? He went to his grave scratching and clawing trying to earn a living."

With sadness flooding his being he'd recall how his family had to swallow their pride and ask the neighbors for help to pay for his burial.

"My dear Mother prayed the rosary daily," he uttered, "and when she'd asked Father Denello why her prayers were not answered he'd hunch his shoulders and reply, 'My child we must…', 'My sister, the Heavenly Father does…', 'My child you must believe….' In the meantime, there was no food in the cupboard, the rent was due, and the electricity was cut off. Again, if it wasn't for good neighbors, heaven only knows what would have happened to us."

Looking at his inanimate friends attached to the walls he concluded, "Well, that way of life was not for me. No, Sir. By hook or crook, I'm going to get mine. I don't know if fear and respect are related and I've given up caring." He mentally stated.

Then sneering and frowning he murmured softly "I'd rather be feared than respected."

Francis had spent most of his adult life chasing that illusive trait called respectability. By opening Eve's Garden, he thought would help him in his quest. It was all for naught. People feared him. They didn't love nor respect him. Of course, for their own personal gain, they prostituted their standards by acting sycophantically, but to all, he was a criminal, murderer, and racketeer; a ruthless and barbarous individual who had committed every crime known to man. He would never be respected.

The media referred to Frank, and rightfully so, as "The Bayou Monster", a mobster who was brutal, unforgiving, and merciless.

On the road to his destiny, many things had come Frank's way. Why respectability had evaded him, he could not understand. If the motionless statues that seemed to see, hear, and discern all, could speak they might have said, "Francis without a conscience, one might never be equipped to distinguish between good and evil or right and wrong."

In his life and business affairs, as far as Francis was concerned, he did no wrong. He defiantly proclaimed to the ivory statues, "I did what I had to do. I played the cards fate handed me. What else could I do?"

In this world, those would be the last thoughts he'd ever have regarding the philosophy of his chosen way of life.

There was a time when his driver, who also acted as his bodyguard, would accompany him into the church. Frank found his presence both bothersome and distracting. That being the case, his orders were to remain in the car.

Now and then a nurse or someone connected with the hospital across the street would enter, walk rapidly to the altar, kneel, and pray; sometimes he'd hear them weeping, watch them make the sign of the cross, rise and leave. Seeing this, Frank would smile thinking they had made a serious medical mistake and had come here to bury it mentally.

Alone in the pew Frank was at peace. He felt protected by the spirits conjured up in his personal belief system. There was no need to be overly concerned, or cautious. After all, he was Francis Anthony Francino, the most powerful crime boss in the State of Louisiana. If anything happened to him, members of the underworld would turn itself inside out until those responsible were found and severely dealt with.

He hadn't noticed the blonde haired, blue-eyed, young man who had been monitoring his every move for over three months. He was as familiar with Frank's daily schedule as Frank was. He knew the time he left his apartment, the time he arrived and departed from Church. He was well acquainted with the time he spent at the club and the time he retired for the day. But, more than anything else, the young man knew the day and the approximate time

Francis Anthony Francino would die.

As he shooed a pigeon away that had gotten a bit close, the young man looked at his watch. It was time. He rose from the bench and took a very deep breath. As the oxygen escaped his lungs, he looked both ways and crossed the street. As he entered St. Paul's Catholic Church, he smiled because he hadn't stepped on a crack in the street or sidewalk. Kneeling at the altar, he checked his watch again; the time was now. He slowly and methodically slipped on the light blue sanitary rubber gloves. He reached into his handbag and retrieved the plastic apron. Putting it on he was certain to make a neat bow with the string as he tied it behind him. He had dreamed of this moment for many years. He had lived and re-lived it a million or more times, now that it was a few minutes away caused him to become aroused. He hardly could wait for Frank to arrive. With a smile as his reward, he patted the bulge in his pants and adjusted the gloves on his hand.

Doing everything to contain himself, he reached into his pocket for the silver-plated surgeon's scalpel. Holding it like a phallus; he was ready. Hearing the Church door open and the sounds of footsteps echoing throughout the sanctuary caused his heart to flutter. Beads of sweat danced on his forehead and his breathing accelerated. He made a quick sign of the cross and rose from the Altar.

As Francis took his seat, a dreadful sensation passed over him. He had found comfort here for years. But this morning, deep within the marrow of his bones he felt an unwelcome presence lurking in the Sanctuary. He took a perfunctory glance at the young man with yellow hair at the Altar and returned to his private reverie.

Coupled with his age, sense of power, and arrogance, Francis had become exceedingly careless. So, instead of acknowledging his internal alarms signaling danger, as the young man wearing an apron approached rapidly, he simply brushed him off as an employee of the hospital across the way. When the young man began smiling, Frank tried to recall where he had seen him. He seemed like such a pleasant fellow. Suddenly, when he was close enough to see his eyes, Frank saw death rushing to greet him. In reaching for his walking cane, he was too slow and awkward to ward off the deadly assault. Like a bolt of lightning but twice as fast, the hand holding the scalpel found Frank's Carotid artery.

As Frank fell between the pews gagging, the young man let out a scream of total ecstasy. He forced himself to discard the blood-stained gloves and apron. Trembling and extremely anxious, he rushed to the vestibule where the container of Holy Water was and paused long enough to try to wash his hands.

Knowing the bodyguard was parked out front; he stopped before opening the door to compose himself. He felt as if the weight of the world had been lifted off his shoulders. He felt calm, refreshed, and tranquil — serenity descended and enveloped him. Checking to see if his fingernails were clean and satisfied that they were, he slowly opened the door and walked out into the cool October air. The Cadillac housing the bodyguard was parked facing east; the young man walked west.

As he turned on Canal Street heading for his hotel, his sense of well-being was short lived. Realizing the enormity of what he had done, he felt polluted, filthy and contaminated. His heart began to pound as he rushed up the stairs of the hotel. He could never share an elevator with others. He thought he would die before reaching the shower. He remained in the shower with water as hot as he could stand it for the better part of an hour, then showered again every thirty minutes for the next three hours.

The clothes he had worn were on the bathroom floor. He could not bring himself to touch them. Each time he tried he became sick. Sitting in the doorway of the bathroom looking at the soiled garments for over an hour, he picked them up with an opened clothes hanger after putting on a pair of gloves. He placed the attire in a laundry bag and threw the contents in the dumpster.

The mere sight of the dumpster caused him to vomit violently. He ran back to the shower panic stricken.

When the news was reported that Francis Francino, The Boss of all Crime Bosses in the State of Louisiana, had been almost decapitated, the news was heard instantly around the country.

The crime bosses in the South were clueless as to the person responsible for this brutal and vicious act. The bodyguard was questioned and tortured for days. He was executed after it was realized he didn't have any knowledge of who was responsible for Frank's death.

Two weeks later, with no leads into the investigation, another major and mysterious problem occurred. About 5 a.m. one Sunday morning someone deliberately set Eve's Garden on fire. The firemen were unable to contain the blaze. It took all their skill and training to save the surrounding buildings. In the crowd of onlookers was the blonde haired blue eyed young man. As the flames grew higher and higher becoming a raging inferno, the young man casually fondled himself. With a sense of complete joy and total satisfaction, he slowly walked down Villirie Street. Reaching Canal, he hailed a cab, opened the car door with a handkerchief, and took a seat.

Not wishing to breathe the stale oxygen trapped in the taxi, using the handkerchief, he hurriedly rolled down the window. He entered the New Orleans International Airport with a calm confidence about himself and approached the ticket counter.

The Clerk smiled and said, "Good evening, sir. Name, please?"

The young man proudly said, "Brandon Anketoes, Jr." "Destination, Sir?"

With a sigh of contentment, he joyfully replied, "Delphi, Greece".

CHAPTER 25

As I reached the bottom step in the hallway and opened the door Elizabeth called out, "Joshua..." trying to conceal the sadness in her voice said, "Don't forget you promised to write. I'm going to miss you."

Not knowing quite what to say and not wanting to tell any unnecessary lies I yelled up to her, "I promise. I'll call and get your phone number and address of the University from Miss. Rita."

Before closing the door, I said jokingly, "I'm going to surprise you. I'm going to make the Dean's list."

With a crack in her voice, she replied, "I know you can." Closing the door, I walked out into the courtyard and was greeted by the chill in the September air.

Elizabeth would be leaving tomorrow morning for Alcorn State University. Alcorn is in Lorman, Mississippi. Students have graduated in Agriculture, the Arts, Business, Human Services, Education, Law, Politics, Medicine, and Nursing. Liz was eager to begin her college education, but she was unhappy that each member of the group was going a separate way.

In a few weeks, I'd be leaving for Southern University in Baton Rouge, Louisiana. It's a mystery to me, and always will be, but I graduated. I had no intentions whatsoever of attending college. Dan and I had a good hustle going in the city. We were making money hand over fist. Not wanting to get involved with drugs and the gang High-Tech, we had no choice but to get out of town. Dan had already left for the Army and soon I'd be departing for college. Whenever I say college I stumble on the word. A lot of money was owed us, but we wouldn't be here to collect. The idea of leaving that money behind broke Dan's heart — mine too.

Walking through the courtyard, I was feeling gloomy and melancholy. I was going to miss Liz and the group. I was going to miss so many things — the fun, laughter, and all the good times. The excitement and anticipation of not knowing what was going to happen in the courtyard or along the Avenue surely would be missed.

I couldn't tell Harold we were leaving nor why because he would have wanted to confront the High-Tech gang and he'd lose.

I gave him the list of who owed and how much. It was a substantial amount. I explained that come payday I needed him to make all the collections. I then informed him to continue loaning the money, and every payday collect the juice. When I told him, the business was his, he stammered and stuttered so badly I couldn't make heads or tails of what he was trying to say.

The things I wouldn't miss were Bobby, the Café, and Rodney. I didn't know much, but I was certain of one thing, Bobby was impossible. He was a complete and absolute nut. Because of the hours, I had been keeping our paths seldom crossed and when they did he didn't say anything. He had thrown in the towel and given up on me. I didn't bother to inform him about college.

It was getting late as I walked out of the courtyard. Feeling restless and not knowing what to do with my time I decided to get a bottle of wine from the Superette and stop by the pool hall. I hadn't been there in a while. It was September, and the night air was rather cool. I stopped, opened the bottle of wine and took a long swig. I placed the top back on the bottle and continued walking. I hadn't eaten in several hours, and the alcohol gave me an immediate buzz. I paused and took another drink.

St. Bernard Avenue never changed. It was the same Spring, Winter, Summer, and Fall, morning, noon, and night. You'd see the same people day-in and day-out. There were those who were struggling to make ends meet and those who didn't give a rat's ass about the ends and even less about those who were trying to make them meet. A block away I could see the Café. The neon lights that once flickered Bobby's Café was no longer in use. Mr. Rodney and his wife were the new proprietors and the name of the place had been changed to Rodney's Diner. I had endured enough trouble when Bobby was the owner, so I wasn't about to subject myself to Rodney's bullshit, so I stayed away — far away.

As I crossed Tremain Street, customers were entering the diner. I could hear the music from the jukebox. It was getting late, and the barbershop, which was next to the diner, was closed. In the darkness, someone was sitting on the barbershop's steps. Probably an addict waiting for a drop, I thought. I proceeded with caution.

To my utter surprise and total disbelief, it was Bobby. He was sitting on the steps rocking back and forth. To my shock and astonishment, he was doing something I didn't think he was capable of doing.

The mighty Mr. Robert Anthony Lange, Sr. was crying. The pain I was privileged to see was not physical. I was witnessing emotional trauma, pure one hundred percent, undiluted emotional trauma.

It was obvious someone had stepped on the old boys' heart. I found that extremely funny because I didn't know he possessed such an organ. I became elated when I realized this was the day I had lived for. My Mother often said every dog has a day, but the bulldog has two. Well, Mr. Bobby was about to learn that I'm the bulldog, and I've come to collect my two days. Partial payments unacceptable — payment in full demanded. In my heart of hearts, I always knew my day would come.

A few months earlier, Bobby decided to retire from the restaurant business, he was sixty-five and had enough revenue from all his rental property for he and momma to live comfortably. Plus, he made a mint working for Mr. Frank and put a large portion on the side. Bobby may have been a fool about a lot of things but never with a dollar.

Looking back at it all, it's apparent the only reason Bobby entered the restaurant business was to establish a future for Rodney. He didn't need it for himself. He wanted Rodney to succeed at all cost.

One of the biggest mistakes Bobby made in life, and there were many, was not respecting Momma's counsel. Whatever she said or suggested always fell on deaf ears. He would not listen to her or heed her advice. So, when he decided to rent the place to Rodney, her begging and pleading for him not to do so was fruitless. My Mother tried and tried, but she couldn't get him to see the gigantic mistake he was about to make.

When Rodney became the manager of his own diner his head became as large as a Bass Fiddle. The minute Bobby released the keys and Rodney's third wife, Miss Lady, put on her apron; an evil wind began to blow no good. They began immediately transforming the Café. The private booths were torn out and replaced with tables. The bar was shortened to make room for a game machine that was supposed to provide a mint in revenue. The wallpaper was changed from lively and inviting to dismal and drab. The red checkerboard table cloths were replaced with plastic ones, though they were washed daily, Miss Lady felt plastic was more sanitary. And of course, the neon sign that everyone had come to know and recognize was taken down.

The family didn't know much about Rodney's lady except that he was from St. Rose, Louisiana, a small town about twenty minutes from New Orleans.

The word on the street was Rodney's lady had a questionable past. It was said, if you had the money she had the time. Emma Mae Coleman was her name was and she hit the jackpot when she met Rodney. He moved her to New Orleans, and like the song says, "The bright lights and the big city went to her head."

They moved in together and soon after Rodney took over the diner she became exceedingly selfish, controlling, and domineering. She became the talk of the neighborhood.

She was not a bad looking woman, but, nothing to write home about. Tall and rather plump, Emma Mae walked with an exaggerated twist to her hips. Under no circumstances was she to be trusted. Emma was cunning, sly as a fox, and as transparent as a cheap negligee. A blind man could see her coming and a deaf mute could hear her footsteps. Whatever she had, and that was questionable, it was enough to dangle Rodney around like a puppet.

From the very beginning Rodney and Miss Lady let it be known that Bobby was in the way. His advice and business experience was not solicited, needed or wanted. His suggestions, proposals, and recommendations were completely ignored. Bobby may have fallen short of the mark regarding his parental skills, his personality may have been flawed beyond repair, and his character may have left a lot to be desired, but when it came to business he was a genius. He instinctively knew what the public wanted. He knew their needs. He had a product, and he supplied it. When it came to business, Bobby was to be envied, he ran with the big dogs.

Bobby tried, in vain, to get them to understand it was a Red Beans and

Rice neighborhood, not a Steak and Potatoes one. His Lady would tell Rodney Bobby was interfering. He'd tell Bobby in no uncertain terms to butt-out. Bobby couldn't believe the blunders they were making. He was biting at the bit. The prices were raised across the board. Once a quarter played six records on the jukebox; the music never stopped. Under Rodney's management, a quarter played three. The music died. Bobby gave all the Churches huge discounts. Rodney and his Lady discontinued that practice. Bobby sold Bologna sandwiches for twenty-five cents. School children would line up around the building to buy them. Rodney said the kids were too loud. He stopped selling sandwiches. Bobby's philosophy was a penny here a nickel there at the end of the day
he had a dollar. Rodney had no time for nickels and dimes let alone pennies.

They told Bobby repeatedly not to bother the customers. He'd engage them in small talk, and for him to tell the help anything at all was a big no, no, and no.

Miss Lady was constantly telling Rodney, "I don't want Bobby in the kitchen. You've got to stop him from undermining my authority." You've got to tell him this, you've got to tell him that, I heard him say this, I saw him do that — on and on she would complain.

They saw Bobby as a liability, interference and simply in the way. He had overstayed his welcome, and they wished he'd go away.

When Bobby began complaining to Momma about how they were running the business into the ground, she'd listen carefully then she'd softly say, "Robert, you rented the place to them. It's theirs to run and operate as they see fit. You can bring a horse to water, and that's all you can do."

She'd pull a chair close to him and holding his hands she'd offer this advice, "Why don't you let them be. Stay away for a while. Find yourself a hobby. Go fishing. Relax. Your health is not what it used to be. Have you been taking your medication?"

Again, her counsel fell on a head and heart made of stone. Soon, very soon, that heart of stone would be shattered into a million little pebbles.

I didn't know how awful Bobby was being treated, and if I had known, it would not have made a difference. The way I saw it, he deserved whatever he got. That fight was between him and his darling son. I found it funny, Bobby couldn't stand the sight of me, and now, the tables had turned. His presence infuriated and aggravated his favored child. No, I don't think that's funny. It's unbelievably hilarious — ha, ha, ha.

Rodney had a penchant for gambling and drinking. The problem was his capacity for alcohol was very limited. Give him a thimble of booze, any kind, and he'd become a raving lunatic.

He'd become confrontational and violent finding himself in many altercations. The reason he was given a pass on the street was for one reason — he was Bobby Lange's son.

CHAPTER 26

Charles "Foots" Laree operated the Red-Light Bar and Tavern on St. Anne Street. Every Monday night he and a few other businessmen would gather to play poker. Foots had a first-class tavern where the ladies were welcome and could feel safe. In the back of the bar was his office where the games were played. When Foots decided to go into the bar business, he had two obstacles in his way. The first was a blemish on his record that prevented him from obtaining a liquor license. The second was he had little capital.

People of color had great difficulty securing a business loan. The lending institutions gladly would finance a Cadillac car but little else. A car was tangible assets and could be repossessed. To go into a business, most minorities had to get financing from the likes of Mr. Frank.

Corporation's like Cerberus, Inc. would loan the money at an extremely high interest rate. Anything that was required to operate the business and get it up and running was provided. There was only one stipulation — failure was not an option. Many men worked themselves to the grave trying to keep their business from failing. The monthly payments had to be made — at all cost.

Foots was much younger then Bobby. Being from the streets he knew Bobby by reputation. He asked for a meeting with Bobby, and it was granted. He explained to Bobby the trouble he had with the law and how he was trying to turn things around, and he'd be indebted to Bobby for whatever help he could render. Bobby was impressed with the young man and recommended to Adamo that Charles be granted a loan and set up in business. Foots' record was purified, and before you could say, "Set 'em up, Joe", the Red-Light Tavern was open for business.

Because foots was obligated to Bobby, he bent over backwards trying to get along with Rodney. Many Monday nights while losing, Rodney would become verbally abusive, cussing Foots and the other men in the game. The more he drank, the more he'd lose. The more money he lost at gambling; the worse that his behavior became. There were times when it was all Foots could do to keep Rodney from engaging in a fight and breaking up the game.

Late one Monday evening the game was under way Rodney arrived later than usual and had been drinking. The guys tried to discourage Rodney from sitting in, but he insisted. Against Foots advice, he continued to drink. Rodney began his normal routine. Not liking the cards, he was dealt he threw them at the dealer shouting obscenities. Foots calmed him down and reprimanded him. A few moments later, losing a large pot, he became loud, disruptive, and argumentative. When Foots tried to reason with him, in a fit of anger, he turned the table over — chips and cards flew in every direction. Without a warning, Foots grabbed Rodney and slung him out the back door into the street.

Standing in the doorway with two men holding him back Foots screamed, "Don't ever come here again. You need to grow up and act like a man. If you ever show face here again, I'll kill ya." He threw Rodney's hat at him and slammed the door.

Leaning against his car trying to maintain his balance, Rodney, slurring his speech began talking to the cold September air, "He don't know who he's fucking with. I'm Rodney Lange."

Getting into his car, he began screaming, "I am Rodney Lange! Do you hear me? I am Rodney Lange!"

He softly said, as he tried to gather himself, "And don't you fucking forget it. I — am Rodney — fucking- Lange."

Rodney drove away from the backdoor of the Red-Light Tavern talking to himself. He had lost a great deal of money. He was drunk, broke, hurt, embarrassed, and humiliated. It matters not how you dissect it that's a lethal combination. Instead of driving home he drove to 'The Place'.

Stepping out of the car, he lost his balance and almost fell. Pushing a customer to the side, he stumbled into the Café. Through inebriated eyes, he saw Bobby with his hand on a customer's shoulder talking. In a heartbeat, Rodney became enraged and furious.

Unable to control himself he began shouting, "How many times do I have to tell you to stay out of my fucking place. I'm sick and tired of you worrying my customers. I'm not talking anymore." He half ran half staggered behind the bar.

The waitress, sensing the seriousness of the moment tried to stop him. "No, no, no, Mr. Rodney." She pleaded, "Please, Mr. Rodney. You've got to calm down."

Pushing her out of the way he grabbed the pistol that was kept behind the bar. Stumbling he started towards Bobby. Ranting and raving he raised the gun and screamed, "Maybe you'll understand this?"

At that moment, a customer slammed Rodney face down on top a table and wrestled the gun from him.

Rodney rolled off the table onto the floor. The silence that fell over the café was louder than roaring thunder. The stillness held everyone hostage. It was as if time had ceased. The patrons looked at one another in total disbelief. No one wanted to be the first to move, or speak.

Sitting in the corner next to the jukebox where he had fallen, the silence was broken as Rodney began sobbing. With his face in his hands, he began screaming and crying. "I'm sorry, I'm sorry, I'm so sorry."

Crawling to where Bobby was standing he wrapped his arms around Bobby's leg and in a voice, that would shame the dead he kept repeating, "I'm sorry."

With tears streaming down his face, he kept repeating, "Please forgive me. I'm so sorry."

Bobby stood in the middle of the Café rigid — catatonic. He was anchored to the spot and locked forever to that moment. He pried Rodney's hand from his leg, and stood there, motionless.

As the customers began to exit silently, not a word was said, yet volumes were spoken, just by gently touching him as they filed out.

He could not make sense of what had just happened. Something inside of Bobby crossed over and shut down forever more. He was a defeated and broken old man. As tears began to form and crystallize in the core of his soul, it became apparent that all the King's horses and all the King's men would never be able to put Bobby Lange together again. With his will and spirit, crushed and shattered, softly weeping he shuffled out of the place, seeking refuge, and comfort on the barbershop steps.

CHAPTER 27

Looking at Bobby sitting on the barbershop steps, I could tell he was emotionally wounded. He was hurting, and I was happy to see him in such pain and misery. It was hard to keep from laughing. If he ever needed a shoulder to cry on it was now,
unfortunately for him, mine was not for rent. I lit another cigarette and deliberately blew the smoke in his face. His agony ran deep because he couldn't stop sobbing. The flood of tears made his black face glisten. I took the last drink from the bottle and let out an explosive belch. Setting the bottle next to the step, I could see a Hooker and a John negotiating across the street. Agreeing on a contract they walked off arm-in-arm, like seasoned lovers.

As Bobby tried to speak he reached out to touch me. I stepped back so he couldn't. I heard fragments of what he was saying, "I can't believe. What did I...?" "I never thought..." "I should never have..." "I don't understand why...?" "I really wasn't listening..." "I was thinking..."

Mr. Bobby, Sir, today just ain't your day. Today is your day to get in the barrel.

The wine had me reeling. My head was spinning like a top. I was high as a Georgia pine. They say a drunken man speaks a sober mind. Well, one thing was certain, I was drunk, and he was about to hear the truth, nothing but the truth; years and years of pent up truth.

I began giggling when it occurred to me Bobby had given the world two sad ass sons. One was useless, the other one worthless, that to me was funny. I wish I had another drink. Ain't life funny? It's one big cruel joke. Here's a man who had more power than any colored man in the City of New Orleans, yet, he was powerless to help himself. As he sat crying and whimpering, he was as helpless and pathetic as a broke dick dog. I tried, but I could not keep from laughing.

The alcohol was entering my blood stream much too fast. I was getting drunker by the minute. I had to get a hold of myself. I couldn't allow the wine to impair my judgment. I had to consider my attack for maximum effect. The question was how to proceed.

The wine began advising me. "Joshua," it said encouragingly, "start with all the times he hit, pushed, shoved, punched and threw things at you."

"No, no." I whispered to the wine. "If I did that he'd get off too easy because that was physical, and physical pain can't be re-lived. A woman gives birth, and that's extremely painful. But, once the baby's born she can't bring that discomfort back to the surface."

"Another thing," I said, to my warped way of thinking, "I was proud I could take a punch. He never broke my spirit, and he never saw me cry. I was wild. Before a wild animal can be controlled, his spirit must be broken. In fact, I felt macho. There were times when I'd provoke him to hit me again. Physical pain is too easily forgotten — scratch that idea."

I began to feel wobbly, and my thoughts began to run together. I put my hand on the wall to steady myself. I had to think clearly.

The wine having come up with another idea said excitedly, "Joshua... Joshua, what about the emotional side of the equation?"

"Now, you're thinking." I responded gleefully. I could hardly stand. Still, I wished I had another drink.

The wine put its arm around me and said confidentially, "Joshua, emotional abuse can last a lifetime. Any fool knows a child needs to feel safe and loved to form healthy relationships. Emotional abuse causes serious behavioral and mental disorders, and more than anything else, it destroys a child's spirit."

The wine began dancing, happy for having come up with a good idea, jumped up on my shoulder and crossed its leg.

Bubbling with glee it said, "Explain to Bobby, how you felt when he called you dumb, lazy, trifling, and stupid. Tell him how it made you cringe when he would announce, 'That boy ain't got the sense he was born with.' And how you wanted to crawl under a rock when he'd say, 'Boy, you'll never be shit.'"

For the first time in my life, I felt strong in his presence — powerful and in control. It felt great — good — wonderful. I always had to choose my words when talking to him. Well, you can bet an English pound, I'm going to select my words very carefully this evening because I want every word, syllable, consonant, and vowel to cut like a hot knife slicing through butter. The time was right, and so was I.

The wine began chanting, "Joshua. Joshua. Showtime. Showtime. Joshua. Joshua showtime."

This was the moment I had lived for, hoped for, and dreamed of my whole life. My heart rate increased, and I became anxious. I took a deep breath and collected myself. I opened my mouth. Everything was silent around me. My words were wingless thoughts that refused to take flight. I swallowed hard and tried to speak again with the same result.

"Joshua... Joshua?" I heard the wine ask, "What the fuck is wrong? You've waited years for this moment; don't let it slip away. Express yourself. Show him your true colors. Joshua, Joshua? What are you waiting for? Open your mouth and talk."

The wine screamed in my ear impatiently. Realizing something was wrong the wine said angrily, "Wait one damn minute. Is that a tear in your eye?"

Jumping off my shoulder to get a better look the wine screamed, "Don't you fucking cave in like a bitch in heat. You know what Joshua; you are pitiful. You've got no balls. You're all bark and no bite."

Calming down a bit, confused and disappointed, shaking its head the wine said, "Bobby was right about you Joshua. You ain't shit."

Pointing its finger in my face and staggering off, the wine repeated, "You ain't shit, Joshua. You - ain't - shit".

Stumbling off it kept repeating, "You - ain't - shit".

Flooded with mixed emotions I wanted to kick myself and hang my head in shame. I kept thinking if revenge is sweet, why was there such an awful taste in my mouth? Every time I tried to speak words would fail me. This was the moment I had waited for all my life. Now that it was here, all I could say was, "You've been through a lot, dad. Give me your hand lets go home."

Now, I had to deal with Rodney I know he'd be expecting me. The rules demanded I show my face. It's all about the laws of the street — honor and respect at all cost. It wasn't about what my relationship had been with Bobby any longer. The entire Lange family had been assaulted and my being the next male in line was expected to address the matter in some form or fashion. I know it's foolish and ridiculous, but believe it, or not, the eyes of the street were on me.

All my life I wondered about Rodney. He was a very strange fellow. He conducted himself as if he didn't have a heart — not even a black one. He cared about only himself. It was as if the world were his, and he was allowing us to reside in it providing we all agreed to kiss his ass — regularly. I didn't know what to do or how to handle the situation.

If I confronted him and simply asked, "Rodney what kind of animal are you? You're not a son. You're not a brother. You're not a Father, and now you're not a human being. In God's name what are you, Rodney?"
If I did that it would serve no useful purpose, none, he'd do what he's always done. He'd laugh at me. To him I'd be a joke.

If I made it a physical confrontation, I'd play right into his hands, and I surely would lose. Hell, I can't fight. My sisters used to beat up on me. In grade school, I had ten fights. I lost them all. The only way I know how to fight, is to get a 2'x4' or broom stick, and knock the living shit out of the person provoking me. In the end, where Rodney and that awful incident were concerned, I did nothing.

When 'The Place' was leased to Rodney, it was on a year-to- year basis. The utilities remained in Bobby's name. A few days after that unforgivable occurrence, Momma had the water and electricity cut off. She then revoked the agreement that Bobby and Rodney had signed. With no regard for what was lawful or unlawful and acting on emotion alone, she had padlocks and chains put on the entrance and exit doors, 4'x8' sheets of plywood were placed on all windows, and "No Trespassing" signs were posted. When Rodney arrived on the scene, the cook and the waitresses were gathered on the sidewalk confused as to what was going on. Seeing his "Place" boarded up and locked tighter than a drum, he began cussing, screaming, ranting and raving. He could not control himself.

In a fit of anger, he got momma on the phone and began screaming into the phone. "If you think I'm going to take this lying down, you've got another think coming. I'm going to sue you for everything you've got. You can't do this to me. I know my rights. You'll be hearing from my lawyer. I'll see you in court. You've treated me like a stepchild all my life. No more! You hear me! No more!" Unable to control himself, he slammed the phone down.

Once the dust settled we were able to persuade momma to allow Rodney to finish the few months left on his lease. It was the legal thing to do.

When Rodney was informed of our mother's decision, he said contemptuously, "It's too late. Tell her to talk to my lawyer. She has violated me for the last time. I'm sick and tired of her. I will see her in court."

We tried, in vain, to get Rodney to understand that the family had been through enough, and momma was getting on in years, and he shouldn't drag her through the legal ramifications of a suit. The strain of it all would be too much for her. Momma had her own health issues and her hands were full seeing to Bobby's needs. All this and more was explained to Rodney, yet, he refused to listen, and all our calls were forwarded to his lawyers' office. He severed all contact with the family. He was hell bent on seeing momma in court.

No one knows how, but Allen Adamo got wind of what had transpired between Bobby and Rodney. It is said that he ordered Rodney's attorney to dispense all legal proceedings on Rodney's behalf, against the Lange family, immediately. He then had two of his bodyguards bring Rodney to his office — pronto.

I'm not privileged to what Adamo said to Rodney, but knowing how he felt about Bobby I only could assume it wasn't nice. What I do know is the very next morning Rodney and his lawyer fell over one another explaining to momma that it was all a huge mistake. To show that Rodney meant well, the lawyer said he would relinquish claim to all the property left behind in the Café. Eventually, the refrigerators, stoves, tables, chairs, etc. were auctioned off. After all the equipment and furniture in the café had been sold, momma felt guilty knowing that the proceeds received from the sale weren't rightfully hers. She sent the check to Rodney's attorney requesting that Rodney cash it immediately. The check was returned with a short explanation, which said, "Refused Under Advisement."

One Sunday evening, momma called a meeting with Gilda, Melanie, and me. She offered the Café to anyone of us, or to all three of us. We all declined her offer. She placed the entire corner on the open market. It was sold a short time later. A gas station and a quick stop now occupy the corner of St. Bernard Avenue and Tremain Street.

CHAPTER 28

Bobby sat in the recliner in his bedroom with his feet on an ottoman. On his lap was the family photo album he began viewing every day. The bedroom was spacious with a full bath and walk-in closet. A huge four-post bed dominated the room. There was a television and radio in the room also, but if momma didn't use either they remained off. Next to the window was a large desk where Bobby once conducted all his business. He had a private phone, but he no longer made or accepted any calls.

Following the ordeal, the family experienced with Rodney, Bobby gradually began to slip into a depression and slowly withdrew from social interaction. He'd remain in his room in total darkness for prolonged periods of time.

Momma had him examined by several different Doctors. In their opinion, he was suffering from a psychiatric syndrome brought on by feelings of guilt and worthlessness. Dr. Bolton, Bobby's personal physician, had treated the family for years and knew the history. It was his belief that Bobby was dealing with a broken heart and as far as he knew there was no drug or medicine known to man that could mend it.

As Mira entered the darkened room, she turned on the light. Bobby never objected her doing so but tonight he quickly requested they remain off.

"As you wish Robert." She said smiling.

"Thanks Cat." He said with gentleness to his tone.

She detected a friendly greeting in his mood and was happy. Hearing him call her "Cat" made her warm all over. He hadn't called her by her pet name in years. The positive energy in the room penetrated every pore in her body.

"Would you like to watch TV or listen to the radio?" She politely asked.

With a pleasant quality to his petition, he answered, "No. If you don't mind, I'd like to talk a bit."

While she sat in the chair next to the bed, she had a premonition that this would be a night to remember.

Catching her totally by surprise, as she was about to speak, he quickly said, "Tell me something Cat, are all your prayers answered?"

Her heart began dancing with glee because of the direction the conversation was taking. In the past, he'd refer to her faith and religion as a bunch of mumbo-jumbo rubbish that made no sense at all.

He didn't see her make the sign of the cross. It was her way of thanking the Lord for this special evening. Gathering her thoughts and trying not to become emotional, with conviction she said, "No, Robert, all prayers are not answered." Then added, "It's best that some are not."

She was about to elaborate when he amiably interjected saying, "I want you to do something for me."

Overjoyed Mira replied, "Of course Robert. Anything you wish of me I'll gladly do."

"I need you to…" he hesitated and rephrased his request. With tenderness in his voice, she hadn't expected he said, "Would you be kind enough to ask your God to forgive me?"

Unable to contain herself, in a blink of an eye she was kneeling next to the recliner weeping. Holding his hand tightly, she said, "I've never stopped praying for you Robert and I never will." She was about to articulate some verses from the scripture concerning forgiveness, but he kept talking.

His voice took on a somber and grief stricken tone. "You told me many times Eve's Garden was a den of iniquity. You were so right. I should have listened. I'll go to my grave regretting the day I laid eyes on Frank Francino."

Shaking his head from side to side, he continued. "Cat, you'll never know the unutterable sorrow that relationship has brought into my life. But the sad truth is", he lamented, "I truly enjoyed the fringe benefits. The few pieces of silver that were thrown at my feet, the company of high rollers, the information I was privileged to, and a sense of power. I became addicted to it all. Every man, woman, and child in the neighborhood knew me. To them all, I was "Mister Bobby". It made me feel important. At the bank and City Hall I was always greeted with, 'How are you Mr. Lange?' 'How may we help you Mr. Lange?' 'It's good to see you Mr. Lange.' I didn't know it, but I was living in a fool's paradise."

Her eyes having gotten acclimated to the darkness she could see what a badgered soul he was. Between sobs, she tried comforting him by explaining that the Lord is just and will forgive all sins.

"No one", she said, "is worthy of entering the Kingdom of Heaven. It's only by the grace of God can that be accomplished."

He had asked everyone in the family never to mention Rodney's name in his presence. Honoring his wish, she simply said, "Robert you've been through a lot. The heartbreak, disappointment, and sorrows that you've had to endure are a lot to expect of anyone."

Having his attention, lowering her head as if in prayer, she explained that the Lord never promised anyone joy without sorrow, or peace without pain.

Squeezing his hand, she said excitedly, "But he did promise us strength, rest, help, unfailing sympathy, and undying love. That's in the Bible, Robert, and you must believe it."

He shifted in his seat but said nothing. After a few moments of silence, he resumed speaking. It was the voice and attitude of a man resigned to his fate.

He grunted slightly and said, "Mira, that's your truth and your belief. I envy your faith. It's unfortunate, but my life, unlike yours, has been like the wayward wind… Unpredictable. It has been a series of compromises, deals, and concessions. And if your God is as wise and judicious as you say he is he won't be receptive to my method of bargaining."

"But Robert…" she protested.

Putting a finger to her lips, he stopped her. Placing his hand on her face with his thumb, he removed a tear. The gesture brought sweet memories back to mind of the times they had enjoyed together before the World took him away. She felt warm all over remembering how the mere touch of his hand would make her thankful she was a woman, and he was her man.

Leaning back in the recliner, he sighed heavily and said, "The only thing

I'm asking forgiveness for is the pain, anguish, and mental distress I caused you. The way I've treated you is unforgivable. But, it's all I ask forgiveness for. All the other blunders and errors in judgment I've made I don't deserve to be pardoned for."

The photo album slipped off Bobby's lap onto the floor. Mira picked it up and placed it on the desk. She walked over and stood behind the recliner and began to massage Bobby's shoulders. As he began to relax a bit she hesitantly asked, "Would you be willing to read the Bible with me now and then?"

He pondered the question a second and finally replied, "Why not?" He chuckled and said, "I might learn something. From this day forward anything that will make you happy I'll do."

She couldn't believe how agreeable and pleasant he was this evening.

As she lovingly massaged his shoulders, he asked, "Can you name one prayer of yours that has been answered that I'd recognize?"

Filled with unbelievable love, she bent over the recliner wrapping her arms around his shoulders with her face next to his she whispered, "You'll never know how many times I've asked the Lord to return you to me."

Kissing him on his cheek, she said, "Tonight that prayer was answered. It's good to have you back Robert."

He stroked her arm gently but was too full to speak. Just then the phone in the den rang disturbing the spirit of the moment.

"Oh, shucks." Mira exclaimed, "Excuse me Robert, but I've been expecting that call."

Holding the door open she said, "I love you, Robert. I hope you know that. I thank God, you're feeling better tonight. I love you so very much."

As she shut the door behind her she didn't hear him say, "I love you too, Mira. As a tear trickled down his cheek, he said again, I love you too."

Alone in the darkness he saw a young man hosing the sidewalk at Tulane and Villirie. Standing at the bus stop was an attractive young woman. He deliberately, but playfully, sprinkled water on her. As she shook the water from her loafers, Bobby smiled, crossed his legs on the ottoman, and wiped the water from his eyes.

EPILOGUE

When this story began to unfold, I was nine years old, just out of short pants. It seems like yesterday.

Gilda, who always had a deep love and respect for animals, along with her husband, owns and operates "The Teacher's Pet Shop" in the Lakeview Shopping Mall. You can buy anything from exotic birds to tropical fish. She talks to those animals as if they're children, and the funny thing is, they seem to understand every word. There are certain animals she cannot bring herself to part with.

Melanie still resides in San Diego. She visits every Christmas and calls often. It doesn't seem as if she's ever going to retire. She travels extensively and says she must continue working to do so. Through the years, there have been men in and out of her life, but she has chosen not to re-marry.

As for Rodney, I'm not sure it was ever clear to him what the world expected. He grew up receiving special treatment and felt he didn't have to obey the rules. He still lives in the city. We don't see each other often but, when we do we're civil. A few years ago, he joined a church and sings in the choir — wonders never cease. He drives a tour bus in the French Quarter and from what I'm told he enjoys it. He was so broken up at Bobby's funeral he had to be sedated.

Eve's Garden, which was truly a magnificent piece of architecture where the high and mighty gathered, was never rebuilt. A medical clinic was erected on the corner of Tulane and Villirie. The public's sentiment was whoever destroyed such a beautiful building had to be deranged.

No one has ever been apprehended in the death of Roy Lee Jordan.

It's a mystery as to what became of Ivan Etorre, or Allen Adamo.

No one was ever convicted for the murder of Francis Francino. The Newspaper stated that from all indications it was mob related.

Harold owns a sandwich shop on Poydras Street. He offered me a part of the business, but I refused. He's doing exceptionally well and has begun investing in property.

Two weeks after meeting with Jaw Bone and members of the High-Tech Gang, he was arrested and charged with three counts of armed robbery. He was sentenced to fifteen years.

While most people long for clear sunny days, Bobby, for some strange reason, had a penchant for cold, rainy, dismal days. He died on such a day. One morning, as Mira, brought his coffee and breakfast to his room, as she often did, she kissed him on his forehead. He was cold as a gargantuan slab of ice. He was sitting up in bed with his back against the headboard. His eyeglasses had fallen onto the bed. On his lap was the family photograph album. He had torn out a picture that was crushed in his hand. When Mira examined the photo, it was of him and Rodney. Rodney was ten years old, and they had been fishing. Rodney was holding up a string of minnows, and Bobby was laughing; one of the few pictures ever taken of him when he seemed happy. Under the picture he had scribbled, 'Daddy's Little Man.'

The day Rodney stepped on Bobby's heart was the beginning of the end. He never recovered. His will deserted him. Rodney was truly his pride and joy. He loved him — maybe too much. The mental impact of that awful night, coupled with other traumatic incidents in his life was too much of an overload. He shut down completely.

When I'd come home from school on weekends, I'd go to his room to keep him company. I'd talk and talk — about nothing. Call it wishful thinking, but I believe he understood.

His eyes would light up and seem to smile. Every now and then a single, solitary tear would trickle down his cheek. As I'd wipe that tear from his face, I couldn't help but wonder, what that teardrop might say if it could talk? It wouldn't have had to say much to brighten all my days. A simple 'Attaboy' would have been enough to sustain me for life.

Momma died on Christmas day several years later. She said goodbye just about the time the turkey would be carved. She made all our Christmases special and her spirit will live forever.

If I close my eyes and listen with my heart I can still hear her saying, "Joshua, when you're nine years old, you'll not have to wear short pants again. I promise."

I can't ever recall her raising her voice at any of us in anger. She'd talk, she'd reason, and she'd listen to all our pleas and distresses. She loved us with an unbelievable love, and because she loved us we were able to learn to love others. Her love was unconditional. Our mother was totally committed to us. Her love will never, ever die.

As for me, I retired from the railroad ten years ago. I'm now what they refer to as a senior citizen. I've been blessed in more ways than I can count. I've been allowed to see many sunrises and just as many sunsets. I have a beautiful wife, three children, and seven grandchildren. Who said you can't have it all?

It took me awhile, but once I was able to come to terms with my self-worth and perception, I was better prepared to re-negotiate my contract with life. I won't bore you with the Psychology of it all, but suffice it to say, I was able to see Bobby, my drinking, and my desire to self-destruct in a totally different light. Who knows maybe Bobby's negativity towards me was his way of molding me into what his concept of what a man should be. As smart as he was, he wasn't wise enough to know that words can penetrate where a sword cannot touch. If he had only known the tongue, is the most dangerous organ in the body, what a difference it might have made. I will never, ever, believe he intentionally set out to hurt me. He was hurting — and a hurt person — hurts others.

I'm nothing much to write home about. I'm a simple, plain, uncomplicated man. My wishes and desires are few. All I ever wanted out of life, was a woman truly to love me, reasons for a child to respect me, and one "Attaboy." If, by chance, you're wondering what's so important about an "Attaboy", look inside your heart, the answer is residing there.

Go with God,
Joshua Edward Lange

ABOUT THE AUTHOR

Spencer Butler, Sr. is a native of New Orleans, La.
He's married and the father of three children and a
Graduate of Booker T. Washington High School, Class of 1957.

Made in the USA
Coppell, TX
07 April 2022

76150850R20118